John Klawitter

.

HOLLYWOOD HAVOC

The Llama Goes Up

John Klawitter

DoubleSpin

John Klawitter

DoubleSpin

Book Layout and
Cover Art by Deron Douglas
www.derondouglas.com

Covers produced for DoubleSpin
By Bronco Bradley Merville
www.creativeroundup.com

Lynnie,
The road less certain
but certainly
more memorable.

AUTHOR'S NOTE

Those of you who remember me from the studios, the indy production companies, the post-production houses, the location and equipment services, the casting sessions, rehearsals, scouting and pre-pro meetings, the Director's Guild of America, SAG & AFTRA, the Writers Guild of America, ASCAP, Disney, Warner Bros, Hanna Barbera, Universal, Paramount...you, who yourself have gritted through the long nights in post bays and laughed it up at the old Hollywood places like Musso Franks, Chasens, Pinks Hot Dog Stand and The Tin Horn Saloon...you may find moments you recognize like an old dream or nightmare. You may see between these pages some heroes, heroines, scamps and wenches you might suspect you have known in your own lives and careers. You may even think you see some reflection of your own image in the well. But in this I must assure you are paging through a work of fiction, and all the incidents, events and characters here are made-up situations and imaginary rascals and fine faux ladies, created from pixie dust for the purpose of telling this fictional story of heart-stopping action and non-stop adventure. You in real life are far more clever, tricky, aspiring, unpredictable and wonderful than any of the pale imitations cavorting through these pages could ever hope to be.

HOLLYWOOD HAVOC: The Llama Goes Up

CHAPTER 1

I woke with fat, dark spiders in my head, painful black crawly things that grew monstrous and evil and then popped cold slime all over me. Now awake, my condition swiftly deteriorated from those first feelings of terror and distress into the nearly unbearable pain of muscular constriction. And that's when the real horror of claustrophobia set in. I couldn't see, I couldn't move, I could barely breathe. I was choking, gasping for each breath and I had no idea where I was or just what exactly had happened to me.

The night before, I'd had a few glasses of a so-so pinot noir and gone to sleep alone in my comfortable bed in my pleasant, if small, condo at Sea Garden Cove, located on Jamboree a few blocks from Pacific Coast Highway in Newport Beach. Needless to say, I wasn't there any more.

I was lying on my side in a shallow puddle of icy cold water. From the feel of it, I was tightly, if not expertly blindfolded, and my hands and feet were firmly bound, my knees pulled up near my chest. There was a rotten, dank smell in the air and the sound of gulls in the distance. And further off, perhaps the dull thud of ocean rollers slapping against a rocky shoreline. My head was splitting and I thought I smelled stale urine and a faint medicinal odor...iodine...no, perhaps—*probably* ether.

My name is Matthew Havoc. They call me Hollywood Havoc, usually sardonically, because I'm a small-time show biz guy. I've worked on about fifty crappy movies for Vinnie Berger, the so-called king of schlock. Vinnie calls me *Hollywood Havoc* for real, because I get things done, and he says that's the real Hollywood, the one that counts. At Berger Royal Pictures we've *dabbled in all filmic genre*, as Vinnie likes to brag, but we specialize in thrillers, sex-and-action pictures, war and martial arts, crimes of all sorts, bullets, fire and explosions, as much violence and mayhem as we cam get on the screen for the budget. And, of course, all that tits and ass.

My job experience means, among other things, that I generally can relate the incredibly difficult and impossible story lines that happen in our flicks to what lately has been happening to me in real life. Sounds stupid, I suppose. Actually, it's what has kept me alive for the past year or so. Until now, of course. Now, I'm pretty sure I'm going to die.

It looked like I had been drugged and abducted, kidnapped from my own bed. And I was pretty sure I knew who did it. My boss, ever one to come up with a shady deal, and my batty old neighbor, Bertrand Berke, had set out to out-fox a Nigerian scam artist named Shamseen Usudman, a slick and wealthy international thug who also just happened to be a terrorist. I'd gotten involved, and this was my reward for being lucky enough to still be alive.

I was trussed up like a chicken for the market, alone and helpless in blindfolded darkness. I knew the people who wanted me dead would have no remorse. This wasn't a clever joke on the part of some jealous show business rivals who might stick a dead horse's head on my pillow next to me for their idea of a joke. (Hey, if it worked in the Godfather, it's gotta be funny. Not too long ago, my favorite terrorist

had plotted to take out half of Los Angeles with a
radial plutonium device he'd hidden in a cement truck
he code worded "Fat Boy." Since I'd gotten lucky and
saved my own life—and stopped his plans in the
process—Shamseen was only seeing to my death as
a matter of honor, one thief to another (show business
people, in his mind, being crooks in our own right and
completely expendable, as well). But this was my life
and my death, and the blindfold had to go.

I tried shaking my head, and then rubbing it on
the floor, catching a nose full of dirty water before I
realized it wasn't a towel or a piece of cloth—it was
duct tape. *Okay, what was my Plan B?* At Berger
Royal, we always had a Plan B, because we knew
Plan A never, ever worked. But that only applied for
situations we, with our experience in production,
figured out might happen. My own kidnapping and
murder at this remote location were not in the master
plan.

I rolled about in a frantic attempt to be doing
something, anything, before death came crashing in
on me. I must have looked like a crazed, giant
amoeba or an earthworm on amphetamines. I rolled
twice in one direction, and hit a wall. Then erratically
rolled four times in what I took to be the opposite
direction, until the final turn brought me up short,
painfully banging my knees and hands into a wooden
stud on another wall.

Okay. I was in the small, unfinished room or
maybe a shack somewhere…somewhere near the
ocean…and maybe there was a highway in the
middle distance, in the direction of the water. The
walls were open to the elements, so it was a house in
the middle of construction…or abandoned before
completion.

I kept telling myself, *I ought to be able to figure this.* I was Hollywood Havoc, and I'd scouted locations everywhere in Southern California. Seaside property was expensive, and unfinished homes, left open to the sun, wind and rain, were rare. There were a few in Laguna del Mar that had been condemned in January after the season's exceptionally heavy rains had caused some hillside instability…and the small project near La Conchita…La Conchita, about thirty miles north of Malibu on the Pacific Coast Highway. It had been on the news several nights before. Officials were debating condemning the entire little hamlet because the crumbling cliffs directly inland from the cluster of modest bungalows were threatening to come down.

Okay, well, that was interesting—but nobody kidnaps a person and then dumps them off in an isolated construction site on the hope that Mother Nature will bring down an unstable hill. Still, the place felt like La Conchita, and that knowledge gave me an uneasy feeling. Here I was, blinded, helpless and near panic. *I had to free myself and get out!* The only action I could think of, the only course open to me, was to roll about some more in the hope of finding some opportunity.

It took another twenty minutes, but I strained and made my painful and awkward way to a third wall. This one caught me full in the shoulder with something sharp, a piece of framing metal or maybe a nail. Whatever it was, I'd rolled into it hard, and it had in turn torn a chunk out of my skin. I felt warm blood seeping down my arm.

A nail! I squirmed around cautiously and moved my head toward it. I am near-sighted, and I'm hyper about the importance of what's left of my vision. Here I was, my eye bare centimeters from a nail I couldn't see, when an engine coughed and roared to life nearby. It sounded like it was right on top of me. My body instinctively jerked in panic and I nearly impaled my eye on the spike.

The engine roar was the deeply congested and uneven rumble of a heavy diesel coming to life. I couldn't tell where it was exactly, but it sounded close, very close, too close. I couldn't help but believe it was connected to my imminent departure from the living. *I had to figure out where it was coming from!* That engine bellow sounded like it was on the side away from the ocean, and somehow up from where I was, upslope on a hill. The engine idled and then raced, idled and then raced, a piece of heavy machinery warming up. I didn't know exactly what sort of machine it was, but whatever this new input meant, it couldn't be good news for Hollywood Havoc.

I went back to work on my tape blindfold with something resembling panic. My first effort rewarded me with a stabbing cut to the cheek. My second, a gash on my forehead. I was out of time. I took a third, desperate stab at the nail and I was able to catch the nail head under a corner of the duct tape and pull a triangle of light into my field of vision. I blinked and squinted.

Through blurry vision, I saw I was in some sort of house without walls. A newly constructed house, but from the look of it, unfinished and abandoned for quite some time. I saw an unfinished stairway leading up to a second floor. I was lying on my side in a puddle of water on cold, hard cement in a small room on the ground floor of a two or three story house. It had sheets of plywood covering the exposed beams on the floor overhead, but no protection from the outside other than the unfinished stud walls.

I rolled over to see what was happening in the direction of the diesel roar. Outside and to the rear the house, a steep hillside rose at an abrupt angle, blocking any possible view of the sky. The engine sound above me was coming from up that hill, but my view was cut off by the ceiling. Even as I squirmed around, frantic for a better look, the engine roar took on a new energy, and I heard the clanking treads of a moving bulldozer.   The machine itself was out of my line of sight, but I heard the sound of rocks and boulders bounding in my direction. I worked with renewed energy to rip away more of my blindfold without poking my eye on the nail. Clots of moist dirt bounced and rolled near me, and a fist-sized rock hit me in the back. There was another minor rip in the tape and I could use about a third of the normal field of vision in my right eye. That was my most nearsighted eye, but fortunately, it also gave me clarity at close range.   Squinting down at my knees and arms, I saw that I was trussed around entirely with duct tape.   That was both good and bad.

I knew from Keg's War, our Rambo-type action picture, that duct tape was strong, but had one weakness—I might be able to rip it using my savior nail. I squirmed around to position my legs against the nail, and frantically began to work on the tape. The bulldozer roared and the dirt continued to fill my room until I was half buried in dirt, but I sawed and probed and prodded at the tape. Seconds that seemed like hours went by, and the wet clots of dirt were replaced by an intermittent stream of thick, gooey mud that quickly enveloped the lower half of my body.   I was making progress. One half of the tape binding my arms ripped apart. But the nail was now under the mud, and worse, it seemed to be loosening. The mud level continued to rise ominously. I gave up my ginger sawing techniques in favor of a more violent tearing motion. Three huge pulls backwards and the nail came out of the wall and was lost forever in the rising sea of mud and clumpy brown clods of dirt.

Lucky for me, the tape ripped with my last desperate motion, and my arms were freed from my knees. Even bound together as my wrists were were, I was able to get a grip with my fingers. I ripped the tape binding my legs and tottered unsteadily to my feet. I wasn't a moment too soon.

The noise from the advancing bulldozer increased in intensity, and then the engine roar became a scream of mechanical rage. There was a snapping noise and a wall of rocks and mud cascaded down on the house. I squirmed out of the room, half climbing over and half swimming through muddy debris that was now half way to the ceiling. The frame groaned, starting to bend away from the weight of the hillside being pushed down on it. And still the landslide of stone and wet soil continued, the sound rising to a roar not unlike that of a waterfall.

I took a last look back and saw the yellow side of the bulldozer itself, now upside down, as it slid into my view and smashed into the near wall of the house. The wooden 2x4 stud frame collapsed in as if it was made of matchsticks. The evil-somebody who was out to bury me had miscalculated, and had started a landslide that was bringing down the entire hill—and themselves with it!.

I would have liked to know who that somebody was, but all I saw was a glimpse of one hairy leg twitching in a frantic death shudder as it was sticking out of the mud under the rusty upside down frame of the bulldozer. Further upslope, the hillside was in motion, the green brush taking on the beautiful but deadly undulation of a python as it made its way as dictated by the laws of gravity. No time to claw the tape from my face and hands or to separate my feet one from the other. I dove out the front entrance and hopped like some crazed kangaroo to clear the creaking frame of the house as it tottered over with a crash. I alternately hopped and rolled until I was well out of range of the collapsing mass of rock and debris, and then paused to rip away the tape binding my wrists and legs. I managed to get the tape from my face so I could see, after my usual myopic fashion, from both eyes. I left my hair alone, knowing I would need to cut the tape out with a scissors later on when some form of sanity might return to my life.

By the time I made it to the road, cars had pulled over on the gravel. A surfer in faded shorts and a Billabong t-shirt pulled a few remaining strips of duct tape off my arms and legs."

"What the hell, dude?" he asked.

"College prank," I said. "Stupid frickin' trick gone wrong."

"Them stupid college idiots don't know nothing about real life," the surfer said.

"Don't bother with the stuff in my hair. I'll have to cut it out."

"Can I give you a lift?"

"Which way you going?"

"I hear there's some three footers down in Malibu."

"A lift that way would be nice."

Things were looking up. My boss, Vinnie, had a nine acre ranchette in Malibu Flats. With a little luck, he wouldn't have left for the studio yet, and I could get cleaned up and bum a ride in to the office.

CHAPTER 2

A week went by and things settled back to what counts as normal at an indy film production company, though I had bought more locks for the door and was carrying the army issue .45 that my dad's old army buddy Halliburton Rooks had given me. We hadn't had so much as a squall in three days. We were still in the rainy season and I was thinking maybe we were overdue. It was one of those glorious spring-spangled early April evenings guaranteed to cause one to be grateful to be alive, living the good life in Southern California, and the producer of a string of cheap and violent but also sexy B-grade movies. And this was me, Matt Havoc, and that was about the way I was feeling. Vinnie and I were playing hooky from the office, *mingling with the natives*, as he liked to say. We were sitting outdoors under the flapping canvas awnings at Pinks on La Brea, gnarfing down a few dogs. The morning had been unseasonably hot, but now the glorious golden California sun had sunk below the rim of the Pacific in the west. There was a cool, damp breeze in from somewhere like the Sandwich Isles or maybe Bora Bora, and Big Vinnie was chewing his way through the Three Dog Night, three hot dogs wrapped in a giant tortilla, three slices of cheese, three slices of bacon, all slathered in chili and onions. I was starting in on my own selection, the Ozzy Spicy Dog, a big, spicy Polish sausage with nacho cheese, American cheese, grilled onions, guacamole and chopped tomatoes. There's nothing else in the world quite like Pink's menu, centered as it is on the treasured national food, the hot dog, and a brick-a-brac of California memorabilia.

Pinks is one of those local Southern California home-grown joints like Mission Burrito, Tommy's Burgers and Bob's Big Boy that started in the Great Depression and grew from sidewalk stand to beloved, if still tawdry, eats place. The legends tell us that, back in those ancient grim economic times, places like Pinks began with a portable grill, and if the cops don't shut them down before they made the transition from nuisance to civic pride, and if enough people liked what they're cooking, they put up a canvas awning and eventually bought the land on which they were nesting, and build a little indoor eating area, with the awnings seats still outside to handle the overspill from busy times. Somewhere in that fast-food history book, some of those early entrepreneurs figured out how to franchise, as Carls, jr., MacDonalds and Wendys, and before you knew it they had about a thousand outlets all over the country. It was a lesson Pink's never really learned, though they did have three or four other locations, a lot of local fame, and they made a really mean, though somewhat complex, range of dogs to please the eye and tempt the palate.

"Christ," Vinnie complained, tossing the paper airplane he'd made out of his menu back over the counter where it nosedived and slid along the floor. "When did Pink's go so fancy? Remember we used to come here and just order a couple of hot dogs?"

Vinnie complained about everything, but most of it didn't mean much. His real and constant game, the sad truth be told, was eyeing the passing scene, on the lookout for starlets and new bed partners.

"Sure is a great season for love," he said, eyeing two teenage nymphets in tight, low-slung cut-off jeans snugged somewhere just north of their hips and cut barely south of heaven. "I appreciate the fact that the good dads of the Southern California wealthy class are presenting their daughters graduating from Hollywood High with boob jobs instead of Mustang convertibles. It's enlightened behavior."

I did my best to get his mind off the passing parade. Vinnie usually had three or four law suits pending regarding his ungroomed sexual conduct that ranged from grab ass at the office to paternity.

"For a while there I thought you were going for the Rosie O'Donnell Long Island Dog," I said.

"Not a chance, Hollywood Havoc," he grinned, wrinkling his nose at the thought.

Hollywood Havoc. Even after my recent kidnapping, which Vinnie more or less believed I'd made up so he'd miss me. My real name is Matt Havoc, but I'd run through a bad patch, and trouble had been sticking to me. Real trouble, and not the production type. Through the unwitting designs of my boss and his sometimes partner in crime, my batty old neighbor, Bertrand Berke, I'd gotten involved in a scheme that had nearly vaporized half of Los Angeles, and me along with it. No joke, no flaky film concept—the real deal. *And now Vinnie couldn't bring himself to believe in a simple abduction?*

"My God, wouldn't you like to get that under you?" Vinnie was nodding toward a beautifully arranged blond and tan piece of sexuality swinging her wonder and delights over to Pinks, probably taking a break from Stage 6 to pick up a Chili Chicken Breast, the Pastrami Burrito, or an obviously rich and overly randy producer like Vinnie. .

In these times, I consider myself to be something of a rescue unit. It's part of my job description. Fortunately, the girl looked a lot like the bimbo from *California Climax* who had taken Vinnie for six figures. It didn't hurt to remind him, "Looks like Angry Angie, doesn't she?" I asked.

He gave me a sour look. Two years before, Angry Angie had my boss up against the rail. Even Marsha, Vinnie's wife, had quietly left for the East Coast, probably selling her furs and jewelry and getting the money off-shore. But that was just one more time Vinnie's steady girlfriend Gloria stepped up to the plate, swearing Vinnie had been with her every when, where and how that Angie said he'd been some incriminating elsewhere. Before Gloria raised her right hand, Vinnie had either been raping Angry Angie's 14 year old virginal daughter from Guadalajara or he'd been slipping around on the snowy slopes of Colorado proposing marriage to Angie with a 4 carat honey yellow diamond engagement ring. Thanks to Gloria, he got everything back. Well, almost everything. He got his swagger and 90% of his fortune back. Angry Angie ended up with 10%, and Gloria ended up with the ring, a 4-carat diamond easily worth twice Angie's take.

"Naw, Angie had a sweeter smile," Vinnie said. "You know, that innocent little-angel-go-fuck look." That's the thing about the head of Berger Royal Pictures; he leads with his dick, and he forgives and forgets, all in the name of a good time, living the high life of a Hollywood Legend. He's as predictable as lemmings and cliffs. One glimpse of a promising new piece of ass and he forgets all the bad things that ever were, are or could be about to happen to him. *He's Goofy, ya-hah-Hoooooie, over the falls!*

I swear, Vinnie's the classic sitting duck, a duck in the headlights, just looking for the next relationship to blunder into. I know it's 'deer in the headlights,' but you get the mixed metaphor. Jumbling imagery around is a disease I picked up from the master, Vinnie, himself. But, getting back to the more serious of Vinnie's bad habits, it's not like he's anywhere near invisible, or even slightly encumbered by any hint of awareness of the modern rules of sexual engagement.. Vinnie Berger is swinging out there in the breeze, one of the few remaining survivors from another Hollywood generation. He's a wildly obvious and oblivious run-away male freight train still on the unsteady and financially dangerous tracks of blatant show-biz lust.

The object of interest hipped up to the counter and ordered the Pati Morrison Baja Veggie Dog, and it was all Vinnie could do to keep from jumping over there to buy it for her. I swear, he was panting.

"Come on, Havoc, what could perceptively be wrong with a sweet little thing like that?"

And he would have hopped to it, no matter what I said, but that was when somebody bounced off the hood of his beloved Bentley, the prime object of his automotive affection that he'd unwisely parked on the street not ten feet away from the outdoor bench where we were sitting.

"What the fuckacious...?" he said.

"I'll handle it," I said, starting to rise. There was reason for concern. Vinnie's had three heart attacks, and here he was, half way through an artery-clogging repast at Pinks.

"No. Hang on to this for me," he said, handing me the dripping remains of his Three Dog Night.

"You should let me..." My voice trailed off because Vinnie was already in motion. The fellow sprawled on the hood of his moss green Bentley Sportster had been tossed there by three Latinos with gang tattoos, glittery Diamonique earrings and shaved heads. They were waving knives around like amateurs, not knowing whether to stick or slash. On the obverse side of the coin, Vinnie is over six feet four, and *overall big.* He does have a presence and a voice. Still, *any knife action can kill you dead*, as Horace Keg always says in his Rambo-esque manner in our blood-and-thunder flicks.

` "HEY, funk-heads!!" Vinnie roared in his stentorian producer's voice. "You're getting carnage on my car!"

He swiftly picked up the big one gallon glass vats of mustard, pickle relish and onions and fired them at the punks with deadly accuracy. Of course, the range was something less than ten feet, so you couldn't really say he was a marksman. But heavy glass shatters with an impressive impact, and he did manage to land direct hits on a brace of the thugs with the pickle relish and the onions. The mustard was also a direct hit. The glass didn't shatter, but the third punk had a huge blot of yellow on his face and chest. He screamed and rubbed his eyes. Unfortunately, the mustard jar caromed off the thug to star the windshield of Vinnie's Bentley.

"That does it!" Vinnie roared. "You sperm-headed pimps want to get catsupped?" He raised the big vat of red stuff two-handed over his head.

And, indeed, that seemed to do it. *Catsup, the ultimate deterrent.* The trio of gang-bangers took off, and the victim, who proved to be a slight little Frenchman, slid off the hood and lay shuddering in the gutter.

"Here," Vinnie said, handing me the catsup and taking back his sloppy tortilla dog, "Flip him over and see how dead he is."

At first the little Frenchie was as floppy as a rag doll, but Vinnie rubbed some raw unions under his nose and he started to come around, cursing magnificently in the French tongue and snorting in a spastic sort of way, like somebody was giving him little jabs with a Junior G-man stun gun or a hand shake buzzer. You know how picky the French are about the culinary aspects of their lives. *Raw onions? Mon dieu!* He had a cut over his left eye and a few scratches on his chin, but nothing serious. We dusted him off and sat him on the bench next to us, and Vinnie bought him a Sprite and a Mullholland Drive Dog, the ten inch stretch hot dog that comes with mustard, onions, chili and sauerkraut. I think Vinnie, ignoring World War II, believed that the new guy, being *a Continental Man*, might go for sauerkraut in the pan-European way.

"What is zis?" the French guy slurred in heavily accented English.

"More hair of the dog that bit you," Vinnie said, handing the big hotdog over.

"Did they get your wallet?" I asked.

"No, I szink not," the little fellow said. He ignored me and the dog in his hand, to fix Vinnie with a vague and yet somehow beady stare. "I come here looking for Vinnie Berger, yes?"

"Well, you came to the right place. But that was a hell of a way to introduce yourself."

"Zactly, so, no? They tell me so at your office. I find you here."

"Sure, yeah. Okay. Who are you?" Vinnie asked.

"My name is Marc Fraper. From Paris, Orleans and Le Mans in the Sarthe Province.."

"Well, that's interesting," Vinnie said, not much liking the geography lesson. "I know where Le Mans is. Steve McQueen shot that stinker of a racing picture there, you know, that thing that didn't know if it was a documentary or a motion picture."

"Zat is ze greatest racing picture ever on ze film!"

"Yeah, sure, and my mother was a nun in the order of The Sisters of St. Francis. If I was making that picture, I'd have booted Steve's ass when Sturgis quit." That shoot was a common Hollywood legend; a production gone famously sour. Highly successful film director John Sturgis, unable to work with Steve's newly minted 'creative awareness', had stormed off the set, claiming it was *the worst experience of his professional career.*

"Eat your stretch-dog, Marco," Vinnie said. "Meat is good for the jitters."

The guy tried, but after one bite he had to set down his Mulholland Dog. He was shaking all over.

"Hey! HEY!!" Vinnie shouted in his ear. It was straight out of the Vinnie Berger School of how things really worked. The show must go on. *You will be okay or I'll yell you back to perfect.* We only have another half hour of daylight, and two more shots to get in the can. You *will* get those shots for me. Don't ask me to stand up there and hold back the sun. And quit that stupid shaking.

`   I sat down between the two of them, and handed our new acquaintance his Sprite.

"Here, drink this."

Marc drained it in three long slurps and a gulp, but it didn't seem to help. He looked around wildly, as if his assailants might be coming back with the rest of their gang.

"Hey, calm down." I patted his shoulder. "Vinnie's packing. If they show their ugly faces, Vinnie will shoot them for you."

"No...?"

"Yeah. Seriously," I said. "Right in the eye. Vinnie's a great shot, practices at the range all the time, and he's always shooting cans and bottles at his place in Malibu. Once he even winged Gloria's horse."

"Hey, you don't have to tell complete strangers stuff like that," Vinnie complained.

"He doesn't have a gun?" The Frenchman said, in that peculiar inflection of the modern Gallic tribe that makes questions out of statements.

"Sure, I do," Vinnie said amiably, his good humor returning. He fished around in one of the pockets in his spacious silk jacket and pulled out a big, ugly 9mm Glock Special. "I would have shot your pals, but it's always trouble in America when you shoot somebody. They never put that part in the cop show. What a pain in the ass. And if you do pull off on somebody, be sure to kill 'em dead—else they sue you in court."

I shook my head, warning Vinnie to be quiet. His jovial banter didn't seem to be having much of a quieting effect on our newfound friend.

"What was so important that those gang bangers were lumping on you?" I asked.

"Yeah, and how come they picked my car to dent?" Vinnie's heavy-lidded eyes slid from the indent on the hood of his Bentley to the newcomer and back again. With my comments about my boss's indiscriminating tomcatting, I may have given you the wrong impression. Vinnie has his weaknesses, but once you get past loose and available women, you've got to look long and hard to find them.

"Oh, zat is just ze accident of nature," Marc said, dismissing the dented hood with a negligent European wave of his hand. His fingers were beautifully manicured. The nails were buffed to a dull shine and there was a big green diopside ring on his pinkie. "Zey see me, zey see my gold watch, my Italian shoes, they szink I have money."

"Well, do you?" That's Vinnie, ever the direct approach.

"Yes," Marc said with a proud nod of his head, "I do have ze money. I am the Big Euros man."

Vinnie nodded and took a big bite of Three Dog Night. "Okay...what you doing over here from Italy, Mister Big Euro Dude?"

"Francaise. I am from la belle France, no? I just said Paris, Orleans, Le Mans, no?

"I guess," Vinnie said, trying to pick up on the way the guy talked. "I got a bad case of the mind-bot, brought on by a dent in my expensive motorcar."

"Mind-bot?" Mark stared at him; with a blank look, as if Vinnie was talking Martian. I couldn't blame him. Vinnie blamed anything he got wrong on mind-bot, a disease he'd imagined to explain how he could possibly get anything wrong.. Mind-bot was a weak strain of mad cow disease, a bottled viruses he was convinced had been strapped in bottles under the wings of light airplanes and released in the free American air by KGB agents. The Berlin Wall may have fallen, but that didn't mean the Russians had somehow miraculously become our brothers overnight. Mind-bot was a concept he'd been developing over the years for a movie of the same name, something with people walking around Washington like zombies while Soviet ships gathered off-shore in the Atlantic near the Potomac River. Even though it was his own idea, spun from his own overly active imagination, I knew he'd come to half-believe it.

"Never mind," Vinnie said, now nervous that some stranger might steal his idea. He wasn't any more crazy than the rest of us; it was simply my boss displaying a prevailing Hollywood attitude at its paranoid best. "So, what you want with me?" he asked.

The little Frenchman brightened. "I come for ze American Film Market," he said, waving his hands as if we might not understand badly accented English. "You know, my interest is ze representation of various Morocco and Algerian clients, I am fill with zis unquenchable desire to fly from Meester Big Euro to be Meester Big Time Hollywood. I go to ze AFM, but no, no, non...zay all small time fry. I say, *Alors, where is ze action?* And zay say back to me, *Go see Vinnie Burger*."

Vinnie gave me his *Isn't life wonderful?* Look, and the minute Marc put his expressive waving gesture down, he wrapped put one massive arm around the little guy's now slumped-over shoulders. "And so, Mr. Marc Fraper, you want to invest in the Burger Six Fund, our incredible new slate of pictures, all prepped and ready to go?"

"Oui. Yes," the little Frenchman said. "Zat is so."

"Manna from heaven," Vinnie said, flipping what was left of his Three-Dogger in a nearby garbage can. I could see he wasn't even going to charge Marc up front for the big dent in the hood of his Bentley or even the scratches in the paint job. Give him a little time to work on the budget; my boss would bury it in the below-the-line.

CHAPTER 3

Of course, as you already suspect, there was no Berger Six Fund. Having lost our last…err, investor, we were in a grim period of non-funding. We had the one picture, *Carnage Days*, on hold while Vinnie scoured the known Universe looking for new…err, investors. But, due to this most unlikely of coincidences and our subsequent rescue of the little Frenchman, *Carnage Days* actually did get funded and after a few weeks began to blossom into the active pre-production stage—storyboarding, scheduling, location scouting, lining up cast and crew—the usual hidden-detail business that precedes the glamour and the glitz of actual on-the-set production and makes it all possible.

Meanwhile, (and I know you don't actually care about this) my own sex life had shriveled away to nothing. I'd been in what I now saw as *the affair of my life* with my fusty old neighbor's daughter, Julia, a relationship I'd hoped would become the love of my ever-after. But Julia, who already was an Oriental arts expert, had unexpectedly accepted an once-in-a-lifetime offer to study Japanese brush art under the last living master in Kyoto. So there went the afterglow out of the ever-after. .

As time went by, Julia's daily emails became weekly, shorter, and finally non-existent. After only two months of her apprenticeship in the ancient Japanese city, her ancient grand master passed to his reward. For a few days I thought things might change for the better and she'd be winging her way back home. Her grandpa, old Bat-Brain Bertrand, was speaking to me again, after a fashion, and we shared a brief ray of hope... but that fizzed out when, instead of returning to the States, Julia set out to travel mainland China by bus, rail and motorbike. She seemed fine and had plenty of money, but somewhere in South China she traded her laptop for a necklace of jade prayer beads, and our correspondence became one-way in the form of occasional postcards with no return address that she'd send addressed to both Bertrand and me. At least she was fair in that she rotated them so I'd get one and then Old Bertie would get the next. They arrived in our mailboxes scratched, folded and wrinkled, postmarked from backwash places where some network producer could have easily held the next Survivor TV series or maybe done a Remote Locations Special on National Geographic or the Discovery Channel.

Old Bat brains intercepted me most mornings on my way to work, usually to growl, in his gruff excuse for a greeting, that there was no postcard. *At least*, I kept telling myself, *I had Carnage Days.* Since Old Bertie had lost faith in the Nigerian scams that had been keeping him spiritually alive, it looked to me like he had nothing.

"She's coming back, Bertrand," I'd say.

"It's your fault, Matthew Havoc," he'd mutter, snipping savagely at the already ravaged remains of the citrus tree to one side of his front door and pouring on a half-bag of grey grains of fertilizer.

"What did I do?"

"You could have married her. Made an honest woman of her."

28

"She is an honest woman, Bertrand. She never lied to you. She never lied to me. She didn't want to get married, and that's the truth."

But I could see the tears starting in his watery old eyes, and I'd hasten to reassure him she would soon be coming home again, and probably then we would get married, if she would have me. I personally didn't believe it, but come on...sure he was a cantankerous and bitter old man, but our relationship went a long ways back, and he was my own personal junior grade Ambrose Bierce, proof that everybody didn't mellow out into smooth peanut butter in their nutty old age.

I myself was still jittery as a clam on crack. It was barely a month since we had escaped atomic annihilation at the hands of a cement truck named Fat Boy, a truck with a radial-type nuclear weapon welded inside, courtesy of my nemesis Shamseen Usudman. Looking back, the unlikely and bizarre adventures that Bertrand, Julia and I had gone through with Fat Boy seemed strange and unreal, and I was glad to put all that behind me. And yet...there was something else, at least for me. *My kidnapping proved it wasn't actually behind me, my business with the mad terrorist was in no way finally put to rest.* Even without my recent abduction, the entire series of events, though scary enough, had felt incomplete, like a movie that ran out of money three-fourths of the way through and never got finished. Maybe it was simply because Shamseen Usudman, a violent terrorist of Nigerian origin with vague Mid-Eastern connections, had gotten away—but I didn't think so. There was more to it than that. The story was unresolved, an unfinished puzzle, something huge that I'd been a part of without understanding the big picture. *I wondered why Shamseen had picked*

Bertrand as the unwitting importer, his agent in the United States. Shamseen Usudman had hundreds of millions of dollars at his disposal. *Why not simply buy his own ocean-going freighter?*

Vinnie Berger calls me *Hollywood Havoc* because by now I've worked on close to fifty pictures for Berger Royal. I'm Vinnie's right-hand man, his go-to guy, the fellow who fixes things, who swipes free location shots on the fly and whisks camera, crew and actors away just before the local cops zoom in with their threats, fees and penalties, the sad sack whose job it is to wet-nurse drunken stars and get them to the set on time, the clever apprentice who sneaks Vinnie himself out the back door of the Peninsula Hotel just as his wife is storming in the front lobby. *Hollywood Havoc, that's me.*

All that, and yet how do I see myself? I like to think of myself as a story guy. I pride myself on my sense of story, on my ability to spin the yarn. Just as an accountant brings an analysis of profit and loss to his daily affairs, I think in terms of character motivation and good dialog, of words that spring fresh and true from the mouths of real actors. Of course, by now, if you've ever seen a Berger Royal picture, you're ROLF, that is, rolling on the floor laughing at me.

Inside his complicated psyche, I think Vinnie's a story guy, too. But he'd be the last to admit it. "Story, shmorey!" he yells at me, "Gimme BIG on the screen!".

The end result? We quite often do pictures with holes in the script big enough to drive a dozen trucks named Fat Boy through, and our characters are so shallow they make my ex-wife, Peanuts—in real life a sexy, if 100% self-centered, film star—seem like a warm and beautiful human being. But at least I like to think I know the difference between a good picture and one that stinks.

And the point here is, I could not get a handle on the one story that had meant the most in my life. *Why did Shamseen Usudman pick batty Old Bertrand, the retired, dried up old husk of a once powerful import-export executive, to help in his attempt to destroy Southern California? Or, more to my personal concerns, why did he choose to involve me?* There just were no answers, and so the story was incomplete…and, even before my abduction, I had been, from time to time, filled with the uneasy suspicion that it was unfinished business. As Yogi (Berra, not Bear) used to say, *It ain't over until it's over.* I'm here to tell you, *It certainly ain't.*

Talking about story, our first pre-production meetings on Carnage Days started in the classic way—that is, with the story, as well a production should. And as Vinnie, Marc Fraper and I sat around arguing about plot and action and character motivation, the endless days that followed our inauspicious beginning swirled around in a muddled way, a lot of smoke and hidden flashes of anger, the atmosphere story meetings sometimes develop when no one vision is clear and so everybody feels comfortable throwing an endless variety of vegetables and spices into the soup. The original script, while not Oscar nomination material, at least had a beginning, middle and an end. Those are the three fundamental elements of any story, and as our days went on they seemed to be dissolving before my eyes.

The Frickin' Frenchie (as Vinnie called him, usually behind his back), now officially our new funding partner, proved to be something of an enigma. His ideas, of which he had bucketsful, tended to the impractical and the outlandish. If he wasn't so

obviously from the original *territory of the frickin'
cheese heads*, I believe I would have long before
come to the conclusion that he'd never done a movie
in his life. But, as you probably know, filmmaking *a la
Francaise* tends to the experimental, the abstract, the
absurd, the dull, and the grandiose, and so I wasn't
quite sure any more just exactly where we were going
with *Carnage Days*. One thing was sure, we were
practically starting over.

For his part, Vinnie was on board with the *grand* part.
Vinnie was always searching for big, *big, BIG*...giant
spectacle, things that were stunning on the screen,
that special unknown happenstance that turns a
movie into an *event.* He most often doesn't know
what that might be, but he's convinced he'll know it
when he sees it. This approach is, of course,
tempered by his strictest of all rules—If you can't do it
for under 5 mil, you're not going to be doing it at
Berger Royal. Ten years ago, that number was 2 mil,
but you know what inflation has done to the nickel
cigar, the dime Coke and the 25-cent hamburger.

So we all were story geniuses, throwing in
carrots, turnips and action scenes, and stirring up the
continuity and the dialogue along with the peas. I
guess, out here, you take it for granted. Just like me,
just like Vinnie, just like the new French guy,
everybody even remotely connected to the business
thinks he or she is a story expert. The kid scooping
ice cream at the cone shop will have a hot new idea
about *The King of KarmalKorn* that he thinks is unique
and original and a big box office beater, and so will
your auto mechanic (a story about a mechanic who
figures out how to turn a Ford Focus into a Le Mans
gran prix car), your insurance agent (A little *shlump* of
a guy scams a giant insurance company for millions
and runs away to Mexico with his secretary) and your

wife (probably something about a wife running away with the mailman). Maybe we all see life through the camera lens and none of us can tell where real life leaves off and the cinema action begins. I'll admit to that in my own days and ways.

And that's why, in that vein of thinking like a moviemaker, there were moments when the Fat Boy Incident gnawed at me, and the unseen presence of Shamseen Usudman fell on my shoulders like the big black shadow of a giant rat. It was unfinished business, and I could see now that, for me, it probably always would be.

Even as the three of us got into grand shouting arguments over *Carnage Days*, I felt like Thomas, the successful young photographer—the David Hemmings character in Antonioni's old 1966 movie *Blowup*. Once I had been awakened to the enormous push and tug of a world of sudden violence and terror, but since then that crazy world of mass violence and death had moved on and left me behind back in my make-believe cinema world…at least until my kidnapping. Now I was nearly paranoid all the time. I kept looking for signs, for clues, for dangerous moments that belonged in that other world, but all I saw was mimes and mummers. Vinnie laughed it off.

"You got post-near-nuclear-disaster depression syndrome, Havoc," he said. "That's N.N.D.P.S."

"You wrote that down," I accused him. "I saw you looking at your notepad."

"Naw, I got doodles down here." He denied it, as I knew he would. Show biz teaches you to deny even the slightest weakness, even among friends. "You should get laid or see a shrink, or maybe both. Hey, put it on the company tab. A trip to Miss Kitty's Ranch in Vegas. I'll come along, keep you out of trouble."

Since the dangerous-looking guy sneaking around Sea Garden Cove turned out to be the pool man, and the swarthy joker who tried to run me off the 405 was probably a genuine case of road rage, I started to lose my finely tuned sense of eminent danger, and even to think I was acting ridiculous. At least that's my excuse for what happened the next time Shamseen actually came back out of his rat hole and tried to get me.

CHAPTER 4

It happened on a day that began as uneventfully as any other. Like every other morning, I woke with a start at somewhere between five and five-fifteen. I'd been dreaming I was tied up inside the tub of a huge KitchenAid mixer with enough cookie dough to bake a million cookies. Somebody with a swarthy complexion was laughing as he poured in bags of radioactive grenades that looked like rancid green chocolate chips. There was an antique alarm clock ticking away on my stomach, and it seemed to have less than a minute left until something bad would happen. After my heart stopped pounding in my chest, I bolted out of bed, threw some cold water on my face and gave my teeth a rude brush.

Feeling a little calmer, I headed for the kitchen and made myself a latte. I took a huge Trader Joe's Pound Plus Bar from the refrigerator. Cold bittersweet chocolate is great for the jitters. The Pound Plus Bar is tough to break when it's cold, but I managed to knock off a line of six heavy chunks by cracking it against the edge of my dark green granite countertop. Then I zapped a square Oatmeal-To-Go bar for 11 seconds in the microwave oven and headed for my study. Slumped in my genuine Herman Miller chair (the chair of true Hollywood movers and shakers), I managed to jot down a few notes on the latest revisions to Carnage Days. After that, I tried to start a letter to the former light of my life. I'd barely gotten past the obligatory *Dear Julia, How are you?* part, when Batty Old Bertrand came banging in my front door.

"Goddamn it, Matthew, you got any decent food?" he shouted.

"Couldn't sleep either, huh?" I asked.

"What you got to eat?" he fairly roared

"I'm not deaf, Bertrand," I said.

"Right, and I'm not senile," he shouted in my ear. I guessed it was better to aggressively exhibit senile behavior than to back down, but I wisely didn't say anything about that. After my most recent brush with my own demise, I was practicing being nice, just in case there was anything to that karmadic coming-back-as-an-ant-or-a-toad stuff.

We moved to the kitchen where he ate what was left of my Oatmeal-To-Go and three of my chocolate chunks before I had his scrambled eggs and Kielbasa sausage on the table in front of him.

"Real food," he grunted. "Thanks, Matthew. I almost wish you were my own son, if you hadn't been responsible for all that vile hanky-panky with my granddaughter and then forced her to run away to the Orient when you refused to marry her."

"Bertrand—" I started.

"Ahh, never mind," he grumped, waving me off with one hand while he used the other to fork eggs into his mouth. "I know you got your own version of it."

At least munching the eggs had reduced his decibel level. Hard to talk through a mouth stuffed the way his was. After a few more bites, he took my plate and fork and what was left of his eggs and started to wander toward the front door.

"Them Buzzards in Burma will be calling," he said by way of an excuse for his abrupt departure. "The X-ray business never quits."

"You do business with Burma?" I croaked. "They have death squads."

"You don't know nothing, Matthew Havoc," he shouted over his shoulder, suddenly back in the imperative mode. "Oh, yeah—I almost forgot. Tell Vinnie I need to talk to him."

"What?!"

"You heard me. Tell your boss, Vinnie Berger, to call me because I need to talk to him."

"Not in this life." By themselves, Bertrand and Vinnie were trouble. Together, they were an unpredictable destructive force, a tornado without a steady direction, guaranteed to mess up anything they touched.

"Tell him," Old Bat-brains repeated a third time, raising his voice well into the thunder range. And then he wandered out my front door, probably heading back to his place to finish his eggs.

Why should I even be tempted to help him? There was the Fat Boy mess, the destruction of Southern California that had been nearly entirely Bertie and Vinnie's fault (except for my small bit-part in it). And, just a few days ago, Bertrand been caught at the local 7-11 in his pajamas, trying to mail a letter to some new buddies in Nigeria who wanted his help to rescue ex-president Abacha's widow's fortune and transfer the loot to the United States. Luckily I hadn't left for Berger Royal, and so I was able to drive over and pick the old coot up before the Newport Beach cops got there.

"Well, they *should* have a mail service," Old Bertrand had said, by way of explanation.

"Shut up, you old fart," I said, by way of an answer.

"You should be kinder to your elders," he complained, pursing his mouth and looking for a moment like he might cry. Too bad he couldn't hold back the quivering sly smile just barely showing itself around the far corner of his wrinkled old liar's lips.

Bertrand could be counted on to not return my plate or the silver. My custom was to wait a week or two, until some time when he wasn't in, and then go over and use a duplicate key to let myself in to collect the stray utensils—usually still dirty in his sink—and to look for my books and film props that had drifted over to his place. I once had to search high and low for my missing .45 automatic, which I found fully loaded under his pillow.

As Bertrand retreated with what was left of the eggs I'd scrambled for him, I slumped into an old yellow wicker rocking chair in one corner of my kitchen. I was feeling simultaneously bored and edgy. The Carnage Days story wasn't really getting any better, and I was drained and weighed down by my inability to get through to the Frenchie, and by my anger at Vinnie for not backing me with a firmer attitude. *Hell, it was Vinnie's picture, too, and it was going to have his name on it, up there on the silver screen lots bigger than mine.* I felt pretty sure I had to get away, so as I was driving in to Hollywood Flats from my condo at Sea Garden Cove I began to plan my getaway. I told myself, *If I could only get even a small break from the endless, howling script meetings that seemed to be going nowhere!* Turned out, it was easy. I was still in my make-work routine of doing location scouting for Carnage, so what I came up with wasn't any sort of a vacation. It was real business…well, real show business, anyway.

38

I was interested in one particular location. It was the top floor of the old Coast Saving & Loan building in downtown L.A. Built in the go-go 1980s, it had a funky style that tried to cross the California Craftsman look with Mies van der Rohe's stark notion that *form follows function*. The result was a blocky and confused little skyscraper, with awkward chunks of concrete and sheets of plate glass that didn't quite know where to go or what they were doing. It was maybe something you might end up with if King Arthur's architect was transported into the present and asked to design something 21st century modern *cum* retro-Medieval…everything but the moats and the drawbridges. In my current mood, I found it satisfying that architects could be as befuddled and wrong-headed as filmmakers. But what really interested me was the wide patio deck near the top of the building. I thought we could do something visually exciting with that. No, not pour boiling oil down on invading Crusaders.

There's a scene in *Carnage Days* where our crazed hero holds off a SWAT team from just such a penthouse patio deck, and a UPM friend of mine from Universal had recommended I head downtown and take a look. We still called it the Coast Savings building, though Coast Savings had long gone to Savings & Loan heaven—that is, merged with somebody else and golden parachutes all around.

The building itself wasn't really tall, maybe 20 some-odd stories, but it was tall enough for what I envisioned. What's more, there was a wide surface street paralleling the downtown Harbor Freeway that we could probably block off for a couple of hours without paying an arm and a leg. And the oddly homely little building had the advantage of being open on one side to the Harbor Freeway downtown. That meant we might be able to fly in from that side and achieve what I hoped would be some incredible helicopter camerawork, dizzying air-to-air aerials with tall glass walls all around, playing nearly as big on the screens in the Orient (one of our major markets) as explosions and bloody, violent death.

I called on down to my favored Medieval blockhouse, and they said they loved location shoots, the space was vacant, and they'd be honored and delighted to give me a personal tour.

"Make sure you lower the drawbridge," I said.

There was a long pause, followed by a measured, "Ahmmm..." from the other end of the conversation.

"Just kidding," I said, feeling more than a little embarrassed. You know it's a bad joke when you have to explain it.

I set up my walkthrough for later that morning and then waited until Vinnie was in the middle of his customary half-a-dozen donuts and a couple of bagels breakfast (six of each) and told him where I was going.

"Oh, yeah," he said, sounding vaguely disgusted as he slathered cream cheese on a plump blueberry bagel. "Leave me with the crap."

"*Merde*, Vinnie. The French word for shit."

"I hate French money men!" He shouted. "They don't know what the hell they're doing!" He did a terrible imitation French accent, "Ve must get our Francs out of ze Cameroon. Krugerands from Sou'Africa. Pounds from ze Brits. Ve must go to Switzerland for ze Euros. Ve must have escargot and bellisimo vino mit every meal!"

By that time, his rant had deteriorated into a French-German-Italian smorgasbord, but I was used to it. Vinnie launched into variations of the same outburst before raping every investor he'd ever conned. The

Germans with their Bratwurst and beer. The Indians with their two kinds of curry. The English with their phony English accents. It was his way of working off his *faux* guilt before he plucked the goose.

"Okay, Vinnie," I said. "I have to go now."

"Yeah, Kid," he said, calming down as if on cue. "See ya later."

But he almost didn't.

CHAPTER 5

I was still driving one of Vinnie's big Ford Expeditions.
I gassed up using the company card at a Shell Station
on Western Avenue and made my way south down
Figeroa Boulevard until I figured out the parking and
pulled into a nearby underground garage.
The real estate people were waiting for me in the big
marble lobby of the building once owned by Coast
Savings & Loan.   I was on time and they seemed
eager. The lobby looked nearly deserted;
encouraging for me, because it meant I might be able
to haggle a good price for a few shoot days on the
site. Promising, indeed.
Generally, when I get into these meetings, it is just
with one person, more often than not a middle-aged
divorcee from the Valley with tired eyes and a sad
smile that said she couldn't wait to get me gone so
she could go pick up her kids or hit a pick-up bar
somewhere, or maybe both, though not in any
particular order.
This time it was three people, and they certainly
weren't your ordinary suburbanites. There was a
50ish lady with dark skin and dark, flashing eyes.
She was wearing a conservative gray silk sarong and
a red jewel on her forehead. And she was
accompanied by a set of buff and shiny guys who
looked like they should be playing Rick's bouncers in
a gay flick, perhaps an updated rip-off of Casablanca.

We sat at a table in the main lobby eating area, which was nearly empty. It was more like a stale fast food joint than a real restaurant; the place was called The Meet & Greet, and it had the cold appearance of a convention center cafeteria. Diners had to take a small, awkward glass elevator or trudge up a circular stairway up to a raised circular slab, a cement statement rimmed in tubular railings, the entire disk elevated half a level above the main floor of the lobby, which was huge. One taste of the coffee and I knew why they had almost no patrons. *Location is not everything, after all.*

"My name is Lefala," the lady said, in an accent that was more Eastern Mediterranean than lilting Indian. The discrepancy set off a little trigger in my brain, but I didn't think too much of it at the time. I guess I should have. "I am the real estate manager for this building," she added.

"You don't sound Indian," I said. After my recent close encounters, I was losing my normal carefree manner.

"Why should that matter?" Her voice was sharp, and her eyes flicked hotly in my direction. It's an awkward age; people get really fussy about little things; they want to dress and talk with ethnic flare, but they resent anybody talking about it. It's almost as if people born and raised in foreign lands have come to believe the United States of America is a small colony of their own culture.

"Nothing, I said. " I do a lot of casting. I'm used to associating certain dialects with certain people."

She looked down at her coffee cup. Her expression, when she returned my gaze, was furtive and angry. "Well, I am not really East Indian, only half."

"Oh…" I said, hoping she'd get off the subject.

"But my husband is a traditional man who insists on the old ways. So I do not get to wear the Anne Kline pants suit."

"Oh…" I said again, really hoping she'd move on.

"He doesn't want me out of the house, and yet he forces me to work for the almighty American dollar."

"I see," I said. *Some getaway vacation!* I was starting to wonder how soon I could get back to my script meetings.

"This is Jeff and this is George. They are my husband's brother's sons. Do not hold that against them." She shot them a quick, unfriendly glance. "They will report everything I say and do back to my husband. Do not hold that against them, either. They must do it or my husband will send them back to the old country."

"Oh, well then, by all means—"

"I have only been on this job for some several few weeks. I hope it will be okay if my two spies tag along. After all, they are in training."

"No, of course not," I shrugged. They were a dark-spirited, surly pair, but I didn't care one way or the other. *See the location, get on back to Berger Royal,* I thought to myself. Maybe I could stop by Pinks on the way back and try out one of those Three Dog Nights that Vinnie favored. I could eat one of the dogs and have plenty left over for dinner.

I wondered how much a couple of kids could learn by tagging along as their auntie showed a penthouse patio to a film producer, but I didn't say anything about that, either.

"You are in lucky," she said politely, "as the office in question is vacant at the moment."

She opened a fat display portfolio with photos of the layout of the penthouse and diagrams of the patio and the adjoining offices. I asked the usual questions about heavy-duty electricity for the lighting and how much the neighboring offices would mind the fuss and bustle of a film production for a week or so.

"It is presently all vacant on the top three floors," she said, reinforcing the rumor around town that the real estate market wasn't in the greatest shape. "So that shall not be a problem."

She picked up our coffee cups and went to toss them in a trash can. *Helping to keep the place neat and clean for prospective renters,* I thought. How little I knew!

"You fellows honestly going to be real estate agents?" I asked. They just stared in my direction with their quiet eyes boring into me like black obsidian.

I waved a hand in front of their unblinking expressions. "Jeff? George? You guys with me here?" Their glares hardened. Sometimes I can be a real asshole. *Hollywood Havoc—he takes nobody serious.*

"They are not bad boys," Lafalla said quickly. "Their English not so very good." She gathered her books up with a rush I took for embarrassment. "Come. I take you up on the elevator now."

But as we passed the cash register she stood back, gravely watching while I paid the tab. That should have been another clue, I suppose, because real estate agents always fall all over themselves to pay the little bills. But it wasn't my money, it was a legitimate production expense and I wasn't paying any attention.

On the quick ride up the swift and nearly silent elevator, Jeff put his arm around George and pulled him a bit away from me. It was an odd, strangely possessive sort of gesture, and unmistakable in the close quarters of the elevator. George smiled at him in a sweetly submissive way. *Different strokes for different folks,* but they were like gummy teenagers, so into each other that being around them made me feel uncomfortable, like I might have to wash my clothes after I got out of the elevator. When two people look like they can't wait another minute to get down on each other's bones, it doesn't matter if they are newlyweds from Sheboygan or two nuns from the Sisters of St. Francis, it can be awkward, particularly if you are trapped in an elevator with your own troubles and are trying to keep your mind off of pure, uncut, raw, naked sex. But Lefala didn't say anything, and so I figured it was just me, missing the affections of Julia, my lost pumpkin sweetie pie princess.

The elevator jolted to a halt at the top, a little disconcerting after our quick ascent. I looked over at Lafalla, but she simply shrugged and murmured, "A minor adjustment. We have someone coming to look at it."

She stumbled slightly, tripping over the hem of her Indian skirt as we got out of the elevator. She frowned and angrily wrapped the loose garment around her. It seemed like nearly anything annoyed her; hardly the temperament for a salesperson. We walked through the penthouse offices and out on the patio. As I'd hoped, the vista was one of those staggering cityscapes. I could visualize our filmic hero, Moroni, smiling his crazed smile as his helicopter rises past row after row of shining windows like a mechanical spider born out of an alien womb, and then spinning around as bullets started glancing off the metal frame and puncturing the bubble windscreen, nearly striking the lunatic pilot. Maybe I was catching Vinnie's enthusiasm for *big on the screen*, but visually this really was something special, and I was impressed enough to want to pencil in some dates and sign on the dotted line.

Jeff and George went off by themselves to perform god-knows-what-I-could-only-imagine in the empty office suites, and Lefala stayed patiently at my side and nodded or said agreeable nothings while I squinted through the fingers of my hands, which I shaped in the customary film director's rectangular frame. She was giving off the general impression that guys like me were really boring and even unpleasant to be around, but, for however long it took, she was there for me like the biblical Job sitting on his pile of offal.

"This is it, Lefala," I enthused. "We're going to do it." She forced a strained smile and nodded. "Yes," she said, "It will be very nice for you." She certainly wasn't one of those typical aggressive hard-sellers. "Where are the papers?" It was my experience that they were right at hand, and that in the next moment she would whip them out and press a pen between my fingers for a ready signature. But there was none of that with our gal Lefala. .

"You will call me when you wish to film," was all she said. She seemed distracted, as if her mind was on more important things. She carefully locked the doors to the penthouse and we made our way back to the elevators where Jeff and George waited. They looked a bit flushed and out of breath, but I thought I could understand how they got that way. We stood in a tight little group, waiting for our ride down.

The gong rang and the door opened…and I felt a sudden rush of horror.

As the client, I was up front, first in line to get on the elevator. But there was no warm and well-lit little compartment in front of me. In fact, there was nothing but a yawing black pit and a rush of cold air. I was standing on the lip of a deadly mineshaft, and the three of them were behind me. And then I felt a hand on the small of my back.

I may not have been quick as Tran Le in Dragonfly Madness, or even my hero Horace Keg in Keg's War, but I did manage to get completely turned around before Jeff yelled, "Allahu Akbar!"
He grabbed me by the front of my favorite Hawaiian shirt, the one with the clashing orange-and-pink hyacinths on it.
A deadly shoving match ensued. Unfortunately for the minions of Allah, George, who was also trying to shove me into the void, was actually getting somewhat in the way.
"Best regards from uncle Shamseen!" he managed to grunt.
Neither of them should have said anything, but people watch the movies too much. In cinema adventures, The Terminator and Rambo are always getting off snappy one-liners before they deliver the fateful blows. But you can ask any real life killer or assassin, they just don't do one-liners. Snappy dialogue sounds great, but even one-liners take too long, actually just long enough to give the other guy the edge.
Instead of frantically pushing back at Jeff as he expected, I gave him a brief little pull, just enough to get him moving toward me, and me moving away from the dark void of the elevator shaft, and then I collapsed to the floor, pulling him down on top of me. As he came down, I managed to ball up and get my feet between us. We were too close to the edge, and I figured we'd both go over, but there wasn't any choice. I straightened my legs and his own momentum carried him over me and out into the black open well of the elevator shaft.

"NO! Jeff!" George called hopelessly, arms stretched after his friend. Before George could gather his wits, I scrambled away from the brink and managed to kick him out as well.

I spun around toward Lefala, and barely got my arm up in time as she came at me with a high-strung cry of rage. I managed to deflect a down-thrust from the curved silver blade she swung at me. It was a pretty, ornamental dagger with a carved ivory handle, all in all over a foot in length, and it gave me a new appreciation for the flowing robes she wore. Joke as I might after the fact, I nearly was a gone goose. As it was, the dagger slashed through the pocket of my Hawaiian shirt, Lefala's hand stopping when the fabric held her fist bunched around the hilt. I managed to punch her in the face, but it was as if she felt nothing. The calm Lefala had been transformed into a mad woman.

"My children!!" She screamed like a banshee, pulling the knife free and renewing her attack on me with the blade raised and her other hand like a claw.

I dove sideways. You would have, too. I was just trying to get out of the way, but she tripped over my legs and went after her offspring, falling without a sound into the seemingly bottomless black pit of the shaft. Well, maybe not bottomless, I thought after a few seconds, as a dull thump reverberated back up the dark and empty void.

I quickly moved away from the open elevator doors. I was feeling shaky and uncertain about what I should do next. The thought didn't escape me that my ex-wife's agent, Horny Hiatt, had been thrown out of a high rise. Horace Keg's rule came to mind: *There were no coincidences*. This was probably the same unconventional hit team that had taken out Horny. I guess you could have hit squads that specialized in long falls of the fatal type. No reason why not. I'd have to talk to Vinnie about it. Maybe we could do a movie about them, call it *The Vertical Plungers*, or *Force of Gravity*. I was delirious, crazy with fear and near-panic. Time to take deep breaths and gather myself. *Was I not an advanced (and probably the world's only) student of the great Horace Keg, master of the warrior way?*

There was a shallow, six-inch vertical cut on my chest and only one button left on the front of my shirt. Not a lot of blood for all that, but I was going to need stitches. I walked to the end of the deserted hallway and found the stairwell. The door wasn't locked so I pushed my way through and sat on the top step. I was exhausted and out of breath, though the drain on my system was clearly more mental than physical. The entire encounter, violent as it was, couldn't have taken more than thirty seconds and yet I felt weak and tired, as if I'd run a fast and hilly 10 K race. This new brush with death brought everything back; the violence and abrupt ending of my previous encounters with Shamseen. My story sense was right— *Nothing had ended.* This was going to go on and on and on without end like the stories about that old mountain man Jeremiah Johnson, suffering his endless stream of violence as his Blackfoot enemies popped up out of their hiding places in the wilderness to come after him with their knives, guns and primitive traps. Somehow it was more entertaining when Liver Eating Johnson did it.
Still, I had to get going, and soon, if I was to get away. Common sense told me it wouldn't do to be anywhere in the building when somebody realized there were three dead bodies riding on top of their elevator. In my mind's eye I clearly visualized a movie scene in an elevator where blood begins dripping on somebody's

head as they ride up to the law officers of Spunk, Lunk and Spidora on their way back from lunch. They were probably eating a Huell Howser Dog from Pinks, and it's a moment before they realize the thick red goop dripping on the bun is coming from above and probably isn't Pink's special house brand chili.

I started my long walk down the stairwell to Vinnie's Explorer, which I'd left in the underground parking lot. I'd been in the building less than an hour, but it cost Vinnie $11. I didn't complain. I handed the attendant a twenty and reached a trembling hand to accept my change from the wizened old Chinaman who made the gate guard bar go up and down. One wrong move on his part and I was ready to smack him with a bottle of Mountain Spring Water or get out and run for my life. There I was, back to imagining assassins behind every flower pot.

I drove over to nearby Chinatown, where another ancient Oriental sewed up my chest while his assistant ran my shirt down the street to sew some buttons back on. The seamstress was out to lunch, so he returned with an aquamarine XXL t-shirt that shouted NEW CHINA WOK *The Lucky Seven Ways of Chicken.*

Once back at Berger Royal, it was as if I'd never left. Vinnie was staring morosely out the conference room windows that looked down at the everyday traffic coming in and out the main gates of the Raleigh Studios, while Marc Fraper, the Frickin' Frenchman, twirled his pencil and stared at the ceiling, undoubtedly thinking deeply artistic filmic abstractions.

I rushed in and shouted, "They tried to kill me!"

Vinnie raised his eyes at my t-shirt. "Which one of the ways is lucky for the chicken?" he asked.

"No! They tried to throw me down an elevator shaft!"

"Hey, I like it," Vinnie said, digging through the script in front of him. "What page is that?"

The little Frenchie shrugged and started leafing hopelessly through the thick sheaf of papers in front of him.

"No! No! NO!!" I shouted. "Real life. Real here, real now!"

Vinnie took one look at me and hooked me by the arm, steering me toward his inner office.

"One moment, Fraper...my associate here has had some hard times of late, and he's – not – quite – all together." These last few words coming as he tugged me along.

"What are you trying to do," he shouted the moment we were free and clear in the next room, "submarine us before we *get the Carnage going?"*

By now he'd closed the door behind us.

"Vinnie. Shamseen tried to kill me!"

"You seen him?"

"No, his people. They said so."

"Yeah, but you're alive—"

        "And they're not! Vinnie, I just killed three people!"

"What, you shoot them? Are you nuts? We don't need cops around here!"

"No, Vinnie! You're not listening! They came at me! They were going to kill me!" I pulled up my big t-shirt and showed him the bandages covering my 26 stitches.

"Yeah? That is impressive." His face bloomed with skepticism, "But, then how come you ain't dead?"

"They fell down the elevator shaft." True enough, even if I'd left out some of the pertinent details.

"Fell down an elevator shaft..." Vinnie repeated.

"Well, maybe I helped a little. Like the fight on the cliff." I didn't have to say any more. He picked up on

52

our shop talk right away.. The cliff fight was one of our kung fu memorable moments. In Berger Royal's own *Dragonfly Madness*, Brave Tran Le had been meditating on top of a small ledge above a shear cliff wall when he was attacked by a baker's dozen of the corrupt Harrigan Matre's thieves, and Tran Le had used his martial arts skills to dispatch twelve of them, except the one he let get away as a living example *Don't Mess With The Tran.* Maybe that's how I visualized the instinctive moves I'd made to send Lefala and her two young accomplices spinning into the void. Once again, life imitates art in the adventures of Hollywood Havoc. Except I hadn't let Lefala go as an example...on the other hand, she hadn't given me much choice in the matter, either.

"You mean that shit actually works?" Vinnie marveled, still trying to catch up.

"Vinnie, they're dead," I repeated. "Three of Shamseen's people. Because of me."

"Hey, I think that's self-defense."

"Anybody see you?"

No, I don't think so."

"I don't think you even have to report it."

That was Vinnie, interrupting my thoughts. I knew him like I knew my own father; he was already visualizing the courtroom scene where his innocent assistant is unjustly accused of Murder One.

"Vinnie, you are definitely not getting it! None of this is over! He's going to keep coming after us."

"You, you mean," Vinnie corrected me.

"Well, okay, me, then," I admitted. "Even though you and Batty Bertie stole his dump truck and wouldn't give it back."

"Cement truck," Vinnie corrected me again.

"My God, Vinnie, what does it matter?"

Vinnie sighed and scratched his forehead. "Yeah, I guess you're right," he muttered. For a few seconds he stared out the window. "Well, it's gotta be over," he said finally. "We got a picture to shoot. Come on, let's go back out and calm our little French pigeon." But when we opened the door and went back into the conference room, it was empty.

Vinnie glowered around the empty room, his eyes bulging in dismay. "Havoc," he growled, "If he don't come back, I'm going to fling you down that elevator shaft myself!"

CHAPTER 6

In the days following my latest run-in with the real dark forces of evil, the sun beamed down on us through the Southern California smog in its usual way. Marginally sanitary water ran from the faucets, expensive gasoline flowed from the pumps at the local Chevron station, and the general population of Southern California didn't become infected with mass mind-bot, at least that I could see.

Somehow, I didn't find any of that comforting. I ran about my life like a mouse in an open field with the hawks circling overhead. I was looking for bombs in the hat rack by my front door, assassins at the 7-11 where Batty Bertie had gone wandering in his PJs, and poison in my latte. Silly as it sounds, I varied my route in to the office, picking up my *grande percent latte* one time in Newport Beach on the Pacific Coast Highway, the next on McArthur Boulevard, and then on Jamboree, all different ways to get on the freeway heading north to Hollywood Flats. But, nothing silly as that happened, and a few days later Marc Fraper returned, looking as if nothing out of the ordinary had gone on. He said something about shifting a second packet of money into the Berger Royal accounts, and Vinnie liked that, so he was welcomed back with a big Berger bear hug.

I came in to Berger Royal a little late that day. First thing, I noticed the new receptionist, a flash-in-the-pan teenager who looked like she might pass for seventeen in poor lighting. She pouted at me and then went back to filing her nails. Then I noticed Marc Fraper. He was standing in the corridor to one side of the elevators, examining the thick slabs of glass that had our regal BR etched on them. This special thick glass served as the front entrance to our offices.

Marc jumped a little when he saw me. My approach had obviously disturbed some moment of deep Gallic thought, probably an insane new way Maroni, the seriously demented hero of *Carnage Days*, could off another dozen or so corrupt members of society before he climbed the top of the Mormon temple in Santa Monica to join the trumpeting angel who was his namesake. Nailing down that location was at the top of my list, but the Mormons were understandably reluctant. They probably didn't realize Vinnie would simply have me film from a truck on the base of the hill outside their massive iron gates, and we'd do our usual filmic tricks and matte Moroni in. Blue sky, blue screen, it made no difference to us.

"Hi, Marc," I said. "Sorry I interrupted the story meeting the other day."

He gave me a wan smile, and that dismissive wave of his royal hand that said it wasn't important in the mighty scope of the French Empire. .

"These doors?" he said, his accented English with its French lilt confusing whether he was asking, or perhaps was making a simple statement. Maybe that was how *la belle Francaise* rose to domination over most of Europe. *Conquest by confusion.* Maybe we could do a comedy about it. I had a sudden image of Marc Fraper as Napoleon, mounting his horse backwards. I would have to talk to Vinnie about it.

"The glass is so thick?" Marc continued.

I shook my head to get rid of the image of the little conqueror falling asleep in his split pea soup. "Vinnie's idea. He got them from *Crash & Burn*, a bank robbery heist flick we did about four years ago."

"How did it go, this *Crash-and-Burn* cinematic attempt?"

"That was an appropriate title—it crashed and burned all over the country. Bad timing; it came out the same week as two other caper flicks. Did pretty good in Manila, though, if I remember right. And Singapore wasn't bad. They love us in Singapore."

"And so Mr. Berger has bullet-proof glass on his doors?"

"Call him Vinnie or he'll think you're mad at him. And yes," I grinned. "We need such security because we are a vault of precious ideas. Come on. I think Vinnie's got some special donuts with raspberry filling. French pastries. He said they're specially for you, but we have to get there soon or he'll gnosh them all himself."

I supposed Marc had considered his options and decided to come back once he realized his funds were committed and he didn't have any choice other than to hang out with his filmmaker buddies at Berger Royal. By this time, he was firmly entrenched as Vinnie's new money partner, and there was no chance his funds were ever going to flow back to Northern Africa or wherever they'd come from..

It was an ordinary Tuesday morning and so he and Vinnie had to put up with my preproduction report. Marc nibbled gingerly at one of two raspberry pastries Vinnie had left for him. Both men sighed and yawned and scratched through my account of locations approved and crew and actors to be considered. In my own right, I have to confess I was stretching out my reports, dreading what would come next.

"How soon do we get to story session?" Vinnie asked impatiently, glancing at his watch as if he didn't have all day to get to his nooner with Gloria. By then it was mid-morning. Even in heavy traffic, it would take under an hour to get to his ranchette in Malibu where Gloria would be waiting. Still, I could see he was visualizing mud-and-rock slides on the Pacific Coast Highway, alternate routes snaking through Topanga Canyon and maybe even the horror of a looping round-about on the 405 to the 101 North, a detour of over sixty miles to get to his sweet hushpuppy.

"Right. Story," I said. "Well, the rest is just details. I guess we could start now." That made Vinnie happy for a couple of reasons; one of the minor details in my report that we now could overlook was the $11,000 for the repairs to his Bentley Sportster that he'd had me tuck away in *Portage & Incidental Expenses.*

I wasn't looking forward to *revisions unlimited,* but I couldn't think of any excuse to duck out. By this time I had come to realize that Fraper, pronounced Frapé, had a heavy hand when it came to story. Like a lot of amateurs—and almost every professional producer— he had tons of strong opinions about what worked and what didn't work in the movies. Worse, he had the bad habit of presenting his ideas in his questioning way, as if they were open to debate. I'd taken the bait a time or two and jumped right in, until I realized these questions had a tenacious quality about them. It wasn't long before I came to the understanding they were really more in the order of demands.

"Hey, why not we could have the Moroni character always dressed always in white?" he suggested.

By now, our story had, after a high-speed rolling Fraper flurry of suggestions, morphed into a wild and erratic tale about the adventures of a poor shlump of a guy who gets fired, dumped on and cheated on by his wife, humiliated and robbed by his friends, and who, under this sort of degrading social pressure, gradually takes on a life of crime and violence, escalating to bigger and more bloody adventures until the final scenes where justice triumphs and he is double-crossed and taken down by the same two-faced friends and associates who shaped him and caused him to rebel in the first place.   Hey, it could happen to anybody.

The story line of *Carnage Days* may seem familiar. In Hollywood, we tell each other there are really only seven different 'root' stories, as we self-righteously go about inventing variations of each other's ideas. I guess in most other places you'd call that stealing, or, putting it delicately, *white collar crime.* But we're a film factory; we've got mouths to feed, babies to put new shoes on, red Italian sports cars to lease, and the biggest maw of all is the production line.

One thing—the blood level was rising. Since Marc had come on board with his big pot of overseas money from sources that were still more than a little vague, the *Carnage Days* script was increasingly awash in a splattering crimson sea of gore. Marc loved blood. He referred to Bonnie and Clyde and The Godfather Trilogy as his ultimate references.

As far as I could tell, Vinnie didn't care that much one way or another. So long as Marc's money was real, he could play Mister Name-Above-The-Title all he wanted. `

Another thing—I don't think Vinnie really believed Shamseen was back in town, or, maybe he was thinking that if the grimly determined terrorist had actually made a reappearance, it didn't have anything to do with Berger Royal.

It wasn't that Vinnie thought I was a liar. He had a picture to make, and he pushed everything else to the back of his mind. The Shamseen that had been his and Batty Bertie's problem back when they stole Shamseen's deadly cement truck was gone. This new Shamseen was my problem, and me being Hollywood Havoc, I could handle it.

Of course, Vinnie didn't know I had skimmed the scammer, diverting a sweet little pot of several million dollars of Shamseen's money into my own offshore account. I figured not telling Vinnie was the safe way—after all, Shamseen might want it back, and he wouldn't be ecstatic to find out I'd gone partners with Berger Royal and blown his scam money on a slapstick Napoleon, or maybe some imitation *Paris Hilton Gone Bad* flick.

Anyway, Vinnie didn't need my money. My boss had run Marc's first check down to the bank and it had behaved gloriously like real money and so, for Vinnie, the good and happy times had begun to roll again. *Don't bother me with crazed assassins, Havoc, I got a picture to make.*

Unfortunately, this new money, which reportedly came through a Moroccan bank, not only put Marc on Vinnie's ever-shifting Best Buddy List, it gave him the status of *a big idea guy* around Berger Royal. If Marc ever was going to put his two cents in, the timing was perfect for him to be tossing off his brilliant *haut artistic a la Francaise* ideas. This was it for both men—that brief, sweet period after the money is committed and before the first frame of footage is shot. The little Frenchman and my fat, impulsive boss were in the honeymoon of their relationship, and Marc, our new idea boy-wonder, was making the most of it.

Vinnie liked *bigger* better than *big*, and he liked *biggest* best of all, and since red splatter was cheap, it looked like *Carnage Days* might actually live up to its title. *There will be blood.*

Moroni, in my opinion, was a sad sack of a hero. The guy was *our moron,* as the original writer had explained when he first pitched Vinnie his script two years ago but in an age that now seemed light years away. That original writer had had one or two "A" credits but he was a little strung out on coke at the time, desperate for a sale, and Vinnie had happily bought *Carnage Days* plenty on the cheap.

"I do not think your assistant is completely on board with my white clothing idea?" Marc said, giving me the unfriendly eye, but directing his comment in Vinnie's direction.

"Naw," Vinnie said, waving one chubby hand and talking around a mouthful of raspberry pastry, "It don't mean nothing. Havoc ain't been getting none lately. It makes him see illusions and act grumpy."

"Delusions," I said. I pointed one hand, dropped my thumb and shot Vinnie with a friendly finger. "Very vivid and real-looking. However, Marc, you do know that Moroni is also an angel in the Mormon religion, and dressing our hero in white could be misunderstood as—"

"Marvelous!" Marc interrupted. "*Tres Fantastique*! I did not know of that connection! How amazing the human mind works! The symbolism is incredible, don't you think?"

I didn't think it was, but it wasn't going to do me any good to say so. White suits were just another a goofy Fraper idea, like his symbolic notion that we should arm Moroni's Japanese gardeners with guns and knives so they could take back the land. But I could see Vinnie wasn't really paying attention.

"Bertrand actually does think the Mexicans are trying to take the land back," he said.

"You still talking to Bat-Brain Bertie?"

"Come on, Havoc, be nice," he gave me a devilish grin. "Bertrand wants to get into show biz."

"You come on, Vinnie—he's a crazy old coot. And you promised to lay off. "

"What of the white robes, yes?" Marc interrupted.

"Yeah, sure. Flowing robes. Very biblical," Vinnie said.

Truth be told, Vinnie didn't care one way or the other about any of Marc's new ideas. They were all just petty details. Vinnie's mind was ticking over like a smooth Jaguar V-12, running on idle with plenty of gas in the tank. It wasn't going to cost Berger Royal anything to put the moron in a white suit and who knows, maybe we would get lucky over in Hong Kong where *Carnage Days* was destined (or was it doomed?) to open. Maybe there would be some unknown oriental ritualistic mystique attached to men in white suits. One could always hope.

"And you'll leave Bertrand alone?" I insisted.

"I'll make sure your old fart pal don't get hurt," Vinnie said. "Now can we just concentrate on *Carnage Days*?"

Vinnie didn't like to pay writers for revisions, so the Coke-headed scribbler was long a thing of the past. I scratched a note to myself on the pad in front of me. As the master revisionist, I was going to have to take a few days to work through the script.

"How is Moroni going to do his secret ninja nighttime scenes in his brilliant white outfit?"

"Well, you have to solve that?" Marc demanded.

"Okay…how about he wears a special dark cape— only at night, for sneaking around?"

"I don't think a cape…?" Marc asked doubtfully.

"Sure, something romantic like Zorro or that French swordsman with the big nose.

"Oh, yes—brilliant, no?" Marc said.

That was my job, doing what I could to make everything stick together as much as humanly possible. It has to be done in pre-production. No matter what you've heard, you can't fix everything in editing.

"White suit, romantic black cape when needed. You want it, you got it," I said, looking across to double-check with Vinnie, who nodded happily. He sat there in his big producer's chair, feet on the desk, hands clasped over his big belly, beaming like some Jewish god of jovial good fortune. His XXXXL Hawaiian shirt was missing a few buttons in strategic places, and he had a big stain where he'd tried to rub out a gob of raspberry preserves…and not for the first time I felt like offering pennies and fruit and burning incense to the great one.

But I wasn't really giving it my all, either; I was doing the meeting by the numbers. After so many pictures, story continuity comes to be second nature. I think my lack of concentration was quite normal, after my realization that Shamseen Usudman was going to hold a grudge. And it didn't help that we were in our umpteenth script meeting. Although the record for Berger Royal scripting was somewhere over sixty meetings, the *Carnage Days* screenplay was getting rather plump and long in the tooth.

Let me explain: The so-called average Hollywood script runs between 114 and 117 pages. That's the way producers demand them, and that's the way the guys who make their living groveling in front of a keyboard write them. One of the first skills a young producer learns is to weigh a screenplay like a green melon and make the classic professional script judgment, "Feels a little light to me." With a little practice, it's easy to tell when any script is under 110 pages or over 120, but the trick never fails to zing the writer, and that's one of the ten commandments of good producing the Berger Royal Way, *Put the fruiting writer in his place from the get-go.* After all, as I've heard Vinnie say a thousand times, *Don't tell me I'm being insensitive. He's just the fricking scribe, Havoc. Writers don't got no frickin' feelings.*

Be that as it may, *Carnage Days* was now close to 140 pages, and Marc's new ideas were still coming in fast and furious. Of course, it was a writer's trick to squeeze the leading between the lines and nip a few pages out that way, but Marc hadn't been particularly nice to me and so I wasn't in the mood to do him any favors.

"Have you thought any more about that dune buggy stuff?" I asked.

The dune buggies army was also Marc's idea. He saw our shlumpy moron hero as somewhat charismatic, and at a key moment Moroni's string of rampages to right wrongs and avenge himself against his enemies—all broadcast in the customary manner on the nightly news—encourages the disenfranchised of Southern California, that is, the blacks, the Orientals and the Latinos, to launch a social revolution using dune buggies they steal from decadent surfers, muscle pumpers, in-line skaters and other perverted beach bums who hang out in Venice. So they could also *take back the land*, I guess, that Fraper somehow was convinced they once had owned. Maybe the only history Europeans studied was their own. He certainly had odd notions about ours.

Marc pursed his lips and frowned, mulling over the dune buggies.

"No, I think we take that back out?" Again, telling me what to do with a question.

"Whatever you and Vinnie decide," I said.

Vinnie shrugged. Marc's frown deepened. I knew Marc was having problems trying to figure out how to graft his great ideas into our script while making it look like they came somehow out of air, a classic technique for washing the hands at that later certain date when disaster struck. But since I had figured him out early on, I was making things as difficult as I could while seeming to agree with everything he said. Bottom line, while I knew a few tricks to hold him at bay in a story meeting, I couldn't figure out Marc Fraper, himself. He said he was a cinema buff, and that he'd worked on pictures before, but he didn't volunteer any titles or credits. I had IMDB-ed him, and I'd come up with nothing. Still, since he was footing the bill and the checks were clearing, I wasn't about to dynamite Vinnie's touchy new gold mine. At least, Marc looked the part of a film guy. He dressed French filmmaker chic, that is, in shiny black loafers, tight fitting black pants, a tight black T-shirt and a casually oversize black cashmere jacket. No socks, and I guessed, no underwear, and a lot of cologne. His hair was tricked up in the spiky Hollywood style of the day, an unfortunate look for him as it accentuated the deep recession in his hairline on both sides of his widow's peak. He was probably in his early forties, trying for ten years younger, and when he wasn't blasting away on his cell phone in whiny, nasal French, he kept at his hobby, adding his personal touches and enrichments to Carnage Days.

"Okay," he said, "We take it out then?"

"The dune buggie suicides were your idea, Marc. You decide."

65

"Well," he said, "Maybe we could take it out then?"
"Out it is," I said. Back down to 130 pages. Still
plump and ragged, but heading in the right direction.
*Too bad. Liberating the land would have gone over
well with the La Rasa crowd.* Of course, the
Rasanites weren't big film buffs. Too busy suing the
cops and rallying for their rights.

CHAPTER 7

I honestly was starting to believe our script meeting was going to stretch on into eternity, but my own cell phone sang out the happy little first chorus of The Bugs Bunny/Road Runner jingle (It's Cartoon Gold/ For young and old/ It's The Bugs Bunny/Road Runner Show/ The Bugs is Hot/ The Coyote is not/ And Road Runner's Go-Go-Go!). I flipped it open and the call was blessed relief in the form of my ex-wife Peanuts, of all people, who said she was on her way up in the elevator with Michael Blastowitz, her new agent. It wasn't like she asked, and she clicked off without waiting for an answer.

"You schedule a meeting with Peanuts?" I asked Vinnie.

"Nope. But it's always a pleasure to see her, if you know what I mean." He gave me his dirty producer's grin and did that feeling-wonderful-soft-round-things gesture with his hands.

"Well, she's on her way up."

"Who is zis Peanuts?" Marc said, giving us a frown that said *I'm an important French person and I am easily annoyed by interruptions*, and I guessed that was a real question.

"My ex-wife," I said.

"I think we should not interrupt—?" Marc began, but he stopped dead in his odd European speech pattern as Peanuts, also known as major Hollywood star Joy

Benefeté, walked in, trailed by a portly man with a perpetual frown stamped across his face. He looked like he could have been her last agent, the deceased Horny Hiatt's, older brother, but I knew he was no relation, other than he was another blood-sucking agent.

And this portly retainer was in turn followed by a small swarm of hustling photographers. Poetry in motion, Peanuts recently in from a film festival in Milano, a big signing at MGM or a meet of celebrities and spaghetti at Spagos, we'd find out all about her day on tomorrow's gossip shows.

The flashes blinked and winked as Vinnie rose and threw open his massive arms and Joy rushed into his embrace and laid her head against his chest like a long lost daughter.

"Joy, sweetheart, baby! Come to papa!" He smothered her hair with kisses. "I was so angry to hear about the Golden Globes! You was robbed, kiddo!"

My ex tossed her magnificent blond head of hair in a way so that every strand fell back perfectly in place, and gave him a brilliant 150-watt smile, "It was just a Globe, Vinnie. New York can keep it. This is an Oscar town."

Marc was nearly standing on tiptoe, all five and a half feet of impatience, waiting for his introduction.

"Oh, yeah," Vinnie said, "Marc Fraper. Vinnie pronounced it as he always did, to rhyme with clapper.

"Fraper", Marc corrected him with a little bow, pronouncing it ending in an "e" that sounded like an "a". *"Enchanté, mademoiselle."*

"Enchanted on this end too," Joy said, wrinkling her nose at me in a friendly way. She ignored Marc and turned back to Vinnie. I could smell something in the wind. Joy wasn't subtle in her wants, needs and demands, and it looked like she was going to be hitting up Berger Royal for something she wanted, needed and was about to demand.

"So, Sweetheart-baby…To what do we owe the honor?" Vinnie said, waving Joy and her new agent to the nearby sofa and collapsing back into his throne at the head of the big conference room table.

Peanuts let her agent gather dust on the sofa. She followed Vinnie and sat on the edge of the dark granite slab as close as she could get without actually sitting on his lap, and came out with it in a rush, "Vinnie. Sweet Vinnie, you've always been so good to me. Since *Intimate Remembrances*, I'm getting offers, darling—lots and lots of offers, and Michael here has some ideas and we've found something we want to do…but…" And here her voice broke with that pathetic little heartache sound of a woman in need. She left it hang there, and would have forever, but my gallant boss took her seemingly frail little hand in his giant, protective lion's paw and rushed right in.

"But what, Sweet Cakes? What? Anything. What can Daddy Berger do for you?"

"I need a loan, Vinnie—but it's not money."

"I didn't say it was, baby. Anything," he repeated, though he seemed reassured it wasn't actual cash.

"I have this little film, sort of a project I fell in love with, and I have to put up my own money to make it happen, and so it has to be perfect, and so I want you to loan me dear, sweet Mattie here to keep me out of trouble."

"Hey, why not?" Vinnie said, beaming proudly, "We're family here at Berger Royal."

"Oh, Vinnie, I knew you wouldn't let me down!" And with that she rushed into his arms for a hug to seal the deal.

Since they were carving me up like roast beef at Newport's famous Five Crowns Restaurant, I thought I'd better get my two cents in. As Horace Keg always says, *It's too late to moo once you're hamburger.*

"When's it start?" I asked.

Peanuts looked over at me with her sweetest smile, all pink hope and rosy invitation to the dance.

"Tomorrow," she said.

That set Vinnie back on his haunches. I could see his mind clicking around like a little hamster running on an exercise wheel.

"Well, wait a minute, sweetheart," he managed to sputter. "We're in pre-production on *Carnage Days*."

"When do you start?" she asked.

"I don't know, two months, maybe..." Vinnie shrugged. He looked at Marc, who was suddenly very interested in studying the shine on his nails.

"Maybe longer," I said. "Not before the absolute end of the rainy season, for sure. Too much outdoor stuff to risk it."

"Well, I guess that's okay, then," he grumbled. I could see he was feeling trapped, rushed and yet wanting everybody to know it had been his generous decision.

Joy beamed and kissed Vinnie on the forehead. "Oh, Vinnie, that will be perfect! We're ready to go right now. We'll be done in six weeks." She gathered her probably imitation but very smart handbag with the little LVs all over it, smiled at her court of followers, and headed for the door before the big man of Berger Royal could change his mind.

I already knew a little bit about the corner into which Joy had painted herself. Like everybody else, I'd read the story in the trades. Peanuts was riding in on a picture that had been ready to go, and then the female star had taken a fatal overdose of instant bliss and the show had gone into limbo. Joy had come along and showed an interest and just as suddenly the picture was back in the green light zone.

"I-I could perhaps help," Marc interjected hopefully, an abject lesson in the pathetic nature of blind optimism.

Peanuts gave him a look that would vaporize a potato at fifty yards. She had a hundred ways of saying no, and, believe me, I knew them all.

"Vinnie…" she pleaded.

He melted like the spring snow up at Mammoth Mountain when the first heat wave comes blistering through.. "Honey bubbles, I already said it was okay. It's up to numb-nuts, here." He gestured in my direction, in the traditional Vinnie Berger way, *pass the heat on to Havoc*.

"I'll let you know, Joy." I said. I'd already decided I wasn't going to do it. You know those romance movies where the sappy guy sacrifices himself three times for some glamourful but thoughtless babe, and the third time kills him and then they do a final scene where she realizes she's losing the love of her life. Well, that's the long way around to telling you, I'd saved her career by taking an early porno movie, *Anastasia in the Barnyard*, off the market, and saved her life a second time when the terrorists came after us. I'd kept count, and there was no way I intended to give her a third shot. Hell, after the way she'd sunk our marriage, I'd been reluctant from the get-go to save her the first time. But my ex never could read me. Or maybe she could, but her career kept getting in the way. Peanuts had stars in her eyes, and she couldn't see anything else for the glare.

"We'll send a driver to pick you up," she said

"Where's the shoot?" Vinnie asked.

Other people's shoots alternately bored him or made him jealous. He had no intentions of tagging along. I figured he wanted to know how far away I'd be when he needed me.

"Somewhere up north," she said. She was already breezing for the door. "Portland, Seattle, Vancouver, I always get them mixed up. At least it's not Canada." Ever since Marilyn Monroe, Hollywood loves Canada jokes. I have no idea why, it's a clubby attitude that has something to do with everything north of Studio City, Universal City and Burbank being nowhere, and, hence, nothing of significance in show biz. By the way, that includes San Francisco, which must drive George Lucas and Francis Ford crazy up there in Northern California with nothing but all their millions, and I suppose the same of the heavy hitters in the film business out of Toronto. Peanuts flashed me another smoky smile full of the usual promise, mischief and mystery, and then she was gone.

"*You* were married to *her*?" Fraper said, eyeing me like he couldn't understand how I'd gotten so lucky.

"It wasn't a good thing?" I asked.

"I do not understand you?," he said doubtfully.

"Must be the language barrier?" I said, giving him question for question.

Vinnie snorted back a laugh and shook his head.

"Havoc," he said, "It's been way too long. You gotta get laid, buddy."

"Abstinence makes him this way?" Marc asked.

"All that's about to change," Vinnie said. "He's going to come back from the wild and empty Northlands a changed man."

Vinnie was right, actually—and in more ways than he knew. But, let me not get ahead of the story. We put the dune-buggy riding ethnic avengers back in *Carnage Days*, then took them out, and then left them as an object for future discussion. Vinnie left for Malibu and Marc disappeared into the ether of his unknown personal life. I sat alone in the conference room, making notes and shuffling pages.

A few hours after our script meeting, I was still firm in my belief that a ticket North wasn't in my future. I was personally over and done with Madge Sacknall, who had been re-minted as Joy Benefeté by her old agent Horny Hiatt. Horny had also been dispatched by Shamseen Usudman, almost as a casual toss-off, just another casualty of terrorism. Joy had moved on and continued to prosper. She was known to the film-following universe as *America's favorite set,* but I knew her as the most ambitious, star-bound person I had ever known. And, with her talent, looks and body, she was going to get there. There was no way anybody could stop her. To paraphrase an old bit of wisdom about inevitability: The way you point your tits is the direction you will go.

CHAPTER 8

Making my way back down south to Newport from Hollywood on the 405 with drive-time traffic, I put on my favorite Bob Dylan CD, Time Out Of Mind. Bob was whining that, *while it wasn't dark yet, it was getting there,* traffic was heavy but not congested to a standstill, and all seemed right in the world. I was thinking of John D. Fool, Class B Detective in the great Moebius Incal trilogy, and wondering if all my heroes were whiners, and if so, what that said about me.

I missed my trusty Land Rover, but it was a vehicle of the past, *totaled by terrorists,* one might say. I'd been behind the wheel when I drove Peanuts, Shamseen and his accomplice off the Pacific Coast highway in a brief nosedive into the surf north of Malibu.. And since the Rover was a total loss, I had pretty much taken over on Vinnie's used (read, one-to-two year old, well-worn and battered) collection of Explorers and Expeditions, parked around the lot and at his ranchette in the Oak Tree area on Malibu Flats. He happily wrote them off to *Chop of Death* and bought a new big Expedition to take their place as his *ranch transportation. A car is just a car, right? That is, unless it was his beloved Bentley.*

Traffic was slow and Bob was going on and on about it until I began to wonder if the dark (whatever that was) would ever get there, and so I switched over to

Talk Radio 790 AM on the radio dial.   Larry Elder, the Sage of South Central, was up to his old tricks, the topic something about gun ownership, in which Larry was taking a serious pro stance. Lots of Rosie O'Donnell types, that is, righteous-sounding eco-libs, were calling in to take verbal potshots and Larry was mowing them down with equal doses of wit he learned from his Mom, common sense from his Pop and outright scorn that was his own unique take on any sort of foolishness that dared rear its ugly head.

I was replaying the recent scene with Peanuts over in my head; I didn't want her to go into one of her superstar rages when I turned her down. If the insider rumors around town were right, over the past several years since we'd parted ways, Joy had transmogrified herself into a self-possessed monster on the set of whatever picture she was starring in. Maybe it was just gossip and hype, but there was no way to be sure. Six weeks reporting to headstrong Joy Benefité in the soggy northlands might be as close to hell as I would get in this life.

So I wasn't paying attention when a low-slung black Honda Acura pulled up next to me, and a guy fired two slugs in my window.

At that moment, Larry had been quoting statistics that a big percentage of victims would never be victims if everybody carried their own piece. I was quietly agreeing with him in an idle, theoretic and therefore abstract way that suddenly became vivid and real as my driver's side window disappeared with a shattering crash. What I supposed was a bullet whipped by invisibly some inches in front of my nose and spider-scarred the window on the passenger side, exiting with deadly force on its way out.

I looked out the space where my window had been and recognized two of the bald-headed Hispanic punks that had been whaling on Marc Fraper when we first met him in front of Pinks hot dog stand. They were in a low-slung black Acura, one of the vehicles of choice for drive-bys. Both the bangers grinned madly up at me like we were all enjoying a big freeway shooting joke.

"How you like that, movie-bastard?!" The punk in the passenger seat yelled.

He had his arm out the window and was happily lining me up in his sights trying to bear down on me with what looked like a snub nosed .38 police special. Of course, he had to look up a little, him in the Honda and me riding high in Vinnie's SUV.

"Hey, catch *this*, baldy-brains!" I shouted back.

The happy times idiot-grin disappeared from his face as if by magic as I grabbed the handle of my army issue .45, jacked a round in the chamber and fired a shot out of my disappeared window in their direction. High speed target practice being the art it is, I managed to put a hole in their front fender. A bad miss, from my point of view, but Larry Elder was right, *The righteous should bear arms—their presence alone may be enough to discourage the bad guys.*

The Acura peeled left across three lanes of traffic, heading for the nearest exit.

A skinny, middle-aged guy in a white Buick LeSabre behind us had apparently seen the whole thing. He pulled up parallel to me, staring across the few feet that separated us. His eyes were wide, his mouth open.

I shrugged, looking across at him out my open window where the glass had been a few seconds before. To a guy just happening on the scene, I must have seemed the ultimate in cool, dismissing a drive-by shooting with a shrug. But I knew two things; first, the danger was past, and second, it was anything but

an ordinary drive-by incident. Somewhere, a small, well-knit man, with features resembling those of an ancient pharaoh, would shortly be cursing my good luck. *Hollywood Havoc lives to enjoy yet another day.* That night I stopped by for a carryout Indiana Jones Special Pizza from Papa John's. (Extra-large, three toppings, all for $13.99. I went for sausage, more sausage, and extra cheese.) When I got home, I slipped the cardboard box on warm in the oven, opened a late model bottle of Woodbridge Shiraz (by Robert Mondavi) and called up my dad's old spook-and-spy buddy Halliburton Rooks on the Black Box attached to my computer. The Shiraz hardly had time to age in the bottle, but at the way my luck was going, I didn't think I could afford to wait. I took a sip, set the glass on my desk and typed into the black room:
TWO TRIES AT MAKING ME DEAD.
There was no wait.
WE KNOW. SHAMSEEN IS BACK.

WHY ME?

FIRST, YOU FOILED FAT BOY. THEN, YOU KILLED HIS SISTER AND TWO NEPHEWS.

I DID WHAT?

LEFALA.

I didn't know how to respond to that. Rooks went on filling the blank screen

WE'RE TRYING TO NAIL HIM, BUT HE'S NOWHERE RIGHT NOW.

WHAT SHOULD I DO?

GO TO PORTLAND.

It seemed I had no secrets. I signed off with

HAVOC IN THE WEST

And then I took my now half-empty wineglass and went to the kitchen for the pizza.   It was a time when bad things kept happening, and all I could do was keep my chin tucked and my guard up. Even so, I don't think I was ready for the next body punch, and if I live to be a hundred I never will be.

As if on cue, as I opened the pizza and slipped out my first slice, I heard the approach of my crusty old neighbor on the gravel walkway. I was savoring that first cheesy, delicious bite when Bertrand more or less staggered in through the front door and threw a tattered letter on the table. The paper was a faded tan color and looked like it was made of cheap parchment, or maybe recycled newsprint.

"Julia sent this," he said. He'd stopped calling her my sweetie pie princess, now that she actually was, or more precisely, had been.

"Jesus, Bertrand, don't you ever knock?"

"Pizza," he said, reaching for two slices which he turned on each other and slapped together like a sandwich. He chewed off a huge mouthful, reached in my cabinet for a big milk glass and grabbed the bottle of Shiraz.

"How about some wine?" I asked rhetorically. I'd become expert at asking non-questions now that Marc Fraper was on board down at Berger Royal.

"Read the letter, idiot-boy," Bertrand said. He tried to hide it, but I could see he was crying. "I tried so hard," he blubbered, "but I failed with every one of them." He was talking about his two sons…and his granddaughter Julia. Even smudged as the letter was, I could see it was her handwriting.

In her urgently slanted penmanship, the letter informed the two of us that our fair Julia was joining an order of monks in the mountains of Southwestern China somewhere near Tibet. These monks, she said, had attained the highest blend of life and art through self-denial and special ritual cleansings. She would love Bertrand and me always, but this new life was a higher goal and she had to attain it. She hoped—no, she expected us—to understand, and she hoped to see us again in this life, and, if not, in the next.

"At least she loves us," I said, trying to hold back the feeling of numbness that was creeping in to paralyze my spirit. I'd always thought, hoped, dreamed that she would be coming back. And now, it seemed, she wasn't.

Bertrand looked at me like I was the crazy one. And in a way, I guess I was. *Crazy with love, overwhelmed with grief, maddened by loss, burdened with the sense of what might have been if I'd just been a little smarter.* I didn't say any more. Bertrand and I kicked a couple of chairs over to the kitchen table and sat there, silently gobbling pizza we didn't taste and guzzling the wine like it was water. After he left, I went to bed where I tossed and turned all night. I guess it was Vinnie's Way that came to save me in my deepest, darkest moment of despair. Vinnie's voice, somewhere in the back of my mind—*Come on, Havoc, get up off the floor, you got a picture to finish!* Bright and early the next morning, I made my way to the kitchen. There were still two slices of pizza on warm in the toaster oven. I yawned and cracked two eggs into my little plastic poacher, dropped a tablespoon of water on each, locked the lid and zapped them for sixty seconds in the microwave. Perfectly gooey poached eggs. I dumped them on the pizza and shook a sprinkle of Jamaican Pickapeppa sauce on top. Breakfast fit for a king. Miraculously, my batty old neighbor didn't show up, and I'd just about finished eating, when Peanuts' limo honked me.

What are you waiting for, Mister Big-time Hollywood Havoc? I asked myself. *There's nothing here for you any more, except maybe more freeway bullets or some other fancy form of extermination.*

"Hey, come in for a minute," I yelled out the front door.

"Why should I?" the limo driver yelled back.

"Cause I got latte and chocolate chip cookies," I shouted in a firm voice of command, grinning as he hopped out of the driver's seat. *Do I know the way to a limo driver's heart, or what?* I held him at bay with a home-made latte and a six-pack of Mrs. Fields finest, caught a quick shower, tossed on a set of production travel-ware and some hiking boots, grabbed my laptop and was ready to stagger out the door. It was a good thing I went, too, because, a few hours later the roof was blown off my condo by an explosion that took out the kitchen, along with my Thermador stovetop, the big, expensive Thermador 42 inch double oven, and my trusty-if-temperamental Rancilio Silvia espresso machine.

CHAPTER 9

It had been raining in Portland for months before
Peanuts and her crew arrived. It was still raining
when she got there, and a day later, when I arrived,
no big surprise, the rain was pelting down again. This
was good, as *Softly The Willows*, was a weather-
drenched relationships drama with over half the
scenes to be shot outdoors under wet skies...*Softly
The Willows*, the picture my ex-wife, known to my now
ex-girlfriend Julia as *The Ice Princess*, had bought
herself into as the female lead.
The production had camped itself in a small group of
log cabins a few miles east of Portland on the banks
of the Willamette River, a slow winding tributary of the
Columbia. Peanuts, confident I would say yes, had
provided me with a packet of information, and I read
the brochures on the plane trip up. The Willamette
Valley contains the fertile farmlands that once lured
pioneers to take the Oregon Trail. The river itself, just
wide enough to challenge a strong arm to throw a
rock across, begins in the mountains near Eugene
and winds north in a sluggish way to dump itself into
the Columbia River near Portland. After filming a few
babbling brooks in the High Sierras and some gang-
banger action sequences and car chases in and
around the concrete banks of the Los Angeles River, I
was impressed.

The log cabins along the scenic Willamette, I found, were nothing like the old split-log and chink variety. They were pre-fabricated in the normal 2x4 wood frame that was sheeted on the outside with plywood, and on the inside with sheet-rock wallboard. However, a thin veneer of what might pass for logs had been nailed in rough, rounded strips to the outer side of the plywood before they were coated in dark red-brown stain. And the roofs were done with genuine sod on top of plastic on top of the plywood, a bad idea as it was a leaky system with water coming at random through any of hundreds of nail holes, and no way to find or prevent them. Inside, the cabins were outfitted with modern conveniences like indoor plumbing, radiant heat and even small propane cooking stoves...but I learned on the first day to rig a canvas tarp over my bed, which made it a little bit like camping indoors. In real life, it was a quaint little cluster of cabins by the river, a tourist and summer vacation destination. However, as this was the soggy off-season, the production had been able to take it over at a very cheap rate.

A truculent taxi driver brought me over to from Portland International Airport to *Willer's Village,* as some wag at the local press had christened our temporary headquarters. *Willows...willers,* get it? No one seemed to be about when I arrived. My taxi driver was a sullen Pakistani who glowered at me from under his turban. I wondered if I   would have to kill him, and if he would then turn out to be another of Shamseen's relatives.

What?" I asked. "I don't eat pork."

"You Jewish, then," he spat out in disgust. "All moviemakers are Jews."

I paid him correct to the penny, and gave him a righteous look. "Tips are earned with civility, not religious conviction," I said.

He focused his angry gaze on me as he dumped my baggage in the deserted parking lot. Then he glared at me again and held out his hand. I shook it, thanking him politely.

"May your children be as many as grains of sand by the sea," I said. I guess that was some sort of tip, though I could see he wasn't taking it well.

For a moment I thought his face would burst with rage, but he managed to control himself, and he retreated to his driver's seat. Seeing he was wringing his hands clean from a bottle of Purell, I pulled out my own bottle of instant hand sanitizer and made a show of purifying my own essence. The look he gave me was one of pure hatred, and for a moment I wondered again if Shamseen had found a way to track me to Oregon. Maybe Shamseen himself had as many brothers and sisters as grains of sand. But, instead of popping me with an ancient musket from British colonial times, the surly fellow straightened his turban and drove off, leaving me to think about cultures in collision and man's inhumanity to man.

My arrival on the location of *Softly The Willows* was nothing resembling a triumphant moment. No marching band to greet me to the production, no high-hat dignitaries standing in the rain to hand me the key to the budget account. Just me, Hollywood Havoc, under my floppy Keg's War campaign hat, dripping alone in the quiet, steady rain. There seemed to be no other recourse, so I left my bags under an overhang fronting a locked and deserted building with a faded sign that read Office. I began slogging here and there through the elements, looking for some signs of life. It took five minutes, but the murmured sound of conversation and clink of eating utensils led me to a striped canvas circus tent that proved to be the cafeteria. Inside, I was greeted with the cool appraisal film crews reserve for new-guys-on-the-set. Peanuts and her support staff—makeup, hairdresser, and two assistants—had been driven via her stretch Hummer limo into Portland, and were nowhere around.

"They went for supplies," a grinning production assistant added vaguely. He was short and bald. He carried a plate of food in either hand, and looked impatient to be about his business.

"Well, I was told to be here for a meeting."

"Nobody's around," the guy shrugged, giving the less-than-grand interior of the tent a sweep with the plate he held in his left hand. They were having pork cutlets. A little of the gravy, which was of a grayish color and lumpy texture, slopped to the floor, narrowly missing my high-top hikers. I was glad I'd wolfed down a small pizza at the airport.

A slight girl with frizzy blond hair spoke up.

"Rags is in his cabin," she said. "Come on, I'll show you." That would be Rags Rogers, our director.

Her name was Norie. She was a student at nearby Reed College, and dressed in the accepted grunge manner popular at her school. That is, she looked as if she'd worn the same throw-on blouse and jeans for a week. Her impoverished-and-suffering student look was accompanied by a lingering odor that suggested bathing wasn't a very high priority, either, but she had a darting, inquisitive look about her, and beggars can't be choosers. I found myself wishing I could have gotten her to give my taxi driver a big, warm hug. She could have laid a sloppy gravy kiss on his cheek and told him all about the great pork chops she'd chowed down on. But, that's the Havoc way, ever too long to hold a grudge over the little, unimportant things.

Rag's cabin looked like every other in the long line facing the riverbank and looking out over the slow-moving grey waters of the Willamette, but Norie cheerily explained it was *The Director's Cabin.* She pointed to a small, makeshift wooden plaque on which someone had drawn a little megaphone.

"Made them up myself," Norie said proudly.

"Great with a can of paint, aren't you…Maybe you can put a clown on my cabin?" I asked in the Marc Frapper way, hoping to get some inkling of what my responsibilities might be. Peanuts, as always, hadn't been interested in giving out any details. *Maybe I was going to be the water boy. No, wait—there was plenty of water. Maybe the dry towels guy.* They already had a producer and a director, and I assumed they had an approved script, or they wouldn't be about to go into production.

Norie's smile broadened, "Just a pair of big, floppy clown shoes. Well, gotta go," she said, waggling the fingers of one hand at me and starting to turn back in the direction of the cafeteria tent. She seemed friendly enough, but my ploy for information didn't net me anything.

Something caught my eye, and I looked more closely at her face. "Wait. Is that a diamond attached to your cheek?

"Diamonique," she laughed. "Starving student, you know."

"And the stud goes all the way through?"

"Yeah. Sometimes I catch my tongue on it. Bummer."

I agreed it was, and, as the rain was beginning to pelt down, hurried toward the cabin with the sketch of the megaphone stapled on it. The door was half-open, so I made my way inside and introduced myself.

"Hi there, traveler from the distant homeland," Rags Rogers said. "Pull up a chair." He kicked one, moving it a few inches in my direction. He was slouched on a rustic Americana sofa, propped by a dozen or so pillows. He grinned up at me, seeming friendly enough. Everybody seemed friendly enough. Production people usually did, during the getting-to-know-you phase, before they figured out whether you were going to cut in on their territory, and, if so, how to fend you off and destroy you.

I'd heard about Rags from the trades and researched him on the internet. It's always good to know as much as you can about the director, because they're a little like postal workers—once you put one on the payroll, you're stuck for the duration, and they can make or break a picture. And, you know, from time to time they do go postal. In spite of all that, from what I'd found out, there was a good chance Rags was going to make *Softly The Willows* something special. He'd been a director of commercials out of Detroit, *the sheet metal business*, as he'd scornfully referred to it in an article in Cinema Today. He'd skillfully shaped his career, parlaying a series of shoots with a famous Ford Motor Company spokesperson and a few Motown music videos into his first feature, and after that he'd never looked back. Now in his early 40s, Rags sported an iconoclastic burnsides moustache and looked more like the Prince of Bismarck or an 1890's hardware store owner than a director of sensitive man-woman relationship pictures featuring just a hint of soft porn.

"Welcome on board," he said.

Other than a young girl Friday with long hair and a serious no-makeup look, we were alone in the director's cabin. The girl Friday sat in her own chair, frowning at a blank notepad in front of her.

"Glad I could come," I said, thinking he had no idea whatsoever just how glad I was to be out of LA, or, indeed, even to be alive. "When do we start?"

"That's up to you," he said. "Want a soda-pop? We've got Diet Coke, Sprite, Root Beer, and Ginger Ale."

"Coke would be nice."

Up to me, he'd said. The plot thickened. The easy way would be to admit I didn't know why I was here or what I was supposed to be doing. But I'm Hollywood Havoc. I don't ever take the easy way.

Rags raised his eyebrows at girl Friday. She glared at me and huffed out of the cabin to get my drink of choice.

"Good help is hard to find," he grinned at me.

Now would be a good time to ask the important question straight up. But, as I usually did, I chose to hedge around it.

"I guess I'm here to help out Joy…?" I left it hang in the air in the classic Marc Fraper manner.   Just another bad habit to add to the Havoc repertory.

"Right. You are. To work on the script."

"Where is it?" I asked.

"Here," he said. I was expecting the usual brass brad bound 118 pages, but what came flying at me was a book.   A hardbound copy of *Softly the Willows* by Miriad Breech.

"This is a book," I said, stating the obvious.

"It's a story," he said. "We bought a story. Classic love story. Simple. Beautiful. Perfect for Joy Benefeté. She will win a Globe for this one…we both will."

"But…where's the script?"

"God's sake, man, didn't your agent tell you anything?"

I examined the cover with its picture of two lovers romantically entwined under a graceful sweep of willows, grey river waters running appropriately in the background. I was stalling for time, and the drawing wasn't that unusual or interesting.

"I don't have an agent," I said finally. "I came here as a favor to my ex-wife."

Girl Friday chose that moment to come back with my Diet Coke and a Crystal Geyser bottled water for herself. The way she stared at me, I couldn't tell if she was more astonished that Joy had been my wife or that I didn't have an agent.

"You're writing the script, Havoc," Rags said. "We've had a dozen scripts, but they're all crap."

It wasn't unheard of. At Berger Royal we were famous for shooting on the run. But we shot the type of pictures where you can get away with it. I opened the novel and started to leaf through it, as if I hadn't read it before. The silence lengthened between us.

Softly the Willows was one of a horde of me-too touchy-feely romance books that followed the success of The Bridges of Madison County. You could say Bridges was responsible for a whole new category of books, a whole new aisle in the bookstores. *Talk about lemmings off a cliff!* Where was craggy, iconoclastic old Hemingway when we needed him? I thought Miriad Breech was an excellent writer, though maybe somewhat a dog of the craft, following wherever his nose told him the publishers and their shallow, craven editors were feeding that season. But then, I can be a little cynical…and (I could almost hear my departed sweetie pie princess Julia's scornful whisper in my ear) who was I to talk, anyway? *Why don't you give*

them a quote from Keg's War or Dragonfly Madness?
There were times when Julia could really be cruel.
Not that it mattered, but Miriad Breech wasn't his real
name, either. He'd written batches of books in so
many different genres and under so many different
nom de plumes nobody was sure what his name was.
I should be so lucky.

But, back to the business at hand. Here I was,
Diet Coke in hand, sitting next to a bucket into which
water plinked at a rate of one drop every two seconds
and my director Rags Rogers was eyeing me
expectantly.

"You got money problems?" I asked.

"Yeah," he admitted. "Big time. *Softly the
Willows* was in development for years before I came
on board. It kicked around from studio to Studio."

` "Miriad Breech get a million?"

` "Two," he grimaced. "With another four million
tacked on."

I knew how that went. *Softly the Willows* had
bounced around from studio to studio, each adding
their expenses plus a little extra greed money. You
may think making movies is an art, but, on the most
basic level, it isn't. *It's just business.* All those
expenses were tied on like lead weights before the
project was allowed to drift on to the next batch of
show biz thieves. That, plus the top dollars the big-
name actors were knocking down, meant there was
less and less money to spread around to the rest of
the people who actually had to make the movie.

"*Softly the Willows* is in its final gasp here,"
Rags said. "This picture gets born here and now, or
not ever."

I nodded my head in understanding. The
ballooning expenses would snuff any reasonable
possibility the picture could turn a profit, and at that

stage, many viable projects simply drifted into limbo and never reached the silver screen. *Ever wonder why Scott Turow's Pleading Guilty never made it? The last time I looked, it had been cut loose from Universal with a dead weight of six-and-a-half million in preproduction fees tacked onto it.* Or, how about some of Stephen King or John Grisham's best sellers you know would be sure-fire box office hits? *Same thing, my innocent young movie-goer friend.*
As a Hollywood insider, I myself had watched it happen a few times before. Not at Berger Royal, true enough, but to people in the business that we knew. Vinnie was too smart to pay for development costs he knew he would have to incur all over, anyway. He'd simply pass and get one of his writers or me to do an unrepentant knock-off, or even better, start from scratch with one of his own ideas.

As Rags had warned, *Softly the Willows* was in its final gasp; the picture would be born here and now... or the ballooning expenses would snuff the reasonable possibility that it could turn a profit, in which case it would drift into limbo and never reach the silver screen. The only reason it had been given this one last shot was my ex-wife's thirst to be recognized for something other than the luminosity and lift of her tits.

"Why don't you use one of the scripts you have as a starting point?" I asked, indicating the batch of screenplay manuscripts all carefully laid out on his desk.

"Assholes," he said, answering my question. "Writers are all assholes."

He saw the corner into which he'd painted himself. "You aren't a writer," he said. "You are a film person who knows how to write."

"I know," I grinned, letting him off the hook. *Just call me easy.* I figured I'd dance to many a tune sung by Rags Rogers and Joy Benefité before I could escape back to L.A., probably just in time for another round of bullets and bombs. "Okaaay….What is it you want, exactly, Rags?"

"Just adapt the damn book," he said. "It's all there. Don't give me nihilistic bullshit, don't give me space aliens or dark forces or political statements. And please, don't give me your own interpretation of the meaning of life. *Softly the Willows* is a romance."

"Sure," I said. "Two people. Passion. Fire on the screen. "

"Yeah, that's it," he said, with a faint spark of hope showing on his noble Prussian features. He looked very tired, like he'd been talking about this forever and nobody understood him. "I need three to five good pages a day. You can do it, right?"

"Shoot page-for-page, the way it's written?" That was the most serious question I would ask him. Hollywood producers force directors to bunch similar shots in the same location, destroying any natural sense of continuity for the director and the actors in favor of the obvious cost savings. Shooting all the scenes in the entire movie that involve any one setup saves a ton of time and hence money, but it wears on directors because they have to carry the mood and tone of the picture in their head. And it confuses actors, who lose their groove and have to struggle to be more than models or talking heads. *Am I pissed off with her in this scene because she's such a bitch, or is this after we've found each other's inner essence?* The practice of shooting out of sequence is one reason Hollywood actors love to do stage plays, the chance to do what is known as *real acting*. But, *Praise the Lord*, Rag's Rogers wasn't going to shoot

91

out of sequence. And with his looming overhead problems, that took guts.

"Page-for-page," he murmured contentedly, with a hint of the devil in his grin.

"You're my hero," I said. "I can do it if you can."

"Fine. Gretchen here will set you up. This is the Director's Cabin. You get the Writer's Cabin."

I nodded, and got up to leave. Gretchen, assigned to show me the way, led me out the door. As we slipped outside into the rain, I tapped the sign with the megaphone.

"Is my cabin the one with floppy clown boots on it?" She gave me a look of total disgust, and I had the sudden illumination that one of the rejected scripts on Rag's desk was hers. *Hollywood Havoc knows these things.*

"We use Final Draft," she said, referring to the software I'd use to write my script. But it seemed a delaying tactic, like she was reminding Rags our conversation wasn't yet over. She was holding the door open, and hadn't left the room, and I got the feeling I wasn't supposed to go yet, either.

"I have Final Draft," I said, grateful for the look of disappointment spreading over her face.

"Rags…" she said, reminding him of some distasteful task yet to be performed.

"Oh, one other thing…" Rags said, his voice carrying past the still-open door. He sounded a little hesitant for the first time.

I ducked back inside, grateful for a respite from the rain.

"And that would be what…?" I asked.

"I'll be sleeping with our star," he said.

"Jesus, Rags," Gretchen snapped over my shoulder. "Can't you be a little more tactful? She was his wife, for God's sake."

Her being behind me, it was easy to hide my grin. *It's always clear on location who resents not getting any.*

Rags was waiting for my answer. I shrugged, "Suit yourself. That's not my affair."

"I just thought I might be doing right to bring it up…" he groped for words, "…I mean, you were married…"

"Does Joy know?" I asked.

"Rags always sleeps with the star," Gretchen said with a touch of her own dogged weariness in her voice. "It helps him stay tuned to his inner ear on the film."

"Joy can be a piece of work," I said, ignoring Gretchen while raising a warning eyebrow to Rags.

"Ohh." He thought about it for a beat. "Then, you're recommending…?" He left his question hang in the air. I was starting to get the feeling that the many Marc Fraper ways of asking questions had somehow mysteriously seeped into the film community at large.

It was an odd moment and when I saw that he was asking for my honest opinion I appreciated Rags for the second time that day. More than your ordinary Hollywood con artist or slickster-turned-director, he wanted to know what effect I thought a roll in the sack with my ex-wife would have on *Softly The Willows.*

"The picture *uber allis,*" I said. *Put the picture first.*

He seemed to want more, so I continued, "On the one hand, she's got a lot of talent. At least, that's my opinion. On the other, Joy's also a very needy person. I found out that, once she got me between her legs, she felt she didn't really need me any more. After that, things get tough."

"How so?"

"Maybe it will be different for you, but I never felt I got a good performance out of her once we went to bed together. After that, she was just a bitch, out of control most of the time."

"You're just saying you couldn't handle her," Gretchen said. "She's an actress. She'll respond to a stronger director."

I shrugged. I wasn't going to get into a pissing match with a feminist lackey.

"Maybe that's true," I said, trying for agreeable. "I certainly could be wrong. The time I'm talking about was just after she signed with Horny Hiatt and she and I were drifting apart and a lot of things were very confusing."

Rags nodded, but asked one more time, "How so? Her performance, I mean."

"Generally over the top. Once she has you, she tends to take the bit between the teeth. I mean, speaking like a director, I think that's more typical than not. But that's when you need your distance."

"And how do you recommend I avoid this…ah, problem?"

I shrugged. "Give her to our leading man."

"He's gay," Gretchen said with a sour smile.

"How about you? You care to volunteer?" Rags suggested.

"Oh, sure," Gretchen snorted. "Make him just another sex slave. After all, he's only the writer."

"Me? Take on Peanuts again?" In spite of Vinnie's joking around before I'd left for Portland, I didn't have to mull over the possibility. "I don't think so." I sang a famous line of doggerel from the old *Way, Way Down East* melodrama, *No, no, a thousand times no—I'd rather die than say yes.* You see, I've already done my time."

94

"You call her Peanuts?" Rags asked.

"Before the implants," Gretchen said with a knowing nod of feminist superiority.

"No, Gretchen," I corrected her. "Joy just likes peanuts. Actually, she eats them, shells and all. Her mother claimed they were good for the digestive tract."

Gretchen snorted again, this time a bit louder, like that was the stupidest thing she'd ever heard, but Rags took it seriously.

"Oh. Well, anyway, thank you for talking it over," he said, nodding thoughtfully.

"Sure. You might get Gretchen here to lay in a few cases of salted jumbos. Like the kind they throw around at Dodger games."

"Make a note of that, Gretch."

"Sure," she said through gritted teeth.

"Get the ones they throw in the stands at Wrigley Field in Chicago," I added, not wanting to let a good moment slide by. "Those are her favorites."

Once again we made our way out the door and Gretchen silently led me through the rain down a short gravel walkway to my cabin.

"Yeah, here it is," I said, recognizing it by the little sign with a sketch of a pencil and a pad of paper. I walked in and Gretchen barged right in after.

"Oh, sure, come on in," I said. "Rude of me not to invite you."

Somehow my luggage had arrived before me and stood dripping and in the way. I walked around it. I kicked off my shoes and lay down on the bed. I cracked open the book while the grim lady bustled about making sure I had towels, bottled water, a basket full of candy bars, and note pads with our *Softly The Willows* logo on top. All the little things producers and directors think script writers need on location to keep them away from drugs and booze. Everything, in fact, but the legendary bolted lock on the door.

I'd had a long day and I couldn't seem to get past the first paragraph without my mind drifting. The writing was flowery and romantic, and I started feel sleepy. I gave out a huge yawn and put the book over my eyes like a little tent.

"You better get to work," Gretchen said. "Call is tomorrow at eight."

"I am working," I told her. "I'm absorbing the story directly into my brain. Close the door on your way out so it doesn't hit you in the butt."

She yanked it shut with what I considered undue prejudice. Once her angry footfalls faded, I jumped to my feet and set up shop on a small table next to the bed. I'd read *Softly The Willows* when I'd heard Peanuts had bought in on the movie, and again on the plane ride north. It wasn't very long, and I've always had an ear for dialogue. I figured it was going to be a piece of cake. By now, Gretchen would be angrily yelling at our director that his brand new prize writer had already fallen asleep on the job.

I opened my laptop, sat down in the hard, straight wooden chair thoughtfully selected to not allow the writer to get too comfortable, typed the obligatory FADE IN ON, and started to bang out the first scene. Miriad Breech had written the book in bold strokes, in many respects clean and simple like a screenplay had to be, and I knew one of the rejected screenplays on Rags' desk was *penned by the author, himself*. That made me wonder where Breech had fallen off the turnip truck. I guessed, in working backwards from the screenplay to the novel he'd had lots of great ideas, but had never bothered to go back and incorporate them in the retro. *Still, that had been his problem, and it certainly wasn't mine.* Another of the maxims at Berger Royal; nothing's sacred. I worked through dinner and before I knocked off at ten o'clock that night. I had hammered out the first shoot day and was three pages ahead into the next, subject of course to Rags approval. *Of course he would approve them. How could he not?*

CHAPTER 10

Gretchen reminded me with a brief and surly phone message at midnight, the morning's call was for eight o'clock.

"Yeah…right…" I yawned.

"You're not in bed?" she yelped.

"Yeah…sleeping…at least, I was…"

"What about the script?!"

"We professionals don't worry about that sort of thing," I said, and hung up on her.

It was seven o'clock when I showered and threw on an outfit more appropriate for the Moroccan desert than the rain that was continuing to fall on the Willamette plain, rain sluicing down in sheets as if it would never end. I tied a garish cotton bandanna around my neck and tucked it in my tan shirt in the manner affected by 17th century dandies, by a certain segment of the gay crowd to indicate they are randy and available, and by a few writers trying to dress like Hemingway might have in his glory days after Paris and before the big C took him down. And then I ran over to the Director's Cabin.

Gretchen was already there, eyeing me like a bright-eyed sparrow.

"Where are your pages?" she asked in her tight-lipped way, her eyes flicking to Rags and then back to me.

"Rags already has them," I said. "I slipped them under his door last night."

She gave Rags, in turn, a scowl that deepened as he tried to explain. .

 "Gretchen, they're fine." He spread his arms wide in a conciliatory gesture, "Everything's fine. They were there when I woke up this morning, under the door. They're great. Mike Coaly had them printed up and he's distributing them to the cast and crew."

"But I am your assistant…"

"So is Mike, Gretchen. And we couldn't wait while you did your nails, or whatever."

"I am your *personal* assistant!" Her voice went up a notch

"Mike is my AD, that stands for Assistant Director, remember? You truly are my personal assistant, Gretchen. You get me stuff like booze and Washington Delicious apples and blow jobs, when I need them."

She gave us both a look of pure hatred, and stormed out of the cabin. I knew Mike Coaly was only a 2nd Assistant Director, and if he was ahead of Gretchen on the pecking order, that made her very low, indeed.

"I wish she'd stop doing that," Rags said.

"Bitching?"

"Naw, she'll always bitch. I mean, giving me that look of pure evil."

"Think she'll quit?" I asked.

"I've been hoping," he said. "So far, no luck."

       The first morning's shoot went off without a hitch. There were some moody establish shots and a little bit of dialogue that established Joy's character, the fragile and yet indomitable Amanda Smythe. It was interesting to watch Peanuts playing *fragile.* I had to admit, and not for the first time, that my ex-wife had talent. That never ceased to amaze me, even though all of Hollywood and anybody who watched Extra Extra knew she'd fooled me for years.

It was noon break and we were huddled away from the worst of the wind and rain in the cafeteria tent when my cell phone gave out its familiar signature call, *Here we go/ With fun in tow..."*

"I'll save your chicken noodle soup for you," Rags grinned.

"Don't bother." I gave him a grimace and headed for the overhang flap outside the front entrance.

Bertrand Berke's voice boomed in my ear.

"Sneaky bastards blew up your kitchen," he roared.

"You don't have to shout, Bertrand," I complained, massaging my injured eardrum. "What sneaky bastards?

"How do I know?" he argued. "They was sneaky. Took out your roof, just a hole up there where you can see the sky. And the whole thing burned some before the firemen came and got water and foam on it."

"My God..." I murmured. "Are you okay?"

"Don't use the name of the Lord in vain, Matthew," my old neighbor instructed, "Of course I'm fine."

"What happened?"

"It was exciting," the old Bat-Brains exclaimed happily. "Fire department came caterwauling and blasting their horns. Three trucks, could barely squeeze past themselves in their joy to get up our hill. You got soppy water and crap everywhere."

"My manuscript!"

"Loose sheets everywhere, like a paper storm."

"Don't let them throw anything out!"

"I know, I know," Bertrand said, in an off-handed way. "What, you think I'm daffy?" He went on before I could answer that one, "But you got bigger fish to fry, Matthew. The Condo Committee's on you like birds on dead meat." This couldn't be good news. Our CC at Sea Garden Cove was the closest thing to living under a communist dictatorship that I could imagine.

"What do they want?" I asked with a sinking feeling.

"They want to tear you down and build a little day care center for working mothers."

"Christ, I don't want that!"

"Me neither," Bertrand agreed. "A horde of yapping little bastards right next door to my place? No thank you! Them women got to resist their lust-urges if they want to rise through the glass cylinder in the working force."

"That's a little confusing, Bertrand, but I think I understand…"

"Don't you worry none about it, Matthew!" he bellowed into the phone. "Them stinking commie-bastard societal engineer-mongers ain't going to tell Bertrand Berke or his friends what to do!"

He hung up, leaving me with a thousand questions and half a shoot day yet to get into the can. *Societal engineers*…Bertrand must have been snagging my copies of New Yorker Magazine again. I once caught him at it, and he said he liked the cartoons. Of course, over the years he'd said the same thing about Playboy.

Rags came out of the red-and-white striped cafeteria tent carrying a Styrofoam cup.

"Tomato soup," he said. "It's not half bad." He gave me a sharper look, "What's up? You look like you've seen a ghost."

"I almost *was* one. Somebody blew up my condo."

"Huh. You sure it wasn't a gas leak?"

I gave him an appraising look. He had enough on his mind without having to worry about my unbelievable run.

"Well, yeah. That was probably it."

I didn't say any more. We had lots of work to do before we could wrap for the evening..

In spite of the interruption, the afternoon's shoot went off without a hitch. My problems in L.A. were a world away, and I pushed them to the back of my mind. And by the time Rags called it quits for the night I could see things were going to work out okay between the director and his writer. He gave me a nod and said, "Good stuff, Havoc." That's all that any writer on set can ever ask for, and more than most ever get.

There were times over the next days and weeks when Rags got close, but he never caught up to me until the day he finished his last scene, which was two days before we wrapped the shoot. That's because I learned my craft in the Vinnie Berger School of Screenplay Writing where Vinnie's motto was. *No ego, no bullshit, just turn out them pages, you frickin' monkey writer.*

It was two days before Bertrand called again. I checked my Goofy alarm clock and the hands said it was six in the morning. We'd done some night-for-night and hadn't broken until midnight. The morning call wasn't until nine, and so I was still in bed.

Caller ID said it was my old neighbor, so I propped myself up with an extra pillow and held the phone six inches from my ear, "What, Bertrand, what?"

"Cranky, aren't we? What, partying late last night with them starlets running around with no panties on?"

"I wish. We worked last night. What's happening, Bertrand?"

"Condo committee brought in a big orange bulldozer to knock your place down. Them pinko bastards declared eminent domain."

"God, they could do that?"

That news shot me right out of bed. I began pacing up and down, a few steps each way in the narrow little cabin, as Bertrand continued his narration.

"Well, no," he said. "I didn't think so, neither, until I actually seen that big, rusty bulldozer with the whites of my own eyes."

"How did they get it up the hill?"

"Clanked right up the road. Made marks right in the asphalt. Even tore it up a little. Committee didn't think of that!"

"So they knocked down my place?"

"Course not. I rammed the sneaky bastards with my Cadillac, that's what! Right in the side. Snapped one of them crawly-tread things. Lucky thing for you, too. Your boss didn't get here for an hour."

"You got Vinnie involved?"

"Yup," Old Bertie chuckled, the pride evident in his voice. "Vinnie's lawyers slapped a big law suit on the commie bastards!"

"What should I do? Should I come down there?"

"Naw. We got the snakes on the run now. Vinnie's pulled together some of his boys. The place is already cleaned up and he's got framers coming in later today. Don't you worry about nothing, Matthew. Living next to you is bad enough, but I'm not putting up with no nest of squalling rug rats."

"Thanks," I said. Then I had another thought, "…Bertrand, what about my papers?"

"Drying 'em with a hair dryer. You sure use a lot of words nobody ever heard of. That better be a best-seller. Paper and notes and crap all over my garage. Got your computer, too." There was a faint clattering noise from the other end of the phone. "Gotta go," my neighbor said, "Here comes Vinnie's crane up the hill." And with that he cut off.

I clicked my phone shut and tried to imagine Old Bertie shaking his fist out the driver's side window as he held off a bulldozer with his prized Cadillac.

All that going on down south, and yet, day after day, I managed to crank out the pages for Rags and Peanuts. For a while, Joy left me to my own devices. We were three weeks into the shoot before she came storming into my Writers Cabin.

"Rags won't sleep with me!" she shouted. She flopped onto my sofa bed without bothering to say hello. "And it's all your fault!"

"You have an exquisite sense of timing," I said.

"What?" She looked puzzled. My ex-wife was a little like a freight train, very impressive once she built up speed, but, at the same time, easily derailed.

"You generally show up when there is food or drink on hand. Not any food. Just the right food." I handed her a *café au lait*. "Perfectly made," I added with a note of pride in my voice.

"Where did you get that?" She was staring in amazement at my large silver espresso maker.

"I bought it. It is a Rancilio Silvia. The brochure says it has one of the biggest boilers in the consumer marketplace. What do you think?"

"Isn't it a little—big?"

I could see her point. The gleaming machine did take up most of my little table.

"Well, yes," I said, "but it doesn't get in the way much as all I do is write and sleep here. Have a chocolate chip cookie?"

"I shouldn't. I'm really mad at you."

"Mrs. Fields," I tempted her. "Shipped in special."

She eyed me, already wondering why she'd come in, and then snatched a cookie. While she nibbled and sipped I began fumbling to make a new cup for myself.

"I've already stopped the toilets up twice with espresso grounds," I said. "I learned I have to dump them in my garbage can."

"You have a special garbage can for your coffee grounds?"

"Sure. Bought one," I said. Her gaze wandered to take in the stainless steel cylinder standing on the floor next to the espresso maker.

"Stick to the point!" she snapped as she remembered why she'd come storming over in the first place. "Since when do you stick your nose in my personal, private affairs?"

"Too often, I'm afraid." We looked at each other, both thinking about *Anastasia In The Barnyard*, the Triple-X film from which I'd recently rescued her. My nemesis, Shamseen Usudman, had threatened to release it, in an attempt to blackmail Joy and get to me. But I'd managed to buy the master and get control of the rights, using Usudman's money, actions which had helped earn me his undying hatred. As Joy remembered, her face reddened and she looked down at her *café au lait*. It took a moment, but then she shook it off. She wasn't going to let our current situation go.

"I'm talking about Rags!"

"Our fine director? By now I thought he'd be putty in your hands."

"Gretchen says you warned him not to sleep with me!"

"She hit on you yet?" I asked, raising one eyebrow.

"What-?" Another derailment. "You don't mean she's a—a buttercup?" My ex-wife's vocabulary swung from Truckstop City to the nunnery, with very little in between.

"I didn't say that." I threw my arms wide, "Look, Joy. You didn't hear it from me." I came over to the sofa and sat down beside her.

"The dailies look terrific, Peanuts," I said. "And you look terrific in them. You were right to go for this picture. It's going to be a huge step for you; you're going to prove *Intimate Remembrances* wasn't just a fluke."

She looked flushed and pleased; she wasn't used to such glowing praise from me.

"I don't understand you…"

"You're in the zone, pal. The vibes are right. You've got it going your way."

"You really think so?" I knew Joy. The only thing in the world more important than sex was how she looked in the dailies. Actresses need reassurance even more than writers. .

"Everything is right, Joy. And it's because of you. You've got it down. Nailed. You are Amanda Smythe, and America is going to love you. Four more weeks, Peanuts. Hang in there, just stay in the groove."

By now I had her by the arm and was leading her to the door.

"You can do this, Joy." I turned the knob and held the door open for her, "I've got pages to do. That damn Rags is good, but he'll never catch up."

A slow smile crossed her face, like we were sharing a secret. And, in a way, as two alums of Vinnie's Shop, we were.

"The Berger Royal School of Writing," she said.

I grinned back, admitting it. "Damn straight. *You vill get those pages done.* Now beat it. And make sure I get that coffee cup back."

And that's how it went. Joy would put up with her lack of personal attention from the director for two or three days and come at me, all howl and claws. I would put a latte in her hand, stick her back together and send her on her way. Praise and espresso were my weapons, my putty, tape and glue, and it worked like a charm. Of course, it helped a lot that most of my flattery was true—she had found the heart of her character and looked golden on the screen. Cher had left Sonny, Barbra had left Elliott and Peanuts had left me, and all three women were the better for it.

Somewhere in all that fluff going on with *Softly The Willows*, Vinnie called.

"We got your roof back on," he said. "Your insurance is paying a bunch and *Carnage Days* is picking up the rest."

"Marc Fraper approve that?"

"Fraper-the-Clapper don't know nothing. He don't take his nose out of that script. He's not happy, though, now that you ain't around to do his continuity."

"He wouldn't know continuity from taffy. He has to type up his new ideas all by himself, doesn't he?"

"Well, I ain't gonna do it." I could almost see the quick grin blooming across my bosses's wide face. "Slows him down some considerable," he said. Vinnie's chuckle deepened, "One other happy stance to report. I got my wife busy redecorating your place. So she's happy, and that makes Gloria happy, and that makes me happy, too."

Gloria, as you probably know, was his steady lay.

"So happiness abounds," I said. There was a pause on his end, long enough so I could see *all* wasn't sweetness and light.

"How soon you coming back?" he growled.
"Vinnie, I've only been here three weeks."
"Oh, yeah. I forgot," he said. "Take care, Hollywood."
I told him I'd do my best to keep it all together, and
clicked off on my end. Vinnie hadn't come right out
and said so directly, but from the tone in his voice, I
think he actually missed me.

CHAPTER 11

Unfortunately for me, like many good actors, Joy assumed the character of the role she was playing, both on and off the screen. They just can't help themselves. It's John Wayne going to the door for a pizza and calling the delivery boy *Pilgrim*, or Katherine Hepburn saying Dearest Darling to some grimy auto repairman. Steal your heart away, entirely by accident. Unfortunately for me, you see, the persona of Amanda Smythe was both attractive and understanding and, as I'd told Joy a hundred times, *she had become Amanda.*

And so, in spite of all the wicked bad I knew about Peanuts, there were times I had trouble keeping my hands off her. And she knew it.

"We were meant to be together, Mattie," she said. It was after a dinner of cold meatball sandwiches and jug wine served in plastic cups by our cafeteria chef, who had taken to wearing a tall white hat that made nearly impossible getting in and out of his mobile cooking unit parked at one end of the huge striped serving tent.

"What are you talking about, Joy?" I barely looked up from the notes I was jotting on the notes and revisions Rags had passed to me, three pages of work I had yet to type for tomorrow's shoot. .

"We were in Spain...Madrid, actually..."

"Oh," I said, still not paying attention. "With Mister Lovely."

"Lintadore," she corrected me. "Fabrio Lintadore."

It was probably just the grotesque tent lighting, but I thought for a moment that maybe she was looking at me with the old bemused look of appraisal, Madge Sacknall's *Invitation to the dance.*

"Hey, I'm working over here," I said. "Don't give me compound sentences. You're in Milano with Mr. Lovely, and so what?"

"Madrid with Fabrio." The smile lines deepened around the corners of her eyes. It wasn't a cruel expression, still just appraising, the seemingly innocent gaze of an unrepentant sexual carnivore. Fabrio was one of those hot flash Italian fashion models who blaze across the silver screen in a single motion picture, gain lots of publicity, and then sink forever into the morass of Hollywood history. Peanuts had picked him up white hot after a remake of *American Gigolo*—incidentally, the week after our split hit the trades—and they had toured Europe, ostensibly to show face at Cannes.

"Yeah, okay—what about it?"

"Mattie, you should take notice. This is me being warm and sensitive."

Joy, complex as I knew her to be, was not a bad person... she had the gentleness and good will of a vulture gauging the temperature of road kill. I made a last mark in red Sharpie on the pages and set them aside with a sigh.

"I am listening, Joy. Europe, Fabrio...what?"

She smiled and leaned forward. "He had to go see his tailor, some new suits or something. Fabrio had more clothes than I do."

"Whatever happened to him?"

"I don't know," she shrugged. "Went to seed, I think."

"Bummer. So none of his clothes fit?"

"Mattie, will you listen?" She was toying with the latte I'd brought over from the cabin, so I pushed it toward her. I'd bought a set of big Chinese delft tea cups with ornate lids. Joy had seen me coming a mile away, and drifted over like a big bass.

"Yeah, sure, go ahead." I pushed the bag of cookies toward her. "Here, have a Mrs. Fields."

"I shouldn't," she said, reaching quickly for the cookies before I might take her seriously. "Anyway, Fabrio had this appointment and I wanted to see some Spanish art and so I took off on my own, swinging along down the streets of Madrid. It was a beautiful Spring day and I didn't have a care in the world."

"Here, give me a sip," I said, reaching out for the coffee cup. "Just a sip," I reassured her. "Share, share."

She reluctantly slid it across the checkered red-and-white tablecloth.

"I have to get back to my cabin," I said.

"Wait, you haven't heard my story," she said. She took the coffee cup out of my hands. "What did your pumpkin princess call you—*rude boy*. You certainly can be rude."

"How did you know that?" I was startled that she had kept track after we parted ways.

"Batty Bertie told me." She gave me the brilliant smile of triumph that had dazzled millions of movie goers all over the world. "And he told me a lot more."

"Like what?"

"Like your sweetie pie Julia called me *The Ice Princess.* You never found me frigid, did you Mattie?" I was just puzzled enough by the fact that she knew intimate details of my relationship with Julia, her replacement in the love department, to settle back in my chair.

"Okay, you're in Madrid looking at art galleries."

"On my way to the Reina Sofia, actually, to see Picasso's Guernica," she said, reaching for the last of my cookies. "They warn you in the hotels, but I never paid any attention, and suddenly I was surrounded by this swarm of street people."

"Street entertainers? Like jugglers and mimes?"

"No, nothing like that, Mattie. Gypsies. They were like a swarm of bees, hugging and patting me and begging for money—all at the same time."

"Were you frightened?"

"Don't be silly. It was exciting, in a way. All that brushing up, a little bit like group sex."

I had to shrug at that one. I'd asked a stupid question. In another life, Peanuts could have been a cut-purse, right off the 17th century streets of London.

"I was overwhelmed," she said. "Overwhelmed is more the word. You know, like those orgies where there's two dozen pairs of hands and you sort-of lose control."

"I guess so..." I said.

"Oh, Mattie, don't be such a prude." She reached across the table and held my hand for the briefest of moments before retrieving the coffee cup. "Anyway, these people were some sort of family, all related. The boss, this fellow with dark, flashing eyes—"

"Like Fabrio?" I asked.

She made a scornful gesture with one of her hands. "Fffft... Fabrio was weak dishwater, compared. Anyway, this guy—his name was Rubinelle—he made them give me back my purse with most of my money still in it, and we went off to this section of the city nobody from out of town ever gets to see, and it was great, this little café with the wine and the violins and the wild dancing."

"Breaking plates and stuff?"

"That's, Greece, idiot. Mattie, listen to me!"

"Yeah, yeah, okay."

"So, it's the middle of the night, and this scary old lady with stringy white hair and hardly any teeth is telling me my fortune and about my son—"

"So you knew right then and there she was a fake."

"No, Mattie, about my *future* son that I was going to have, and she described the father, and it was you, right down to the way you wear that funny Keg's hat and practice your stupid karate that you don't do very well and try to write your Great American Novel and make movies—she actually said you make movies! It was you, Mattie."

That was just a little too much, and I had pages to finish before I could crawl into bed. "So you didn't tell her that we'd gone our separate ways and that her prediction had been disrupted by show biz?"

"You don't think what I'm saying is important, do you?" She sat back suddenly folding her arms and giving me the cold stare I knew so well. Did I mention, my ex could turn the charm off like a broken water heater?

"Did you get to see Guernica?" I asked.

"Yeah. Bunch of howling stick-people. Don't change the subject, Mattie."

"I'm not. I don't believe in fortune tellers."

She folded her arms, the cold spell deepening into an ice age.

"So. I tell you one of the experiences of my lifetime, and it all just means nothing to you?"

As usual, I found myself explaining. "Joy. Think us over, start to finish, you and me, the whole potato:

You came, you saw, you conquered—and then you left."

"It was the times, Mattie! We parted ways! It was a mutual thing!"

"Yes, of course, Joy. I read all that in the trades."

"Oh, don't be so bitter. I got over it—I moved on."

It would have been easy to comment on the lightning speed and the ease of her recovery, but we had a picture to make. *Let the past bury the past.* I took a long count before saying anything. I found that after a few moments I was able to smile. It was a weak attempt at the familiar and even famous Hollywood Havoc grin, but I'm sure it was there, the gesture if little else. "We had some good times, Peanuts. But the point is this gypsy fortune-teller you happened across one drunken night in old *Espanola* was wrong. We had no off-spring, lucky thing for the poor kids."

"What?" She yelped, "I could be a good mom! I could mom with the best!"

"This isn't getting us anywhere, and I foresee a spell of typing in my immediate future." I got to my feet and collected my pages, wondering that the conversation had gone so wrong so fast. "Make sure I get that coffee cup back."

"Oh, sure, just run away from me...like you always do!"

That, of course, was another of my ex's little mini-mind-traps. In another lifetime, I'd have jumped to the bait with some remark like *You're the one who ran away to Spain with the likes of Fabrio and Rubinelle.* But... she had moved on, and we were both better for it. I shook my head, saying nothing.

As I walked away, I saw we'd created something of a scene. The few groups still gathered at tables here and there were eyeing us with varying degrees of bored amusement. I turned and looked back at Joy, giving her a little *See now what you've done?* expression. She was still watching me, her steady gaze not leaving my face. She didn't respond to my gesture. But the *Glacial Age* had melted into something else. If I didn't know her so well, I'd accuse her of, in that moment, looking genuinely thoughtful.

CHAPTER 12

Vinnie, long distance, kept me aware that I was just on loan. He had a thousand questions about the pre-production on *Carnage Days*, and I only had one answer—*There is no real way to tell until we have an approved script.* He set business aside for the moment.

"You sound so much better, Havoc," his big, booming voice intoned over the tiny speaker, "Now that you're getting some on a steady basis."

"I don't know who's worse on the phone," I replied. "You, or batty old Bertie."

"Come on," Vinnie said, trying to sound injured. "I'm only looking out for you."

"By the way, how's the decorating job going?"

"My wife's having a ball. You like pink flock wallpaper? Little cherubs and stuff, heartsy-artsy-fartsy, like all over?"

That provoked the anticipated yelp from my end.

"Ahh, settle down, kid. I was just pulling your chain."

"What's this about you and Bertrand?"

There was a significant pause—I could visualize Vinnie on the other end of the conversation, furtively looking around before he answered.

"He's getting it on with my wife."

"What?!"

"Hey, just kidding...though, tell the truth, I'd be grateful, take the pressure off me, you know?

I said I did know.

"Bertrand got his Caddie patched up, good as new, after his run-in with the law."

"I thought it was a bulldozer."

"Yeah, well things got excitable and he put it in reverse and took out a Newport black-and-white.

"Jeez, that's another one I owe him."

"Naah…we buried it in the budget. Fraper-the-clapper don't know nothing….anyway, Old Bertrand squires my missus around to designers and tile places and stuff. She tells me she thinks he's gay."

"She better not let that slip to Bertie."

"Yeah, I know. I don't open my trap. Anyway, say hi to Peanuts for the gang."

So even long-distance, Vinnie and the good folks back at Berger Royal were sure I was getting it on with my ex. That's real faith in the good old Tinseltown *way of romance.* Showbiz Cupid's arrows are erratic, but the nights on location are long and lonely, and they have plenty of time to find their mark. Three days later, Joy came storming into my cabin. It was right after lunch time. We'd had a long lunch break, due to the helicopter she'd hired showing up forty-five minutes late with the steaming hot Papa John's pizza.

" Inclement weather," the pilot had said.

"You helicopter jocks have trouble getting it up, just like everybody else," Joy had responded.

"No, seriously," he said, trying the serious professional approach.

"Yeah, yeah." Joy cut him off like a true Berger Royal alumni, "I don't want to hear it—we got a picture to shoot. Where the fuckin' crap is our pizza?"

She'd had her fill of Pappa John's finest, her favorite being the Tuscany Six Cheese Special, but when she showed up in my cabin, she wasn't finished with the shouting.

"You have to fix the damn script, Mattie!" she yelled, throwing the afternoon's pages on my bedside desk. They slid across the surface and fluttered to the damp wood plank flooring.

"Hey, don't throw them on the floor," I complained.

"You're lucky you don't have a fireplace," she stormed.

I sighed as I bent over to pick up and sort the pages. I'd observed that the people who hung around with the person who had become the great Joy Benefeté did sigh a lot. *Well, just a few more weeks and I could kiss her lovely behind goodbye.*

"Rags approved them, Joy," I reminded her.

"Well, Rags can be wrong, too," she pouted. We were set up to shoot a pre coitus scene, the foreplay being that Amanda, playing against *the gay blade,* has to morph from cool appraisal to warm interest..

"It doesn't feel right," she complained, shaking her head no when I pointed suggestively to my silvery plump and rounded Rancilio Silvia.

"Well, maybe the problem is Humphrey Thomas," I said. I gave her the one raised eyebrow look.

"Matthew, this is *me* we're talking about. I could arouse a sexually ambivalent tree frog, the rusty Tin Man from Oz, or a dead Benedictine monk about to enter the pearly gates. Don't blame *Mister Gay Blade.* This dialogue sucks!"

"Well, it's right out of the book." I busied myself with Rancilio, emptying the still-warm grounds from the last cup of the morning.

"Here, Havoc," she said, moving between me and the espresso maker. "Just get your ears tuned." And she started in as Amanda Smythe.

Frosty, the first line: " 'Oh, I don't know. We tried and we tried in Paris. And then that time in the Canary Islands. We went to Rio…' "

She shoved the script in front of my face, and I read Humphrey's line: " 'But darling, that was before I'd discovered who I was…say, remember that place we found by the waterfront, the fireworks going off in the background, people trooping by, heading home from carnival, still in costume but everybody looking spent and lonely…' "

A little heated, her second line: "That's all past…none of that is now, you-stupid-man!"

And Humphrey's line: " 'I don't deserve this, Amanda. Sure, I made a mistake. I didn't know what I had…everybody makes mistakes…' "

She softens a little: " 'That was some time, that night in Rio…' "

By this time, she was six inches from me. She reached up to touch my face, as if seeing me for the first time.

I put the paper between us, reading my next line, " 'Yes, my darling, I'll never forget it, for so many reasons…' "

She took the page out of my hands. Those huge, soft, innocent grey-blue eyes of hers were looking at me with an intensity you couldn't get from anything other than a tiny key light placed at just the right angle, or from maybe the soul of a really great actress, and she had me caught up in the moment and leaning forward when the phone rang.

I took a quick gasp of air and turned for the phone, which was across my bunk.

Joy Benefeté, never one to break her concentration in a scene, moved forward to cover, pushing me smoothly back on the sheets and smiling down at me.

A voice bellowed in my ear, "God damn it, Havoc, that Fraper is driving me crazy!"

"I thought you had it under control, Vinnie," I said.

Peanuts moved onto the bed next to me, leaning over me and whispering in my ear, "Oh, Humphrey, I had no idea you remembered..."

"He wants sailplanes," Vinnie complained. "You know those ones with the little motors?"

"That was such a glorious time for us both," Joy whispered, her lips brushing my ear.

I paused, not sure where I was any more.

"Well, Vinnie, give him the sail-things. They don't cost very much, do they?"

There was a pause.

"You alone, Hollywood?" I didn't say anything. Joy breathed some more in my ear. "You're not alone, are you."

I sighed and shook my head.

"Put her on, Havoc."

I handed the phone to Joy and she lay down beside me on the little bunk bed.

"What, Vinnie?" she said. She managed to sound pleased to hear his voice and peeved that he'd interrupted us. She ran one hand over my shoulder, then across my chest, feeling for first one nipple, teasing it just for a moment, and then the other.

"When do I get my boy back?" the voice from Los Angeles asked.

"But Vinnie," she teased, "I'm not done with him." Her hand had moved down my belly and was fondling the rising heat at the base of my tightening abdominal muscles. And there was a rattle of the doorknob and then an impatient knock on the door. It seemed I needed not one, but two rescuing angels.

"Hey," Gretchen's peeved voice carried in from outside. "This door is locked!"

"Don't say anything," Joy whispered, her eyes dancing as she tried to reach between my legs to stroke the insides of my thighs.

"I know you guys are in there! We're ready on the set! Rags is waiting!"

Well, Joy may have been ready and willing, but that was it for me. It was the old Berger Royal mantra, *First, get the shot in the can.*

I rolled off my side of the bed, falling on the floor with a thump. Joy let out a merry laugh. "Gotta go, Vinnie!" She snapped the phone shut, and stalked me across the room.

"What about the script," I asked.

"Oh, Mattie, you proved to me that it works. You're such a genius!"

"I hear you in there!" Gretchen shouted, now hammering with both fists on the door.

"Hey, get a grip, bitch!" Joy yelled at her. "We're still rehearsing the scene."

"Rehearsing, my ass," Gretchen yelled back.

Joy went to the door and threw it open. We must have both looked disheveled and flushed. Gretchen backed away, wide-eyed and a little open-mouthed.

"What, you've never seen real professionals rehearse?" Joy snarled at her.

That set Gretchen back another step or two, and she staggered on the lip of the small porch and fell backwards on her butt in the mud.

Joy slammed the door in her face and grinned at me.

"Okay, five minutes, then," Gretchen's voice said from the other side of the door.

Joy winked and headed for the bathroom. In a few minutes she returned, for all intents and purposes ready for her scene. By beef stew and potatoes that evening, the entire crew was buzzing that we'd gotten it on...but I guess you could call me the first course…for the main entree, the great actress, glowing with sexual promise, devoured her lines with an appetite that was going to arouse males in movie houses across the land and make them glad they took their dates to a chick flick.

Two days later, Vinnie unwittingly rescued me again. Right after the first shot of the morning, one of the tripods unexpectedly gave way and the camera recording our main shot fell over in the mud.

Rags was the boss on set, but our masters down south, the studio people who were co-investors in *Softly the Willows* with Peanuts, had fired many of the below-the-line crewmembers in favor of locals, who were on a lower pay scale, and didn't need per-diem, to boot. Unfortunately, the standards were somewhat erratic and, for every dollar saved, time was lost as the relatively inexperienced gaffers and grips struggled to keep up with Rags, his cinematographer and lighting director. When the camera tipped over in the mud, it looked for a moment as if Rags was going to have a heart attack.

"Can we shoot pretty soon," Peanuts asked. "My makeup is starting to run."

"That is our main camera," Rags said through clenched teeth.

"Yeah, fine. Well, lets get another one."

"There isn't another one between here and San Francisco."

"Well, wipe it off, Honeybunch, and let's get going." Peanuts stood there, tapping her foot and glaring at Rags.

"What?" he asked. "The camera falling over is my fault?"

I was sitting in the writer's chair, an ordinary chair six inches lower than the director's chair. It said WRITER on the back of it. I felt safer there in situations like this, hunched over in my chair and pretending to be invisible.

"Mattie," the female lead of *Softly The Willows* implored in that somehow sweet but nettling way that I knew like my own breath, "take me on a hike up the river."

By now, Rags and I had agreed she was trying to get to him through me. Gretchen had told him she'd caught us making love in the daytime while the entire cast and crew was ready and waiting to shoot, but the silly wench had broken down under our director's intense questioning (with me present) and had to admit she hadn't seen anything.

"But they were in a suspicious circumstance," she blurted out, trying for some sort of recovery.

"Oh, Gretchen—get a life!" Rags had dismissed her with a toss of his head, his long hair and Prussian mustachios flaring. '

Rags and I exchanged a quick glance. He gave me a nod and a twitch of his shoulder, indicating he'd be delighted if I could get the unpleasant Joy Benefité out of his hair for an hour or two. I threw pebbles at the water waiting for her to change into a halter top, shorts and a pair of hiking boots. I loaned her my floppy Keg's War hat and we took off in the warm rain, walking up-river toward a cove she said was a favorite local get-away.

The place turned out to be a deserted fisherman's lean-to, really a two-sided cabin on stilts, half way out over the water, with a high, sloping roof that kept most of the rain off. We sat with our feet dangling about a foot over the water, watching the muddy brown current ebb in little swirls below us.

I'd brought along a bar of my favorite on-location chocolate, the triangular dark chocolate Toblerone bar with bits of honey. Peanuts automatically held her hand out and I ripped off a chunk and handed it to her.

"I told you we'd be back together before this picture was finished," she said, her voice a soft, throaty whisper.

"I have to take you with your hiking boots on?" I asked.

"Any way you want me, Lone Ranger."

"Not a good idea, Princess White Flower."

"So what are we doing here?" She got to her feet and found a long stick she could use to swing around like a bratty kid.

"Hey, be careful, you're going to hurt somebody," I protested.

"Nobody here but us chickens," she said, taking a playful swing at my head.

I grabbed her wrist and made her drop the stick.

"Oh, white man so strong…and handsome," she said, giving me her innocent Indian-maiden look as she collapsed against me.

"Joy, we shouldn't—" But before I could figure out what we weren't supposed to be doing, we were kissing and in the next moment we were on the floor of the hut. In fact, a family walking along on the opposite banks of the Willamette spotted us and quickly hustled their two little children away, yelling across the water, "Go rent a room, you goddamn tourist-perverts!"

That didn't bother Joy at all. She sat up and waved at the dad, who had taken a last, longing peek over his shoulder. I couldn't blame him. Her breasts were every bit as full and beautiful as advertised. She smiled proudly, following my gaze.

"The only set of tits in town that don't need to be air-brushed," she said.

And in that moment, my cell phone rang with the familiar happy chant, "Here we go/ with fun in tow / it's the Bugs Bunny/Roadrunner Show…"
I snapped it open, barely avoiding Joy's effort to grab it and throw it in the river.
"Hollywood Havoc here," I said. "This better be good."
"What," Vinnie's voice boomed, "You getting' laid again? Jesus, man—don't you ever have time for business?"

Peanuts grabbed the devilish instrument right out of my hand.

"Vinnie," she bubbled in that marvelous, throaty way of hers. She listened to whatever he had to say, and then replied. "Funny you should ask, dear heart. The naughty boy just about had my blouse off when you interrupted us." She paused again, and then broke into merry laughter, looking over at me. "Oh, no problem, Vinnie. You know the boy can get right at it at a moment's notice. One sight of my world-famous set and—" She frowned at me and gestured with the hand not holding the phone, indicating I was to scratch her back. I felt a little like the designated widow in a black widow spider mating dance. Joy had a thousand moods and moves, but I knew from experience that rubbing her back generally didn't stop there. Her frown in my direction increased and she gave me a curt nod of command.

As I moved close and reached around under her arms I could hear Vinnie complaining on the cell phone. It sounded like Frapper-the-Clapper, had gotten arrested by Homeland Security for asking questions about poisoning the local water supply. Joy was keeping the conversation going and working on my hiking shorts at the same time.

"He sounds weird, Vinnie," she said. " I think you
should dump him." She had the belt unbuckled and
the zipper down, and that was enough of an entrance
for the hand of hers that wasn't busy with the phone
and seemed to have a mind of its own.

"Harder," she whispered greedily. "Use your
nails."
I worked on her back with renewed fervor.
"How's that?" Vinnie said. "I didn't catch what you
said."
"I said maybe you should get rid of that crazy cheese-
eating surrenderist—you know, the Frenchie."
"His money spends real good, sweetheart," Vinnie
said.
Joy could give graduate courses in multi-tasking.
"Oh," I said, giving out a little gasp as she smoothly
circled her thumb and forefinger and moved them to
capture me gently under the rapidly growing head of
that thing of mine that was swelling out of all
proportion. One gentle but firm move like that, and I
was hopelessly snared in her noose. Say what you
will about my lack of willpower, after that move of
hers, any control I had over the situation was
history…and she knew it.
When I was a high school sophomore, we had all
scoffed and chortled in biology class over the plight of
the male elephant, a poor fellow doomed by instinct to
throw down the log he was carrying or to surrender
the fine meal on which he was dining, and to trumpet
and trample his way across fields and through villages
standing in his way, all to be the first to get to a lady
elephant in heat. Humbling to realize how similar we
men are to the pathetic grey pachyderm with the big
trunk and the ears.
"Oh, Vinnie" Joy said into the phone, as if he was the
only man on her mind, though now that she knew she

126

had me, she pushed me on my back so she could watch me while she began to operate with a more languid touch. "Well, sweet Vinnie," she said, "in that case, if the frog mixes you a drink you make sure he takes the first sip, darling. Or is that the Italians, sinister like that?"

My breath was coming in little gasps. I turned my head to one side, away from the river, and saw Gretchen in the distance, huffing her way toward us, head down and following our tracks along the muddy path

I shook my head—*unbelievable rotten timing! Oh boy—here come the Nazi Panzers! We had to quit!* I shook Peanuts by the bare shoulder, frantically redirecting her attention by waving my hand in front of her face and gesturing back down the trail the way we'd come. I guess somebody has to be the adult in these situations. Joy's look went from wonder to annoyance. Her gaze followed where I pointed through the heavy greenery along the riverbanks to where, in the middle distance, we could just make out the solitary figure of Rags' assistant plodding unhappily along in our direction, stubbornly following the way we'd come. *Gretchen the Grim, come to fetch us for her master.* Joy gave me a sad smile and a little shrug, and then circled her thumb and forefinger again, but this time to give the object of her attention a sharp and efficient flick with her fingernail, a quick and painful little gesture with the magical effect of an instant shrinking potent.

She indicated I was to hold the phone to her ear while she strapped her halter top back on. She said later she'd have had me do it, but I would have taken too long to admire the view. She was probably right about that. Regardless, by the time the grim lady of the river made her appearance, Peanuts and I were both prim and proper. The star of *Softly The Willows* was chatting merrily on her cell phone with some famous Hollywood person, while the untrustworthy worm of a writer was giving the water a series of frustrated slaps with the wooden stick that had started it all.

"So long, darling, sweetheart, Vinnie-baby," Joy said as Gretchen huffed up to our waterside retreat. "Duty beckons, and we must heed its dreadful, ugly call." There could be no doubt, the *dreadful and ugly* she was talking about was Gretchen, herself.

CHAPTER 13

So I was under the spell of one of the world's most beautiful women, even though I knew from our failed relationship that it held the potential to be emotionally devastating for me. I swear—you would be, too. She came over to my cabin for a latte, and I sat behind my small writer's table like a schoolgirl having tea with a sexual predator just out of prison.

"It's crazy, Joy. We shouldn't start this. We shouldn't."

"Why not, Mattie? We're both adults."

"You've got the picture going. Your career is riding on it."

"And you think denying myself a little of *Havoc's Heaven* is going to do what?"

"Joy, look around you!"

She gave me a cold look.

"I don't do it with gaffers or grips," she said, gathering her few pages of script and storming out the screen door without her coffee.

I actually started counting. I made it to the count of seven before she banged her way back in, collected her favorite big tea cup with the lid on it, and banged back out again.

"Make sure I get that cup back," I said. .

Amusing, I suppose, and even heart-wrenching, but no good would or could come of it. I was a dalliance, a bone she might gnarl in memory of the good old days. But I knew in my heart of hearts that the best way to be destroyed by my ex was to give in to the idea that there could be something of a real and significant relationship between us. Of course, knowing that and still holding out the hope that there might be something else were two different things.

I might be the only available person on the set that she considered worthy of a nod, but I had to get myself back to the tough old uncaring Hollywood Havoc, the love 'em and leave 'em guy who lived to make the best pictures money could put up on the screen. Nobody had ever knocked me off that ridiculous, self-inflicted pedestal of isolation until Joy had come along, and now she was back, swarming my self-confidence and the renewed sense of who I was and what I wanted with her warm smile, her quick wit and the promise that we might renew that undeniable unique sense of completeness we had once shared together as the show-biz couple on the way up that everybody had to watch out for.

For the past few weeks I had been vulnerable to Joy's advances. *How could I be so stupid?* Vinnie had inadvertently saved me not once, but twice, from becoming a brief throwback fling, a gesture to the past she had left behind. I had to face the truth. I was a retread. I had wallowed down this path before. I should have learned my bitter lesson the first time around, but as BR Pic's Rambo-esque warrior, Horace Keg, was always telling Tuy, his Southeastern Asia hooker-with-a-golden-heart, *Sex makes men stupid.*

The days dragged by. Joy got over her cold miff as if by magic, and I was considering a quick run to the red light district of Portland to take the edge off my continuing stupidity. There was finally a moment when I had to actually thank the Lord of Relationship Train Wrecks for Gretchen—of all people—who came steaming in to my cabin to drop off some revisions. "Oh. Did I interrupt anything?" Gretchen asked with a lip-curling look of disdain, studying the scene with Peanuts and me in each other's arms. I could see by the expression on her face and the furtive way she was acting that Rag's little assistant was actually feeling around for her cell phone with the camera in it. Somebody was sending pictures to the Hollywood Insider, and I had my suspicions.

"Yes, you did interrupt us," Peanuts said, matching scorn for scorn. She had that superior, hateful lilt in her voice that meant *I'm Joy Benefeté and you're not.* "We're working on my big romance scene with the gay fish and it would be nice if you would quit interrupting us. Just take your little papers and your randy, skinny little ass and get out of here."

Oil and ground glass in the same sentence, and more—Joy managed to get a slap in at her co-star, whom by now she'd tried and failed a dozen times to convert to hearty if not healthy bisexuality. That was Peanuts in a nutshell. Still, now that I was trying to dodge *the big nasty* with Joy, I owed Gretchen for that interruption. Once she'd made her grim appearance and left, the mood shifted. Joy and I actually did work through a scene, but it was a tough one where she has to tell the male lead she's had an abortion and it was his child. Nothing like a little dose of harsh reality to take the edge off the unthinking excesses of mating, Hollywood style.

So I did get through that one, but as the days followed one another and slowly piled up into the second month, I found my mind wandering again and again to Peanuts. It's those pheromones, you know. There's nothing any man can do about it, other than accept a two year contract as entertainment manager at Antarctica or sign up long-term at the Benedictine Monastery. *Come on, I would tell myself, of course Joy could be very attractive, she didn't get to be America's Favorite simply because of her stellar boob rating.* One moment I'd be remembering all the bad times we'd been through…our arguments were legendary for their crazy, thoughtless intensity and absolute nonsense over everything and nothing. Once, in a fit of anger over how to spell the word *popsicle*, she had actually pushed me off a cliff at Grand Canyon, lucky thing it was only a steep roll of a hundred feet or so. We'd been fighting, but Peanuts told the skeptical Park Rangers that I was wearing the wrong shoes. Never mind that we were twenty yards on the wrong side of the safety rails.

Of course, we were different now, almost ten years older. My fingers would go quiet on the keyboard and I'd look up see the dark faux wood walls of the cabin and realize where I was, and in the next minute I'd be on my back on the rough planks of that two sided fisherman's shack by the river with her hands and the light in her eyes and her warm smile all over me, and I'd be thinking that, if the worst thing that happened was a roll in the hay, that wouldn't be so bad now, would it? *How stupid is that?* I even had begun to rationalize that, since handling Joy on the set was the director's problem, there was no reason the writer couldn't enjoy a little dalliance with no ill effects.

There were a few more close calls, a few sparks, but no fire. The *will* was there, but no *way*. It wasn't that she had adopted a vow of chastity or found some other love interest, say a salmon fisherman from upstream or a beet farmer from the valley. Fate and a killer schedule conspired to keep us apart. And then, with only three shoot days left, time was running out on our admittedly lusty, lonely-heart's-club daydreams.

But just when I thought principal photography was over and the end of the production would be spitting us all back to La La Land, the predictably rainy Oregon weather turned against us, and the days dawned bright, sunny and clear and stayed that way until dusk and through the cool, starry nights. And that was a disaster.

The way Rags and his camera crew were painting the screen, the palate of *Softly the Willows* was entirely light pastels.

"We don' want no *steenking* sunlight," the frustrated cinematographer shouted, raising his fists to the heavens.

"I want everything a touch somber," Rags had told the smart-looking (if somewhat shop-worn) lady reporter down from the Calendar section in the Times, giving her his sincere directorial look and a belligerent flare of his Prussian mustachios before he took her off for a private session in the Director's Cabin.

"I want things looking like a reflective and appropriately weary late Spring season. It's been raining too long in our story. When will the rain ever end?"

The next morning, the sun, oblivious to our intent or desires, continued to shine in through the small window in my cabin. Rags took the fresh cup of latte I handed him and frowned up at the cerulean sky.

Up until that last unlucky stretch, the Pacific Northwest had treated us perfectly with an endless procession of overcast and rainy days and fog-drenched dripping nights. But just as we arrived at the final climactic scenes, when we would have preferred sweeping torrents, violent winds and buckets and barrels of rain, the clouds overhead did an unseasonable disappearing act and the sun bounced out to burn all day long with brilliant intensity in a brazen-bright, clear blue sky. Frankly, I don't think the state of Oregon was ready for the climate change. From horizon to horizon, confused birds fluttered about without their grey cover of clouds, cows lumbered around looking for raindrops on their heads, and finally the dripping landscape shrugged and then began to wring itself dry. All that may have been wonderful news for the farmers and the local people thinking about starting a nice tan and some crops, but it spelled pure disaster for our own little enterprise, the fog-bound and gloomy little world that surrounded the troubles of Amanda Smythe, heroine of *Softly The Willows.*

    The cheaper new crew members, dubbed 'the locals' by the original workers from LA who were still left on the picture, saw it as easy money. They sat around and played cards, and moved reluctantly to do any work not directly connected to their job titles. If you asked a gaffer to grab a first aid kit out of the cafeteria tent, he'd go do it, but with a sullen look and a slow walk that made you wish you'd gone yourself.

    We waited a week, marking time by playing five dollar limit poker and eating pizza. I finished pecking out my final scenes, had them approved by Rags and the pages copied in quantity. I packed my bags, and still not a cloud in sight. Mother Nature was playing dirty tricks on us. Not even an early morning fog, and the TV weathermen had background maps of a Pacific Ocean devoid of weather fronts all the way to Russia.

    I was getting itchy to get back to *Carnage Days.* I could only imagine what Marc Fraper had done to the script while I'd been away. By now, I feared, the moron would be the Mormon angel reincarnate, wrathful but holy, bloody but unbowed. I brought up the subject that I might drift on back to LA as casually as I could, but Rags wouldn't let me go, and I could understand that, too. When you're directing a feature, there's a comfort in knowing there's someone on the same wavelength that you can talk to and to hammer out revisions, just in case something unexpected might come up, because on a picture something always does.

Rags stormed around for days until he also had finally had enough. We were in the Director's Cabin, throwing darts for quarters. He was up about 20 dollars, but I was resigned to it. He was a better darter than I, and it was as good as any way to make the time pass.

"Mother Nature's toying with us," he screamed, shaking a fist at the window.

Gretchen, who seemed happy her director was in such anguish, gave him a superior little smile. "I told you, we've been lucky so far."

"Shut up, Gretchen," he snarled. "That's *it*—I'm not waiting another day!"

"You have to wait, Rags," she said, slyly egging him on. "Up here, everybody waits on the weather."

His next dart stuck in the wall, missing the round board entirely.   He threw his last dart across the room to where it stuck in a picture of a dancing bear hanging on a far wall.

 "Gretch, where's Arnie?" He meant Arnie Control, our line producer. A line producer, as you probably know is considered by the movers and shakers of Hollywood to be something less than a producer. He does all the work, carries the production responsibilities on the set, but is paid less than the 'real' producer who is busy back in Hollywood schmoozing up his next picture. Then you have Executive Producers on top of the 'real' producers…but don't get me started. Hollywood can be a fun place, but I never said it was nice or fair. Gretchen shrugged, looking at her nails. "It's lunch hour. I imagine he's in the lunch tent."

"Well, would you run fetch him, please? That is, if it's not too much of a bother?"

She gave me a glare, as if it was my fault, and flounced out of my cabin.

Fifteen minutes later, Arnie showed up, all bald-headed fluster over his meat loaf, the last serving of the day, and getting colder by the minute. "I don't care about your meatloaf," Rags said. "You shouldn't be eating that for breakfast, anyway. I want a crane. A big, big crane. Big. Red or yellow or orange." He stretched his arms wide for emphasis. "So big they have to put it on the back of a big diesel truck."

"Rags, we don't have the money—" Arnie started. Rags took him by the arm and they started out of the cabin, heading for our next outdoor setup with me walking behind.

"You NEVER have the money! I said *red or yellow or orange!* GET ME MY FRICKING CRANE!!"

Arnie turned to me. "Can't you talk some sense to him?"

I shrugged and jumped in a shallow mud puddle to see if I could splash any on Arnie's tan Dockers. He was a little too far away, and I missed by inches.

"Director wants a crane, Arnie," I said. I moved a shade closer and took another leap. This one had the desired effect, and Arnie started cursing me.

"Now you see why we don't allow fricking writers on the set!"

" 'We don't care what mamma don't allow'" I chanted.

"Christ, quit fooling around, Havoc!" Rags shouted.

"Arnie, don't you see, we're burning big bucks every day that I don't get these last shots in the can! What the hell's a few thou for a lousy crane?"

Arnie sighed in resignation, "And what do you want a crane for?"

"I'm going to gobo the whole fricking scene. God won't give me fricking cloud cover, so I'll make my own!"

Arnie was our line producer, and at that moment he could have said no, but he knew that would only delay the inevitable. Rags would sell Joy, and she would give Arnie hell for not hopping to in the first place. He gave us both a look that said he'd chop us in little pieces and dump us in the muddy Willamette if he thought he could get away with it, but then he turned away and made his way toward the line producer's cabin (it had a small wooden sign with a picture of a clothes line painted on it.)

"Where you going?" Rags demanded.

"To get my fricking meatloaf—and your fracking crane—and in that order," Arnie said, preserving what little dignity he had left.

CHAPTER 14

Rags Rogers crane showed up as the sun was setting. It was big, it was red and it was wonderful. "Righteously awesome!" Rags said as he watched the driver back it into position. "Hey, can I come up there and see how it works?"

The driver was a swarthy little guy with a bald head, hairy arms and a pot belly. He just looked at us, not saying anything. I guess I was automatically on guard, thinking *Middle Eastern Terrorist,* but, after a moment, Rags yelled over at Arnie.

"Hey, Arnie, tell the *paisano* I want to go up in the cab!"

The crane driver responded with a string of words that might or might not have been *Mange m'gatz,* that is, *Eat me,* in garbage-mouth Italian.

Arnie gave us his own dirty look, but he went over to have a confab with the driver to settle things down. After five minutes he came back, wringing his hands. "No deal, Boss," he said. "Some branch of the Teamsters."

"Fricking unions will be the death of us, yet," Rags raged. "Okay, let's get to work hanging that flyswatter."

"But that will get us into golden time," Arnie complained.

"Jesus, Arnie," Rags yelled, suddenly furious all over. "Pinching pennies, again—while we're losing a fricking fortune!"

"We're already on time-and-a-half, and we didn't do nothing today except wait around for your big red Tonka toy."

"Shall I go talk to Miss Benefeté about your attitude?" Rags asked.

"I'll gladly do it," I volunteered.

"No. Naw. No. Go ahead." Arnie waved at us over his shoulder and walked away muttering his own string of not-so-vague obscenities.

A flyswatter is a big, heavy square of fabric framed in light-weight magnesium alloy tubing, a gadget that hopefully blots out a big patch of sunlight directly over any fairly tight scene we wish to shoot. By fairly tight, I mean a medium shot with up to five or six people in it, and maybe the side of a cabin for a background. In this next set-up, we were going to recreate a scene between Joy and her co-star Humphrey, that takes place in a rustic picnic area by the river. It was one of those sad scenes; Amanda Smythe has to reveal to her lover that their son died in childbirth. Although the emotion of the actors in the scene was critical, we needed lots of tables and individual little circular barbecue grills built out of stone, and, of course, the rain that wasn't there. It's the drawback of filming artistically—once you establish a color palate and the mood of the picture, the slightest deviation pulls the audience away from the story.

First thing the next morning, Rags pounded on my door to get me out of bed.

"Crane's ready, I'm ready, camera's ready, your ex will be ready in ten minutes," he bubbled, a cheerful smile lighting his noble Prussian features.

I'd taught him how to use my espresso maker, so he made his own cup of mocha extra while I threw on a shirt and a pair of Dockers and laced up my hiking boots.

"So you end up doing Peanuts after all?" He gave me a quizzical, amused look.

"A couple of close calls," I shrugged. "I've been trying to avoid it."

His smile broadened.

"Why? Because of me?"

"Well, there is that. You know, mood on the set, all that..." My voice trailed off and it was a moment before I could continue the thought. "She's the single most self-centered person I've ever met. Make the mistake of caring for her, and it will rot your heart from the inside out."

"Woo. To me, she's just another broad."

"That's what I keep telling myself. Keeps me sane, you know?"

Rags allowed as how he did know. He warmed up his latte with a little hot milk left in the pitcher, and led me out the door to get a closer look at his new creation. He pointed proudly to the huge silk square hung from the giant crane's massive outstretched arm.

"See, my dear Hollywood Havoc, We have our own cloud cover," he said. "Fart on you, Weather Gods."

"It's not nice to piss off Mother Nature," I warned, quoting a popular margarine commercial. I was watching the crane operator, the swarthy little guy with the pot belly.

"What the hell's wrong with that guy?"

"What guy?" Rags asked.

"That guy on the crane. He keeps staring at us."

"Don't be such an egotist. He's staring at me, waiting for orders. I am, after all, the lord and master of all you see about us."

"Well, he sure doesn't have on his happy face," I said. But Rags wasn't paying any attention. He was eyeing his jerry-rigged set-up with a critical stare. "I don't think it's enough," he decided. And with that, he ran off to find Arnie. Within an hour, they'd hired a second crane, even bigger than the first. Rags had the crew rig another big flyswatter behind the first one, higher because it had to be up and out of the shot. They screwed together a series of hoses and nozzles and rigged them up under this second silk square. Rags lost another day doing this, and that drove Arnie a little crazy.

That evening Joy hired a limo to take her out somewhere for a real dinner. Rags and I had the misfortune to be sitting across from Arnie in the meal tent.

"You just don't give a rat's ass," Arnie said to me. He was stirring a fork through his cold rigatoni, searching for stray pieces of Italian sausage.

"What gave it away, the grin on my face?" I said in the appropriate Marc Fraper manner.

Rags looked up from the script on the table in front of him, frowning as he took a sip of cheap red wine from a plastic cup.

"Arnie, you're the guy who sent the real chef back to Los Angeles," he said. "Jesus, what swill." He spat the wine in a little stream on the gravel floor.

Arnie ignored him. He was looking to pick a fight with me. It's a common game on location. *Pick On The Writer.* "Why should you care, Havoc? You got your pages in. You're done, here. But you could show a little support for the rest of us."

Too bad for Arnie, I didn't report to him, and so I didn't care what he thought. I grinned across the table at the bristly little fellow, "Arnie, stop being such a dip-shit. I love Rags' idea, two flyswatters and the

sun can go suck eggs. *Mon frere*, here, is going to save your butt and all you can do is bitch about it."
"Frickin' lot you know, Havoc. *Not one, but TWO giant fucking cranes!* I'll be the laughing stock of Hollywood."
"Yeah, where? Is there some bar where drunken old line producers gather to gum over their failed manhood?"
Arnie shot me a look that probably was meant to kill. When it didn't have the desired effect, he scooped up his tray and headed off toward a table stacked with dirty dishes.
"What's the hurry, Control? I yelled after him. "You going to peddle your bicycle downtown for a hamburger before Jack-In-The-Box closes?" Arnie, who wasn't in the best of shape, had improved his mobility with a battered old Schwinn he'd picked up somewhere, probably stolen from some local kid.
My comment got half the people in the tent looking in our direction. The quality of our mess hall grub was sliding from fair to bad, and any rumors of a foray to civilization for real food perked up ears all around. Arnie had his talking-points, and when he got back to Tinseltown, he would blab it up around town. On the other hand, two cranes may sound like over-kill, but directors who shoot commercials learn lots of helpful tricks. The constant gloomy weather had painted Rags into a corner. He had to come up with a look that was a convincing match for the rest of the film that he'd already shot, and the ordinary night-for-day shooting, or darkening the footage in the lab wasn't going to work.
Extraordinary problems demanded extraordinary solutions. From what I could see, Rags was proving to be somewhat of a genius in his attempt to take on Ma Nature. Most clear-for-cloud shooting looks

phony because the sun glints and glistens off the falling water and the ordinary little things like trees and telephone poles in the background just do not look right. They've got a false shine on them. But as Rags had rightly figured, with his extra crane, the background rain could be under a cloud cover as well. Sounds simple, but it isn't and I have to give him credit for thinking that through.

There was going to be a drawback; we'd have to shoot slower. Every time we wanted to change our setup, say for reverse-angles, we'd have to swing the second crane around behind the first so that the mist-makers and our little, make-believe shower would still be in the background. And, even after all that, our Von Bismarck look-alike still wasn't happy, so he rigged a smaller shower system under the first swatter so the actors could get naturally soaked like they were supposed to, but controlled so they wouldn't look ridiculous. Complicated, awkward and slow going, but we all could see it was going to work.

CHAPTER 15

During my weeks in Oregon, I'd come to understand that, when it came to survival in their damp climate, native Portlanders adapted like ducks or beavers. They were like a sub-set of humanity shaped by climate with special tiny feathers instead of hair follicles and with pelts like muskrats. They had special oils to keep off the constant moisture, and, who knows, maybe primitive gills like frogs for breathing in the really heavy downpours. They scurried in and out, running from doorways to overhangs to cars, dashing around in their ordinary clothes in all but the most severe downpours. They didn't seem to mind wet clothes and drippy hair. Once we established that early on in the film, it just seemed right for our actors. When in Portland, run around in the rain, do as the natives do. Even if it's fake rain under huge drapes hung from cranes.

It was mid-morning, going on eleven o'clock by the time we fine-tuned our final adjustments and had a fine fake drizzle coming down on our actors and a light but steady fake rain in the background.. Rags had worked out the last of the bugs by shooting everything at a slight down-angle to minimize any possible hint of that damnable blue sky. Now he squinted through the lens, muttered a few things to his director of photography, who in turn flogged his camera crew and—finally, finally, finally, they were just about ready for his first scene. I was standing next to Rags, really doing nothing but marveling at his ingenuity and staying out of the way. Invisibility on the set; it's an art-form in itself, not unlike caddies learn to stay out of the line of sight of the golfers while they're putting.

The thought occurred to me that I might not have turned off my espresso maker.   Once the word had spread about my big shiny Rancilio Silvia, six or seven members of the cast and even a few of the original crew members had started to drop in on a regular basis for bitch sessions and free lattes. I couldn't remember if I'd turned it off or not, which was a problem because the milk residue would cake on the steamer.

"Gonna check something in my cabin," I said to Rags.

"Get me a refill," he said, automatically handing me his empty cup. "Double jolt, double chocolate, light on the cream."

"Aye, aye, Captain," I said.

I took the cup, turned from him and took two or three steps in the general direction of the Writer's Cabin— and at that moment there was a snapping noise, a sound like metal breaking. I looked up just in time to catch a glimpse of the heavy crane arm that supported the flyswatter over our heads as it gave way and came swinging down in a ruthless arc towards us.

The white silk of the swatter was framed by light aluminum tubing and strung with wire, but the crane arm itself was a massive metal girder.   It was this heavy metal arm that came swinging down like a giant club, aiming directly for the spot where we were standing.

I took a quick step and dove across the space separating me from Rags. I caught him full on in a hard tackle that drove us both backwards. There was one scream of terror that was cut suddenly short, and a moment of crazed bewilderment, and Rags and I scrambled to find ourselves under a wooden picnic table as the crane arm crashed down on top of us. After that, everything was mass confusion. People were yelling, and all that shouting was nothing more than background walla for that one sharp, horrible scream that had ended so abruptly. There must have been a dozen members of the crew who were now shrouded and floundering around under the silk, covered by the cloth that instantly obstructed our view like a dense white fog. Rags and I were under the splintered wooden table, pinned by the massive arm, and by wires and aluminum tubing, which were proving much heavier than they looked.

I was finding it hard to breathe. There was the huge weight of the table, and a portion of the crane arm on top of that, all pressing on my back, and Rags was crosswise and partly beneath me. First, a cement truck named Fat Boy, and now a big red crane that looked like a monster Tonka toy—I was having a run of bad luck, of being pinned to death by heavy metal objects. *Unbelievable. This had to be more of Shamseen Usudman!* As Horace Keg always says, *There are no coincidences. .*

People screamed and yelled and ran aimlessly about like drowning ants, trying to reassure each other that everybody was okay. For all that wasted motion, nobody came our way with a pry bar or a tow truck. I didn't hear the crane engines start up and Rags and I both remained stuck under the picnic table, the legs of which had collapsed. Fortunately for us, one end of the heavy wooden slab that made up the table top had wedged itself on the nearest stone barbeque grill, and that was the only thing preventing us from being crushed to heaven or hell or wherever film people go. "You okay, Rags?" I grunted.

"I – think – so."

"I'm stuck," I said. "I can't do anything. Trouble breathing."

"I can breathe okay," he said. "Can't feel my legs, though."

"Hang on. They'll have us out in a minute."

There was a moment's silence, and then he spoke again, "You know, with that rain coming down inside, you know, that last little bit we rigged up, I think we have it licked. I really do."

"Sure. We'll be – up and running this afternoon. But you lose – the bet."

"What bet?"

"I finished the script – last night. No way you catch up now, Mister – Fancy Pants – Hollywood Director."

I didn't say anything more, but from my angle under the flapping silk I could see the bottom half of Rags' body. His left leg disappeared under the edge of the crane arm where it sank into the dirt. From where he was, he couldn't see the bottom part of his body, but I could see his left boot, with his foot still in it. It was lying about a yard away, cleanly cut off from the rest of his leg.

The crane arm shifted, but it seemed to settle down rather than lift off of us. I found it harder and harder to get any air, and after a minute or so I passed out. The last thing I remembered, I was once again thinking of the final words attributed to the dying Gertrude Stein, *The fog rises.* It looked to be just another poetic ending for Hollywood Havoc, a not-very-poetic guy.

CHAPTER 16

I can't tell you how much later it was that I came back to the world of the living, but come back I did, with a ringing headache and darting black spots in front of my eyes. I remembered eager hands pulling Rags and then me out from under the debris and the arrival of an emergency ambulance. I staggered around for a while, but, aside from the headache, spasms in my lower back, and a few scrapes on my arms, I wasn't much worse for wear. Mentally, of course, I was a wreck.

They rushed Rags to the hospital with a belt wrapped tightly around his leg. His severed foot with the shoe still on it was packed in a cooler full of ice cubes, and it made the trip along with him. Actually, he was hugging the cooler as if there was a chance somebody might misplace it or throw it out. He didn't let go until half way to the Willamette Falls Hospital in Oregon City when he went unconscious. There was a chance the Portland area docs could sew it back on, but nobody would guess how successful that might turn out. Still, they were going to try.

Mike Coaly, Rags' 2nd Assistant Director, didn't get off so lucky. It was his scream we'd heard as the crane arm caught him squarely across the back. Believe me, it's a hard way to get your name up full screen, white letters on mourning black, on the end of a picture, with the header *In fond remembrance of*.

The police did their customary due diligence, but there wasn't much they could find out. I had my own belief that the accident had been no accident, but there was no solid or real evidence pointing in that direction. Except for the joint pin that had snapped, the crane itself seemed in perfect working order. Experts came out and argued over the pin; most thought it was a simple shear fracture—one engineering professor from a local city college thought it looked like the pin had been hacksawed, but experts with better credentials hooted him silent.

And the swarthy little guy who'd been operating the crane was nowhere to be found.

I stopped Arnie Control on his way to the mess tent.

"Arnie—the crane operator!"

"Yeah, yeah, we know, Havoc. Expired Teamsters card. Actually, he lifted it off a dead guy."

I felt guilty and about ready to spill the beans. My dad, Jack Havoc, had been a writer on location in France when a high speed camera rig had taken out a camera operator. He told my mom that it had affected the mood of the entire shoot in a somber, serious way…everybody saw their role in making the picture with a clarity you don't ordinarily achieve. Not that people set aside their animosities, and not that the usual hi-jinx and on-the-set tricks didn't continue to some degree…but after a death on set, everybody worked harder *to make it all worthwhile.* I knew it was going to be the same with *Softly The Willows,* but for me there was something more. Mike Coaly had died because of Shamseen Usudman's insane desire for vengeance against me.

Maybe I could just share my fears with Arnie and get on an airplane heading back south. But Arnie cut me off with a tirade about his own fears. He was afraid people were going to call him incompetent.

"Look, I know what you're getting at, Havoc," he said. "But, I swear, it ain't my fault. I do my job. You were there. Rags wanted that crane instantly, that moment, right then. We didn't have time to sit around and take our pick of crane operators. This guy showed up with the big red machine, and he flashed that card around when anybody asked. Nobody knew much about him, but that's what happens when you hire on the fly like that. He got the assignment, he showed up on time, he screwed up and he disappeared."

"You don't think he meant to drop that crane arm on us?"

"Are you nuts?" I didn't say anything while Arnie gave me a long, critical stare. "You really are seeing space aliens, Havoc. You writers are all fuckin' wacko. You ought to stick to porking horny stars."

I'd lost my momentary urge to unburden myself to Arnie Control.

"I'll tell Joy you said so," I said.

"Yeah, why not snitch that, too!" His face went beet red and he huffed off toward whatever slop they were serving in the mess tent.

I followed after him and pulled up a chair next to Joy's co-star, who was staring down at a chess board on a lap top computer screen in front of him..

"Hey," Humphrey said, looking up from his game with the slow, appraising smile that was his stock in trade both on and off the screen. "You missed our star's *Let This Not Be All in Vain* speech."

"Fill me in," I said.

"She did a good job, considering...."

"Considering what?"

"Well...Mike Coaly was Rags' assistant, he was a bright—nay, brilliant—young man, and yadda yadda." Humphrey stared at the electronic chess set and his fingers flicked over the keyboard. One of his knights did its little "L" move. He studied the screen for another moment and then looked at me again. "Truth is, the guy kept to himself, nobody really knew much about him, and I don't know anybody who honestly liked him. So, with that sort of material, our stellar Joy gave a most brilliant performance." He eyed me for a moment, the humor lighting his eyes, "I hear you almost got squished, yourself."

"Not funny, McGee."

"Geez, I haven't heard that in...well, actually I have never heard it, except on old recordings of classic radio shows." He looked around at the people quietly waiting in line for warmed over *chicken alfredo* and cold green beans. "Nothing sobers up a crew like a death on the set. Doesn't seem to bother their appetites, though. Where's Gretchen?"

"I haven't seen her," I said.

"Nobody's seen her. My guess is she no longer cares to hitch her wagon to a one-legged director."

"He's going to lose it, then?" I asked.

"Nobody knows for sure. Hope not. He's a good guy."

"Good director," I agreed.

"That, too...I'll miss Gretchen. She gave a good blow job."

"I thought you were gay."

"Like the frog always says, *Sex is complicated.*"

"What frog?"

"You know, in that famous short story, *Hemingway And The Bullfrog.*"

"No, I don't know that one."

"Hemingway's in Europe, fishing for trout. One cold night he's sitting around a campfire and this big bullfrog, who also just happens to be a New York literary agent, tries to sell him on writing genre novels."

"And that's why sex is complicated?" I asked.

Humphrey wrinkled his nose and the slow, predictable grin spread over his face as he morphed from a sort of complex and intense relationships expert into another of his practiced personas, everybody's loveable big brother.

"I guess you have to read the story," he said.

"How's it end?"

"Hemingway throws the bullfrog in the fire."

"Because he was gay?"

"No, idiot. Because he wanted Ernest to put happy endings on his novels."

"Oh," I said. But my mind had wandered, and I found myself wondering how much Bertrand had been able to save of my own desperate attempt to write *the great American novel.*

One of Arnie Control's assistants hurried back from the hospital to give us the cryptic report that Rags was 'still in surgery.' Arnie had a second helping of chicken pasta and huffed and puffed around for a while, red-faced and looking close to a heart attack. He finally called a production meeting in the cafeteria tent, which was a good location, as most of us were sitting around playing cards and reading the local newspapers, anyway.

Arnie never could stand an empty quiet space and after dinking with a stylus on his electronic notepad for a while he got up and started blathering in solemn tones. It seemed out of place; it didn't seem like it was his place. I couldn't make much out of it, and when I looked around, everybody else seemed to be ignoring him, going about their own business or talking in hushed little groups.   To me it looked like Arnie was marking time, reading out loud from pages in his notebook. Or maybe, showing he was in command, should anybody dispute his claim. On the set, the director is always in charge; but Rags was gone, and here was Arnie, talking loud.

"Tell me if I'm forgetting anything," he said.

"Why?" somebody piped up from a far corner of the room.

"Because we're *family*, God-Damn it! Coaly died for this project, and Rags has been brutally maimed, and we have to finish this picture for them!"

"But what does that have to do with helping you do your job?" Somebody else asked.

"A fine, decent man—a young professional with his career ahead of him—died for this project, and your own director loses his leg, and we have to finish this picture for them!

I could see people around the room were shaking their heads and looking puzzled, but nobody said anything more. Arnie continued reading from lists of equipment and their due dates, and then he went through a shots list, and percentages of costs spent as against projections, and after that my mind drifted and I lost track.

My mind was on Peanuts, that bull elephant fixation. I was in measurable bad shape. I'd gone from the sincere and firm conviction that getting involved with her was the wrong idea to rationalizing that a casual fling with my ex couldn't be all that bad, particularly since Shamseen Usudman was going to take me down, if not the next time he tried, then surely the time after that. I was Hollywood Havoc, the Tinseltown Cat with nine lives. But I'd been using them up at a phenomenal rate. I couldn't have very many left. Surely, the gods of fate would snicker if I shied away from a roll in the hay with one of the world's most attractive women. It was that old warriors mantra, straight out of Dragonfly Madness, our Oriental martial arts extravaganza, whose hero always said in his quiet but joyful way, *Eat, drink and make love with Mary—for tomorrow we die.*

CHAPTER 17

Some time in there while Arnie was droning on, the object on which I lately had been projecting my hopeful lust returned to the tent and sat at our table, across from Humphrey and me. She'd apparently forgiven Humphrey his *personal weaknesses,* and she returned his automatic welcoming smile with a tentative one of her own. She gave me a nod and resumed reading somewhere in the middle of a worn pulp novel with a picture of a sensationally naked couple on the cover. That Peanuts—when she wasn't doing it, she was reading about it. She was a perfectionist and *practice makes perfect,* as Tuy, Horace Keg's virtuous but sly reformed Saigon street hooker always said with a wink and a knowing smile. The entwined folks on the cover of Joy's bodice ripper appeared to be a long-haired, dark-skinned guy from Italy who had an Indian band around his forehead and a blond *Lady from Baltimore.* They looked to be in the act of blithe coitus while slipping with abandon over a foamy white waterfall. Peanuts looked up at me and whispered, "Can you do sex upside down if you were tied upside down like a captive of violent and perverted savages who had you hanging from a tree branch?"

"You mean me personally?"

Arnie frowned and shook his head, glaring in our direction, but Peanuts ignored him.

"Mattie, if any man alive could—"

"I don't honestly know, Joy. I never tried it."

"Maybe some time we should. Might be interesting."

"I know a tree branch that might work," Humphrey added.

Joy wrinkled her nose at him. And with that, she went back to her sex instruction novel, only pausing from time to time to turn a page and give Arnie her best *why-are-you-still-talking?* look.

"Hey," I said. "Cover for me and I'll whip you guys up some lattes."

"You can whip me up any time you want," she said.

"Me, too," her co-star added.

Ten minutes later, when I returned with a lacquer tray with three lattes in my special extra large teacups with porcelain lids on them, Joy was still reading, Humphrey was still involved in his chess match, and Arnie was still talking.

"Wouldn't it be *impossible* getting it on underwater?" she whispered. "I mean, naked and everything, but that scuba gear has to get in the way." When Joy whispered, half the people in the tent could overhear her, which was what she wanted. She liked seeing Arnie's face go purple. She had developed what she called an Arnie-a-meter, a scale she could use to judge how close he was to a heart attack by the color of his face.

"Yeah, and watch out for sharks," Humphrey whispered. "They're attracted by that delicious pearly white jazz."

"No, not really?" Joy looked at him with sudden interest.

I nodded in Arnie's direction, "What did I miss?"

"Absolutely nothing," Joy said. " Where's the Mrs. Field's chocolate chippers?".

"You ate all the cookies, Sweet Pea," I said. "How about a dry bar?"

Dry Bar was our nickname for Nature Valley Oats n' Honey Bars. They weren't too bad, dunked in a hot latte.

"I'd die first," she said. "Gimme some chocolate."

I slipped her a Ghirardelli 72 percent dark chocolate bar as Arnie turned his attention in my direction, now acting as if he hadn't noticed me before.

"Oh, there you are, Havoc," he said. He tossed his look of fierce professionalism in my direction. On him it looked like he was working on a difficult bowel movement.

"Just how much did we get in the can before that crane arm gave way?" he asked.

"So then, you were on the set, Arnie?" I replied in my best Mark Frapper question-the-questioner manner.

"No, I was not on the set," our line producer retorted with an angry snort. "I was in my cabin, on the phone to L.A. trying to save your lousy, free-spending asses."

"Well then, I've got bad news for you, Arnie. We don't have anything. Zip. Nada. We were prepping for the first shot when the thing came down on our heads while you were safely tucked in your bed."

"Okay," Arnie said, close to hyperventilation. "We got nothing." He tapped the back end of his pencil on the table. "It's a sad thing, losing Mike. But what we do is keep going."

"Keep going?" There was a chorus of startled responses from around the room. "Why would we quit?"

Arnie had to think fast.

"Yeah," he said. There was an annoyed pitch to his voice. "I mean…in Mike's honor. Mike wouldn't want us to quit."

That quieted everybody down a little bit. It was awkward, but Arnie had managed to bring up the subject that was on his mind. He frowned down at his notepad and then nodded as if he'd come to a difficult decision.

"Havoc can sit in for Rags until we get another director up here," he said. He looked out of his element, forced by the moment to spin out the first things that came to mind.

I could see my ex's eyes lift from her pulper, flick over to me, back to Arnie, and then back down to her book again. I thought I saw a brief smile flicker across her face.

"Could you do it in 40 seconds free-fall with a parachute strapped to your back?" she said in a giggling whisper.

I shrugged doubtfully and whispered back, "I'd think the chute straps that go around your groin would get in the way." My own comment was too loud to be deemed discrete.

"Groin. I love that word," she said. "You mean vagina, right?"

"Like working your way through a chastity belt," I said.

"It would be easier if it was two guys," Humphrey chimed in.

"Oh, *ick*," Joy said.

"Don't tell me you haven't thought about it," Humphrey said, his big-brother smile assuming a slightly superior edge.

"Havoc ain't DGA," the DP muttered grumpily, reacting to Arnie's decision. He was making the point he thought I wasn't in the Directors Guild of America. Arnie paid no attention to him, choosing instead to glare at me. It was obvious some of us weren't taking the proceedings seriously enough.

"Come on, Arnie," Humphrey said, "Don't give us the *everlasting grief* crap. It's not a happy thing, but Joy already did the *fare thee well* moment, and Coaly's been shipped south for his final rites.. He wanted to do the Neptune thing, so by now he's probably damp ashes floating ten miles out from Santa Monica Pier. Nobody here knew him well enough to wear black and go into mourning for more than six or seven minutes."
"What does that have to do with Havoc not being in the guild?" the DP asked.
"Nothing," I shrugged. "I've been DGA for ten years."
"A bloody hyphenate," the DP shrugged, the reluctance evident in his gesture. "Well…okay with me." Clearly, it wasn't, but then, it wasn't his call.
If it had been Vinnie, I'd already be lining up the first shot, but I didn't trust Arnie. It wasn't that he didn't know what he was doing. Being an okay line producer isn't brain surgery, and he'd worked a bunch of pictures without messing up. The way I saw the situation, out here on location, Arnie could make all sorts of promises to keep the cameras rolling, but I knew he didn't have the authority to make it stick with the guild or with the studio guys.
"You clear that with anybody?" I asked.
"I don't have to," he said.
"Woow. A little testy, there. Come on, Mister Control. You know you need a waver from the DGA." The Directors Guild was sticky about forms and formality, and you don't just automatically replace the director on a film, even if he gets separated from his leg. If Arnie didn't get a new deal memo for my services approved by the DGA, they could come after the production. And if I didn't sign a valid copy, I could lose my deal, or worse, my membership in the guild.
"That will take me all of five minutes, schmuck."
"Hey, no name-calling," I said mildly. "Just do it."

I turned back to see if Peanuts needed any more advice or information on unusual mating positions, but she'd drifted away out of the tent, taking one of my ornate ceramic covered teacups with her, as usual. The cafeteria coffee was the worst. They'd turned the electricity off, and it was lukewarm. I was sure my Rancilio Silvia was still hot back in my cabin, so I yawned and got up, figuring I'd make myself a latte special, cream on top and laced with some caramel syrup shipped up from Ghirardelli's that I'd ordered on the internet. .

"Where you going, Havoc?" Arnie yelled after my retreating backside.

"Writers Cabin," I said over my shoulder. "Where the writer hangs out."

"Hey, you're on stand-by!"

"Oh, I'll be ready, Arnie." I smiled at him. "Ready when you are, AC."

Vinnie would have already shoved me into the breech, or slid into the director's chair and picked up a megaphone, himself. On the other hand, I wouldn't have insisted on a deal memo from Vinnie. I always trusted him to be fair. But this wasn't a Berger Royal production, and I knew Arnie Control couldn't be trusted to jelly up plain bread, much less carry out his function with anything resembling honor.

Arnie hadn't gotten his nickname *The Weasel* without due cause. He was one of those grim-faced guys who reduced filmmaking to a factory assembly line. He was good with numbers, but bad with people, and it was just one of those things. As for telling the truth, with him *lying was just another occupational skill.*

It wasn't hard to figure the bind he was in. The guys back in L.A. were looking to him to finish the picture. The shots we still needed to get in the can were vital; we couldn't just wrap with what we'd already shot and then cut around the missing scenes in edit. Pictures that try to get away with that short-cut are monumentally unsuccessful. You might remember the failed movie Brainstorm, a great concept, but the unfinished footage stuck together after Natalie Woods' untimely departure from the planet. And I was sure Rags wasn't about to miraculously get up off his bed and walk. He wouldn't be in any shape for a while, and we needed a director *now*.

Arnie's big hope was that he could get me up and directing without a contract. That way, he wouldn't lose a production day while he went about wheeling and dealing for a replacement director from Hollywood. I would be slaving for guild minimum wages and no guarantees while he was conferencing with his bosses, the studio execs, and with various agents around Hollywood, jousting about to line up another director to finish the picture. It would be great for him if he could say he'd gotten Havoc to keep things going in the interim, *hey, maybe even save a half day or a day on the schedule*. The studio guys would be happy, it was an emergency. No questions would be asked, and if anything did come up after the fact, *Fuck the union, it was a crisis and what the hell's a fine or two on the ass end?*

I could see Arnie's point of view, which was strictly about saving money and finishing the picture, *no matter what*. On the other hand, those of us close to the creative process on *Softly the Willows*—Rags, Joy, Howard, myself and maybe the DP and a handful of others—were convinced we were creating something special. But Arnie didn't have a creative bone in his body. From Arnie's point of view, there wasn't anything magical about production; the world was full of directors and most of them were out of work most of the time. I could see him hitting speed dial on his cell phone before I'd even left the tent.

I found out later that afternoon that Arnie's call to the studio had bordered on hysteria. Any time a production grinds to a halt, the producers either have to declare hiatus or the money continues to disappear at the same fantastic burn rate as when things are actually getting done. *Softly The Willows* was now dead in the swollen and muddy waters of the Willamette river, but production monies continued to fly off into the ether for salaries, location fees, rentals and a hundred other miscellaneous items like laundry and the limo Peanuts hired to take a run to the nearest Subway for sandwiches for everybody. And if Arnie did declare a hiatus, he'd have to ship most cast and crew back to L.A., and then back to Oregon when the picture started up again.

With that sort of situation, the studio guys down south were quick to make up their minds. In the next few hours, they struck a deal with a director out of Hollywood by the name of Buddy Baker.

CHAPTER 18

Later that afternoon, Buddy came winging in to Portland from Tinseltown. Peanuts limo was unavailable for him—not a good sign—and so he caught a ride from one of those surly Portland cabbies to our location on the river. Our operation had dried out some in the past few days, but the new man hit the location complaining the weather was unpleasantly soggy compared to Southern California. I don't know how I felt about it. Disappointed, I guess, that we couldn't have finished up without him—and a little fearful that he might find some new *directorial interpretation* that would leave his footprints all over the film. I furnished him his pages, and, after locking himself in the Director's Cabin for forty minutes, he emerged with a confident smile and declared himself *ready to have a go at it.*

I wasn't exactly waiting around for him, so Arnie had to send his assistant downriver where he found me skipping round river pebbles. The new creative team gathered around the light from a solitary lantern over a table in Arnie's favorite place, the mess tent. The group consisted of Buddy Baker and Buddy's assistant, a hairless fellow named Chummy. Then, there was Arnie, Arnie's assistant, the DP, whose name was Phil Miller, and me. Joy had begged off, complaining she needed her beauty sleep, and

Humphrey grumpily declined as well, saying if Joy didn't have to be there, neither did he.

One of the chefs sleepily rolled out of the sack and scrambled Arnie some burnt eggs. Arnie had unwisely given Joy an ultimatum, and he delayed the meeting until it was abundantly clear she wouldn't be attending.

While we waited, Arnie sprinkled a liberal dose of Senior Pico Mexican hot sauce on his eggs. The Senior is a moderately hot sauce, but some wag, knowing Arnie was the only one on the set who used it, had refilled the Senior Pico bottle with Hurricane Jenny, a dark reddish sauce that ranked a lot higher on the chili pepper heat scale.

"So you can shoot without your prep days?" Arnie asked Buddy for the third or fourth time, as took a huge bite of the eggs. A shocked look came over his face. He reached for his water glass, which, unfortunately, was empty, and then ran for the bottled water dispenser, which, unfortunately, was also non-functional, having been cleaned for the night. It was some time before our line producer was able to collect two warm beers and return to our table.

"Sure," Buddy said as if there had been no interruption. "I intend to start shooting tomorrow. I promised the guys in L. A. But you pay me for the prep days."

"Yeah, yeah," Arnie said, rinsing his mouth out and spitting warm Coors on the gravel floor. "Okay with you, Havoc?"

"I'm out of it, Arnie," I said. "My work here is done."

"Don't be a sour ass," Arnie said. "Everybody knows you wanted to direct."

"No, Arnie. I don't need the credit or the grief. Buddy here can handle it."

"Then what did you mean—" Arnie started, giving me a cold stare.

"The script is re-written and it was approved by Rags. I was just hanging around because he asked me."

"We don't need the writer any more," Buddy said.

I knew a little about Buddy Baker. His real name was Jonathon Sparge Baker. He insisted people call him "Buddy". Nobody was sure why. The cast and crew on his pictures called him "Budsey-Boy", mostly when out of his hearing range. I'd read a bio-promo on him in the Reporter, and there's always the scuttle-butt the crew kicks around from picture to picture.

Buddy dressed a little odd, but directors like to do that. His special look was natty *Eastern Preppy*—a rumpled sky-blue pork-pie hat with a red-and-black band, a sports coat and a tie, no socks and special white gym shoes without laces, the kind worn by Sunday afternoon boaters while sitting on their yachts in the harbor. Buddy had done one or two cinema releases that hadn't gone anywhere and a handful of Movies-of-the- Week and made-for Cable TV movies, so I figured he could interpret a script, move fast and get it done. *Let it go*, I was thinking. *Buddy can do it and I can catch the next airplane south out of Portland!*

But Arnie scuttled that plan. "I say you hang around, Havoc. You never know—we might need you."

"Arnie, the script is finished."

"We got a clause," he said.

I knew he did. It was called *extenuating circumstances.*

"Okay, but that's a re-write," I said, meaning *He had me, but I wasn't going to work for free.*

"Day rate, minimum," he said.

"Triple-scale," I countered.

"What?!" he yelped.

"I was getting double before. You want more, it costs more. You doubt me, go talk to WGA."
"Yeah, yeah, okay."
Arnie saying things were *okay* was a nice starting point. I scribbled a three line agreement on the blank backside of an 8 x 10 inch flyer advertising Cheaper Carpets Installed Faster, and I made Arnie sign it.
"Witness," I said, shoving the flyer across to Buddy.
"Do I have to?" he complained.
"Just do it," Arnie said, rolling his eyes and giving off a big sigh. His breath smelled like Hurricane Jenny.
He looked like he wasn't feeling too good. Of course, he always looked that way. A guy like that should be in a quieter business, something like librarian or a color commentator for snail races at county fairs. At least, that's what I thought.

CHAPTER 19

. It wasn't until after breakfast the next morning, and, in fact, a half hour after the eight a.m. call that I realized Peanuts wasn't thrusting forth with her normal fanfare from the Star's Cabin (the one with the little sign with the star on it), and that led to the sinking feeling we weren't just going to be able to run through a smooth last two days and get out of Portland.

Phil Miller gave me an appraising glance.

"What, Havoc—you still here?"

"Not my choice. Arnie extended me."

"Now we got two directors?"

"No. As the writer. Nothing's happening here. Come on, I'll make you a latte."

The DP shrugged and agreed.

"What are you thinking?" he asked as we half-walked and half-jogged off the set.

"About Buddy? He looks okay to me."

"Yeah, but is okay good enough?"

"Not my call, Phil."

He didn't say much while my Rancilio Silvia puffed and steamed.

When our lattes were in the cup, we stood outside my cabin, waiting for the coffee to cool and watching the brown waters of the Willamette slide by.

"At least you *care*," he said finally. "And you were close to Rags. You know what he wanted."

"It'll be okay. Buddy's a good-natured guy from
the I'm Okay-and-You're Okay-So-Long-As-You-Do-
It-My-Way school of directing."
"Ain't they all that way," the DP said. He was looking
across the river. "Is that a guy with a ground-to-air
missile on his shoulder?"
I think I turned more grey than Arnie about to have a
heart attack, but I swung my Bushnell compact
binoculars on him and it turned out to be one of those
kids with a 'popper', a toy fishing get-up that looked
like the old army grenade launchers.
"Just a fishing gun," I said. "You pump it up and shoot
the line out in the water."
"Dynamite's more a sure thing," he said. "Jesus,
Havoc, what's wrong? You look like you seen a
ghost."
I gave him the first silly excuse that came to mind,
and we walked back to the set, but Peanuts still was
nowhere to be seen. The sun was again bright and
shining, and we were ready to go with the
complicated rig that Rags had inspired us to create.
The offending red crane had been carted away,
replaced by a big orange one that loomed overhead
like the giant flyswatter it had been named after. Still,
as the morning stretched toward noon, the crew sat
around on towels and caught the fresh sunlight on
their cheeks and Joy Benefeté showed no indication
she might be coming out of her cabin. She had her
own lunch catered in, proving somebody was alive
and probably healthy in there. I had a cold slice of
pizza and hung around in the cafeteria tent with the
cast and crew, playing chess with Humphrey, who,
gay or not, could really move those rooks and bishops
around the board.

"I think Arnie's secretly gay," Humphrey said.
"You think everybody's secretly gay," I said.

168

"Not you, Hollywood Havoc. You're legendary dick never strays to the wild side."

"Reticent genes," I said.

"Retarded," he retorted.

Arnie Control and his new director sat by themselves at a table near the door, both on cell phones pointed south toward the cavernous oak-lined studio conference rooms where powerful men were puffing expensive cigars and feeling cash draining from their pockets like warm honey through a sieve.

"No, really," Humphrey said. "He's a very precise, controlled guy. Obviously doesn't know himself. Probably dominated by his mother, picked on as a kid."

"That what happened to you?" I asked.

"You should pay more attention," he admonished, neatly wiping out one of my knights.

"Here he comes," I said. "Maybe you could ask him."

"Are you a closet homosexual, Arnie?" Humphrey asked him in that friendly, curiously All-American way that had boosted him to Hollywood fame and fortune.

"Talk to her, Havoc," Arnie said to me, completely ignoring our male lead.

He was looking exhausted, the bags under his eyes appearing even darker than usual. His apprehension was easy to understand; quicker than you can say 'unemployment line' he'd gone from being two days ahead of schedule to a day and a half behind. In his job, staying on schedule was silver and being ahead was gold. But I was out of sympathy for Arnie Control.

"And say, like, what?" I asked.

"Look, Havoc, we're in a jam here, and I don't much like your attitude."

"And say what to Miss Benefeté?" I repeated.

"Goddamn it, I okayed you for this gig, and now you give me nothing but shit!"

"Arnie, the lowest gaffer on this set knows you pushed for a big-time "A" writer instead of me. Christ, it was in the trades. And you hate shooting in sequence, which somewhere along the line you got into your thick head was my idea."

Arnie's face sagged and he looked around for a dog to kick or a snub-nosed .38 police special with which to shoot me.

"She's got to finish this picture, Havoc," he said.

"She's got her own money tied up in it. You say you care for her, so why don't you prove it?"

"I say your ordinary closet type…repressed, bitchy, devious and fork-tongued," Humphrey nodded to me.

"You knew what she was like when you signed on!" Arnie howled at him, suddenly furious at the interruption, or maybe the universal lack of respect he was getting..

Humphrey gave me a triumphant glance, checkmated my king, and ambled away. "I wasn't talking about Joy, Arnie," he said over his shoulder. "I have to go to the bathroom. Care to join me?"

"No-I-do-not-care-to—"

"Calm down, Arnie," I said. "Sit down for a moment." I didn't actually want him joining me, but I didn't know much about heart attacks. I thought it might somehow be better than dying standing up. He plunked himself in Humphrey's vacated chair and swept the chess board and the little wooden brown and beige figures to the floor.

"Hey, that's not helping anything," I said mildly. I picked up the checkered board and then got down on my hands and knees and began to collect the chessmen. "I don't get it, Arnie. What's her problem?

You pissed her off, didn't you? Come on, level with me."

"His problem is," Buddy, who had sidled within hearing range, said in a softly nasty voice, "the god-damn actress is telling the pussy-foot producer what to do."

"Which is exactly what?" I asked. "Get that knight by your foot, Buddy.. The little horse-head thing."

Arnie flashed a frustrated and harrowed look around the tent, but he didn't say anything. He stood and kicked at the knight, giving it a little boot under the table. I sighed and went over to retrieve it.

"Okay, don't tell me," I shrugged. "Buddy, why don't you go talk to her yourself?"

Buddy shot me a dirty glare, then looked down at his white Keds, which were already caked in mud.

"If you insist on wearing those boat shoes on our picnic set, you're going to need a new pair every half hour," I said, trying for casual conversation..

"He tried," Arnie cut in. "He did try to talk to her."

"And?" Getting straight answers from this pair was like pulling taffy.

"She said no," Arnie said.

"Well? What does she want?"

The two men looked at each other and then looked away, not answering my question. I looked out from under the table, and nobody said anything.

"Anybody see two brown rooks and a beige pawn?" I asked.

This was becoming stranger and stranger. I could hear Vinnie's voice in the back of my head, *Sure, these guys are rummies--But what's their fricking motivation?*

"Okay," I continued, "you want me to talk to Joy. And what exactly would you like me to say to her?"

171

"Tell her to get her famous and fabulous set of tits out on the set—pronto!" our new director said in his own sudden, unexpected flare-up of rage.

"Gentlemen," I said, standing and setting down the chess pieces on the table. "We're all under a lot of stress here, but are you sure that's the message you want to convey?"

Buddy was seething, a royal ego in full bloom. "She gets her big fat lazy butt out on that set *right now!*"

"Well, alright," I said, heading for the folded back flap that served as an entrance to the tent. "May I quote you?"

Buddy jumped to his feet, puffing like an angry animal that tries to frighten its foe with a show of strength—a feather-rattling peacock maybe, or an agitated puffer-fish.

"What, Buddy? What?" I moved in close and grinned at him.

"That's it!" he said, "That's it, that's *it!* This is, bar none, absolutely the worst experience of my entire career!"

"You haven't had that many," I reminded him.

But he was already storming out of the tent.

"I'll sue you people for every dollar you own!" he tossed back over his shoulder. "You too, Arnie! The whole fucking lot of you miserable losers!"

I was getting into the spirit of the thing. I happily yelled after him. "Hey, Buddy—you're supposed to be directing, and you're not. We'll get you for non-performance. How will that look in the Hollywood Reporter? Budsey-Boy Baker can't get actors to act."

"God-DAMN it--!" There was a brief, indecipherable howl of rage from the other side of the canvas, but Buddy didn't return. I found out later he'd tripped over a guy wire holding up the big tent and slid a foot or two on his belly in the ever-present mud of Oregon. "Now what do we do?" Arnie wailed. With Buddy gone, our line producer was concentrating his petulant glare on me.

 "Not *we,* Arnie. There ain't no *we,* sweetheart. It's your problem. I'm just the writer."

Arnie got up and then sat back down again with a heavy flop and a weak sigh. Then, when that gained him no sympathy, he got up again and walked angrily back and forth, brows lowered and glaring in my direction.

"What, Arnie? Want me to leave so you can make some more important phone calls?"

He tried to gather up some sense of personal dignity.

"A little common courtesy would be nice, Havoc," he said in a low voice.

"Sorry, Arnie, I'm entirely out of common, today."

I took a short walk to the chow line for an energy bar, came back to the table and sat down right next to him.

"Why do you have to sit right here?!" he shouted.

I took a chew from the bar. Raisins and peanuts, not my favorite.

"I was thinking maybe I could pick up some tips on how the big time line producers do their business. But I must be missing something. So far, all you seem to be good for is speed-dialing long distance numbers on the phone and listening a lot."

I wandered away for about thirty seconds, but I returned in time to see he had the cell phone to his ear again. He impatiently tried to shoo me away with his free hand, but I shook my head.

"Free country, Arnie. You want privacy, go to the Producer's Cabin…you know, the one with the little quarter moon drawn on it."

I guess he could easily have gotten up and walked away, but he seemed too distracted, or maybe he was just tired of the hassle. After all, with his problems, I was just one little mosquito, hardly worth a swat. He ignored me while he said 'yes' a lot, with long spaces of silent listening in between. Then he clicked shut the phone and stared vacantly across the tents to where the cooks were cleaning up the now-deserted cafeteria line and getting ready for the next rush.

"Rags wants you to finish up the picture," he said with a hollow ring of defeat in his voice. "And your precious ex-wife is siding with him."

That Peanuts, what a wild card! You could go along with the critics and say she was shallow, heartless, selfish, and self-absorbed and lots of other negative things. But in her own way, she was true to her own, and, when all was said and done, you just never knew which way *America's Favorite Set* were going to point.

CHAPTER 20

Arnie demanded we start filming immediately, but by then it was pushing towards three o'clock in the afternoon and so I had to disagree. I suppose there were smoother ways to dissent, but our line producer wasn't on my "A" list at the moment.

I shook my head. "Nope," I said

"What do you mean, 'nope'?!" he screamed. "You get a golden shot to the butt of your lousy fucking going-nowhere career and you say 'nope'?! We're two days behind!! You can't say 'nope'!! We're fucking losing a ton of money here, Havoc!"

"You know the rules as well as I do, Arnie." I shrugged like it was out of my hands.

"No, why don't you tell me!!"

"Right. I will. The Director's Guild says I get a prep day before we shoot. That's a full prep day, which would be tomorrow, followed by our first shoot day, which would be the day after."

"You can't be serious! You're just a fucking-nothing piss-ant-nobody who's fallen out of the sky and lucked onto the chocolate cake and we're on location and you're talking goddamn stupid DGA nonsense rules to me!"

"Highly poetic, Mr. Control," I replied. "Why don't you get on your cell phone and tell it to the DGA."

"God DAMN it!" he yelled. He was so mad he looked purple.

"Tell you what I'll do, Arnie. Because I'm a good guy, I'll forget you called me an insignificant insect. And to show my good faith, I'll count today as my prep day—make a note of it." I tapped his faithful Palm Pilot. "I intend to be paid."

"We start tomorrow?" he said doubtfully, caught between anger and hope, and unsure he'd heard correctly. I could see the cogs whirring in his brain. I could have asked for anything—a cool hundred and fifty thousand or even a quarter of a million dollars wasn't out of sight. Yet I wasn't holding out for money, which meant he would only have to pay me scale, maybe a couple lousy thousand bucks a day plus a few hundred for health and pension. Less than triple scale as a writer.

His brain hadn't caught up to the full equation, and I wasn't sure it ever would. What he thought didn't matter to me; the truth was, I didn't need a big pay out; bottom line, Peanuts had her own money in the picture, and I wasn't about to hold her up for cash. And I knew what Rags wanted. With me directing, we might get away with this thing yet.

"Tomorrow morning, Arnie. Eight o'clock call. See to it."

I sat alone in the tent as he ran off to make the arrangements. Actually, I wasn't thinking about his schedule, but what might be best for the picture. I'd been listening to the weather forecasts, which, unlike our prognostications in La La Land to the south, seemed fairly straightforward and clear. There was a big front moving down the coast from Alaska. It was supposed to arrive sometime before midnight, and if the indications were correct, the rain was about to pelt down, and if that happened we wouldn't have to rely on Rags Rogers ingenious giant flyswatters to finish the rest of the picture. Call me superstitious, but I figured I'd be shying away from cranes for the rest of my life.

Late that night, there was a soft knock on the door of the Writer's Cabin, where I'd chosen to remain, rather than moving in Rags' old digs. Ignoring that call was one of the harder things I would ever do my checkered career of amoral choices and roads better not taken. The knock on the door quickly increased to the level of a hard and impatient pounding. That was followed by the sound of someone impatiently rattling the knob. And then a kick, the words, "Ow! Owww! God DAMN you, Matthew Havoc!" and some muffled swearing. *Peanuts, for sure, and just as randy as ever.* I rolled over in my lumpy mattress and put the spare pillow over my head. My advice about my ex-wife had been good enough for Rags, so I figured I'd follow it myself.

Still, lying there alone in my bed, I couldn't help thinking about my ex. I wasn't sure what I still felt for her beyond the old emotional bond and the ever-present physical attraction. She was an interesting cross between serious talent and an alley cat, and she'd come a long way since she was Madge Sacknall, newly baptized with a drama degree from Long Beach State University. I remembered the first time I'd seen her, standing awkwardly on Vinnie's doorstep with a VHS tape with few commercials and a bit part from General Hospital resting on the seductive curve of her hip. And she'd come along from even further back than that; I knew, from a picture in the tattered high school yearbook she kept for good luck. She'd lost the ethnic bridge to the nose she was born with, and her naturally straight brunette hair had been converted into dancing ringlets of honey blond. Still, the wide and luminous eyes that gave her a screen presence not seen this side of Betty Davis were all her own, even if the blue was augmented just a subtle shade or two with contacts. Forgive me if I sound analytical; those are just details and the truth is, like most men on the planet, I could all too easily lose myself in her smile or—to the unknowing—what looked to be her simple, innocent gaze. At that moment I was realizing that it was a lot easier to give Peanuts what she thought she wanted than to try to be her friend. But that's the thing about us Havocs, father and son...we don't ever seem to take the easy way.

I lay there thinking until a chill wind came up and it began to rain. There was a soft patter on the roof of the cabin and then a steadily increasing drumbeat. For a while I listened to the tinkle of the water dripping from the leaky ceiling into the plastic cups and bowls I'd stolen from the meal tent, and then I finally drifted off into a restless sleep where preteen terrorists wearing Elvis Lives t-shirts and Tropicana bath towels around their heads came after me with multi-colored plastic grenade launchers.

Lucky for me, for the next few days, Joy was still in that marvelous zone she had displayed since we first started rolling film on *Softly The Willows*, and, as far as I was concerned, she was the key to the picture. She was so far into Amanda Smythe that I was printing practically everything we shot, and the next two days went off *with nary a moose-fart*, as an old cowpoke narrator like Gene Autry's sidekick Pat Buttram might say. Since Rags and I had been in agreement every step of the way as to our interpretation of the original book, I let the DP block out the scenes the way Rags had indicated in his notes. I said 'Action' and then sat back and let the magic happen. And the gods of cinema rewarded me. The climactic scenes of *Softly The Willows* unfolded with the exact dramatic intensity that I believed Rags would have wanted. Several times Joy went a little strong and edgy, but she was listening and so it was easy to pull her back just a little, the way a jockey does with a powerful racehorse.

It took us two long 12-hour days to finish, but that was only because the rains were intermittent and I chose to override Arnie's frantic calls for moving things along, and to film only during the heaviest cloudbursts. These were, after all, the climactic scenes, and dramatic weather best suited the mood of our picture.

"You'll thank me, Arnie," I told him, "When you're up there on the big stage waving your golden statue in front of all those jealous stiffs in tuxedos."

"Right, sure, yeah" he scoffed, but when he saw how powerful the dailies were, I think he more than half-believed me.

And then, at the end of the second day, just when we were all thinking this was an endless journey through hell that would go on forever—just about at that point, we finished our final shot. We all looked at each other, the miracle shot and in the can, and yet none of us ready or prepared to believe what we had accomplished. .

Regardless, I jumped on the moment and intoned the all-important phrases, "Thank you, Ladies and Gentlemen. Print everything. Everything. And, incidentally…*Okay, that's a wrap*."

Joy's eyes locked with mine, and I thought for a second she might rush over and we would share a significant moment, but then everybody swarmed everybody and the more customary form of end-of-the-production madness moved in to sweep us away like some sort of low budget makeover replicating the famous separation scene in *Doctor Zhivago*. It was the madness of the throng—Hollywood hugs and the sudden flurry of show biz *Mmmmwah!* kisses all around.

We had crossed the finish line. This was it, the end of principal photography. *Softly the Willows* would soon begin the complicated post-production process that could still make or break the picture, but that was to be in another time and another town, and clearly my gimp buddy, Rags Rodgers, problem. For now, there were cheers and the pop of champagne bottles. Expensive bubbly was gulped down from Styrofoam cups, the on-location traditions intact. Styrofoam, cheap plastic or cut crystal, we didn't give a hoot. *We were done, we were free!* We could get out of the soppy mess of this Oregon wilderness and go home. By the time we wrapped, it was past 8 o'clock in the evening, but the catering people, wise to the ways of production, had seen the moment coming. They immediately brought out a spread, and the wrap party started practically before the last roll of 35mm was out of the magazines.

The party was a rushed affair, as they always are, with the bustle of everyone packing and blowing kisses and trying to line up air transportation so they could get out of town and back down south to their real lives and their significant others.
The now-actual possibility of departure from the slog and slop of our location shoot was at last undeniably in the air. You could smell the anticipation and the joy. Everybody was happy, much of it having something to do with what we'd done, and equally as much with the thrill of finally getting away from the banks of the Willamette River. The general opinion was that we had something extraordinary in the can.

That said, both cast and crew were eager to gulp a glass of bubbly and then pack and grab a cab and shoot on over to Portland International. Some few lucky souls had already snagged reservations and drifted away even before the shrimp, fruit slices and cheese plates arrived. The rest milled about, gnarfing down brie and crackers and giving out their email addresses and phone numbers, promising to write and stay in touch, show biz pals, buds and lovers forever.

Peanut's agent, Mike Blastowitz, had shown up the day he heard Buddy was replacing Rags, but for reasons nobody could figure she'd had banned him from the set. The moment we wrapped, Mike figured out his ban was lifted—or, at least, that nobody would care--and so he showed up at the party to claim his star client and hustle her back to L.A..

Some agents feel they have to deify their clients in order to earn their 15%. It could have been that Mike was one of these. I knew a little bit about him. We'd bumped shoulders around town. He came from somewhere in the Midwest, Pittsburgh or Cleveland (unlike Horny who had been born in Hollywood, rumor was, backstage on the Universal lot). Blastowitz & Menchen was a mid-sized, very hungry agency, hovering uncertainly neither here nor there in a business where you generally had to keep growing or languish in semi-poverty and disdain.

He was bald, but unlike Horny, who'd had a weak chin, Mike had a lantern jaw and an arch and superior manner that he groomed to serve the elite of Hollywood, that is, the top layer of superstars, hot directors and powerful studio execs. Since Berger Royal Pictures was stained with the words *low budget*, Vinnie was not on his A, B or even C list. And I personally was even lower than that, an unfortunate and regrettable footnote to his biggest client's early sexual misadventures.

Mike may have been physically more imposing than Horny Hiatt, but Joy picked her agents for results rather than class and there was a certain similarity if not resemblance. A hard working, hard knocks agent, looking out for his client. Actually, to me, the guy looked a little worn down at the edges, like he took a lot of punches and scrapes and still bounced back, ready for more. That's why he reminded me of Horny. He showed up, peering in to make sure he was welcome, and then made his way around our hurried little get-together, feeling out the few actors who might be worth a tumble and handing out an occasional matte gray business card.

He finally got around to me.

"You owe me, Havoc," he said.

"Mike, hi. How you figure, big guy?"

"Hey, pal. I got you this gig."

"I thought Joy wanted me."

"She's my client."

"You're her agent," I said, defining the relationship without getting into the details. I just wished he'd go away. It had been a long day and I was tired.

He glared at me through his fish-eye glasses. I wear fairly thick glasses, too, but his looked heavy as leaded glass.

"Arnie told me about you," he persisted.

"I'll bet he did," I said. "I'll bet you and Arnie had several phone calls about me."

His lip curled, "What's that supposed to mean?"

"You're a liar and a schmuck. You didn't recommend me, Mike. You came out against me."

"You don't know that…how could you know that?"

"Peanuts told me."

That knocked him back a step or two, but he wasn't going down for the count.

"Don't you ever call her Peanuts. Her name is Joy Benefeté.

I'd wanted to leave it alone, but he was getting me riled.

"Tell it to the press, Blastowitz. I'm family, you're not and that means I'll call her whatever I want. The problem with you agents is you say you're doing what's best for your clients, but you don't really give a crap. I heard she did this picture in spite of you, and I'm here to tell you it's the best thing she's ever done."

"You don't know crap yourself, Havoc," he said, his voice rising a notch. It was starting to sound like a drag-out bitch fight. I saw Humphrey grinning at me in his bemused way from across the room. "You're a cheap, no-talent hired gun. Nobody in Hollywood will touch you except Vinnie Berger, and do you know why that is?"

"No, Mike, why is that?"

"You don't show respect."

I had to give him that one. I was angry and was about to say a lot more and so it was probably a good thing we were interrupted by my ex herself before I could solidify the enmity of someone who could do me plenty of harm and who might even some day do me some good, in his own behalf, of course.

"Michael," she said. "I thought you were handling my bags." *That was Peanuts. You worked for her, you did whatever she asked.* I didn't know how long she'd been standing there or what she'd heard, but then, neither did he.

183

"Right," he said, looking flushed and irritated. He turned and positioned his thick body so he was facing her while standing directly between Peanuts and myself. "Look, Joy, I've got you tickets on the last flight out of Portland tonight, but you've got to shake your butt if we're going to make it."

"I put you in charge of the luggage, Michael," she said. "Don't worry about me, myself, the person."

"You're saying you're not coming tonight."

I wondered for the thousandth time why Hollywood people made such a big fuss over every nothing that came along. It wasn't just that Joy was a difficult person; any fool could see Blastowitz was blundering forward onto the really thin ice with a professional predator. All he had to do was keep at it and she would be shopping for a new 15-percenter.

"No, Michael," she said, "I'm saying I want my bags to be on that plane. And it's your responsibility to make sure that happens. Is that so complicated for you to understand?"

I didn't have to say anything. He was the big Tinseltown agent in charge of luggage. I gave him an amused look that he couldn't have misunderstood.

"You'll get yours, Havoc," he muttered angrily as he moved towards the exit flap on the tent. In the distance, I saw Humphrey silently mimicking the words, *You'll get yours, Havoc.*

"Already have," I said.

"Matthew." Peanuts was frowning at me, shaking her head and talking like a disappointed schoolteacher, "do you have to irritate and offend every single person in Hollywood?"

I grinned at her, "Michael thinks I lack respect."

"Boy," she said, her stern expression melting as she broke into a grin to match mine, "he doesn't know the half of it, does he?"

184

CHAPTER 21

I walked across the indoor gravel to the portable table and snagged Peanuts a fresh glass of champagne. We sat on metal folding chairs and put up our feet, watching the dwindling party dwindle and wind down as various members of the cast and crew paid their compliments and took their leave, presumably to make a mad dash to the airport.

"So I owe you twice," my ex said, eyeing me over the plastic rim of her wide glass.

"Not at all," I said.

"Anastasia…and now this."

I was about to deny it in stronger language, but she held up one hand.

"Don't start," she said. "You do go on with all that stuff about me living up to my God-given talent."

She gave me her quick, practiced Amanda Smythe smile, and I had to try and remember who she really was.

"The only trouble is," she mused, almost as if speaking to herself, "I'm starting to half-believe you."

"You have it in spades, Joy. Look what you've done here. Great, incredible stuff. On the money, on the mark, on the trail of the big golden idol. The dailies don't lie. Don't let up now. Listen to Rags; work with him in edit. You're gonna get an Oscar, Peanuts."

"Yeah, maybe, I guess…but it's so hard to believe that… what I've always wanted so badly… could finally, really be happening." She shook her head, looking at the bubbles climbing in her champagne. .

She wasn't disagreeing, and in a way, she wasn't even talking with me. From the look on her face, I knew she was thinking back over the years, maybe thinking about the times we'd had, maybe further back along the trail of her career. We'd shared some real madcap moments, first down in Mexico and then later, playing Hollywood's newest love-y twosome.

The next thing she said surprised me. "You have every right to hate me, but still you come through for me, time and again. You and Vinnie are the only people I really trust."

That made me, in turn, say something out loud that I thought I'd never admit. "You did the right thing, getting away from Berger Royal…and me, too, for that matter. I wasn't ready for somebody like you."

She shook her head, tossing the light golden hair back from her forehead in a characteristic Amanda gesture.

"I think there was no question about dumping Vinnie," she said. "There's no denying getting away from Berger Royal at that time was the right move for me…but you and me splitting, that's maybe a closer call."

"Yeah, maybe. We did have something, at least for a while, didn't we."

"It was real for me." She seemed to be waiting for my admission.

"Yeah. Me, too."

So there it was again. The undeniable *us*, those times, the commitment, the things we'd shared, all back on the analyst's table for yet another look. *Play it again, Sam. One more time for old time's sake.* I shook my head, trying to pretend it was old, inconsequential stuff, all blown away by the winds of time like last year's dandelion seeds. That was the past, locked down, faded, gone.

"Let's not go back there, Joy. Just see how far you've come. You did the right thing and nobody got hurt. Not you, not me. No harm, no foul."

She was eyeing me, and I could see she wasn't buying it. We both knew nobody gets dumped without feeling the pain.

"No. I got over it," I said. "I did—honest. Maybe it took a while, but I'm okay, you're okay."

"Let's go for a walk," she suggested. "Down along the river."

"It's raining," I said.

"No it's not. We're between downpours. Come on, Mattie, don't be a chicken, it's our salute to *Softly The Willows*."

"You've got a plane to catch."

"No, I don't," she said, taking my hand and pulling me up from my chair. "And I've got some serious questions to ask you."

"Not about us, okay?"

"Not about us," she laughed. "I promise, not about us."

I could tell from the amusement in her eyes that she was Madge Sacknall or maybe Joy Benefeté, up to her old tricks. Or she was Amanda Smythe with some new ones. Or maybe even my once beloved ex, Peanuts, who just needed a friend to take a walk down by the river. Anyway, we ducked out into the damp evening and she was all and not any of those things, and she ended up changing my life, yet another time.

We walked on the path that curved along the near bank of the river. The wide stream was moving in a slow, dark ripple, its low murmur and dark liquid body a solid presence we heard and felt rather than anything we could see. We stayed on the curving path, crushed stone laid down by our crew before we'd begun the shoot. Water dripped from the branches of the trees and our footfalls made a crunching sound as we walked along.

The air was still and silent, a few minutes of calm before the next storm. There was an occasional puff of air, a few lightning flashes and a low, distant mutter of thunder on the horizon.

Finally, she turned to me.

"That wasn't a virus, was it Matthew?"

She was referring to the first time I had run into Shamseen Usudman. He had tried to take most of Southern California out with a nuclear device welded inside an imported cement truck.

"The thing at Vinnie's ranch? No, it wasn't." The cement truck had ended up at Vinnie's ranchette in Malibu, and Homeland Security had moved in to save the day.

"The National Inquirer was right, weren't they...?"

"They usually are," I said. "As long as they stay away from aliens from outer space and Elvis sightings."

"And the world's fattest babies," she agreed. But then her expression took on a serious note, "...and Horny dying?"

"...was a part of it," I finished her thought. "Horny was being paid five million to get Horse to re-release your old barnyard tricks film."

"But why?...and...what happened to him?"

"My guess is Horny got greedy. Those people are not playing around."

"Present tense?" she said, looking up at me with a worried expression.

"Shamseen is back in town. And I don't think Rags was an accident," I said. "That crane arm was meant for me."

"What?! Why? Why you?"

"I'm not sure, Joy. I can't worry about it. We just go forward. We both have stories to tell, pictures to make."

"Right," she laughed, "the old Berger Royal mantra, *You got to kill me to stop me.*"

"That's right," I said. We eyed each other for a moment, neither of us laughing.

"Poor Horny…" she said finally.

"Yeah, and poor Rags…" I added.

She linked her arm in mine and we walked on, thinking our separate thoughts.

The first fat drops of the next rain shower started to pelt down.   Peanuts looked at me and smiled. She was the ultimate Pandora's Box; I knew from experience she brought a new depth to Humphrey's use of the word *complicated.* She looked radiant and somehow fragile in the dim light from the infrequent antique lamp posts we'd installed, perhaps vulnerable because of her concern for the trouble we'd gotten into, maybe even a little of it for me. I knew her skills as an actress, but this, I felt, was maybe even a touch towards the genuine. She had nothing to gain from me. She was gone and we were no longer an item. She had made her leap and transcended; she was up there with the super-stars.

"We've got to go, Peanuts."

"Where?"

"Forward. On to the next thing."

"No, we don't, Mattie," she said. "Not right away. Where's your old sense of adventure?"

The flash of a smile and a brush of her lips on my cheek and then she turned and ran back down the path the way we'd come.

"Come on, Mattie Slow-buns!" she yelled over her shoulder. "You're going to get your butt wet!"

"Slow Buns!?"

And I took off after her. Her Star cabin was the first we came to, and we tumbled inside just as the real rain came pelting down. Her luggage was gone, but the bed had been newly made up.

I knew it wasn't right or the smart thing to do, but we were both flushed and excited, and in another moment our lips touched and the fire that, over the past weeks I'd tried so hard to keep from igniting, suddenly flared up and I took her in my arms and could think of nothing but the smell of her hair and the silken feel of her skin. I'd like to say we gradually built the emotion between us with tender and loving care, but the truth is, we more or less ripped each other out of our clothes and fell together in a soppy, clutching and yet somehow emotionally charged embrace. We didn't even make it to the nearby bed. The rain pounded on the roof and we laughed like poor, starving fools stranded at the last oasis of love, laughed even as we savagely grappled and pulled and wrenched at each other's clothing, and finally naked, devoured each other on the floor like the desperate lovers that we were. I found myself bursting deep inside her and heard her cry out in happy desperation and for that brief moment all was right in the world.

There was time enough later, when we were lying warm and cozy under the covers together, to linger and explore the familiar curves and places we had known so well ten years before. And after a long and slow time of exquisite tenderness, her loins were throbbing over and over and I ran my fingers gently over her stiffened nipples and pushed inside her warm, wet opening at the base of her taut belly a second time, and I'm not sure why but we both were crying, happy and sad, empty and fulfilled at the same moment.

Hours or minutes went by. I stirred, aware that she was watching me.

"You should have never left me, dearest Mattie," she said softly, breathing in my ear and kissing my neck.

Nice, except that I hadn't left her, she'd run out on me, off to an exclusive Alpine ski resort with sleazy Freddy Driver, an up and coming drummer with a hot rock and roll band. The guy I'd been ten years ago would be up in arms over an innocent-sounding but dynamite-charged comment like that from her.

Even in the present, after all this time gone by, my first reaction was to jump up and start yelling, but then I realized that was just what she wanted. In fact, I knew those exact words, *You should have never left me, dearest Arnold,* as the opening lines from a scene in *Purgatory Passion.* That was the last BR picture she was slated to star in before Horny Hyatt snatched her out of Vinnie's nest. Of course, professional that she was, she'd learned her lines, I suppose just in case something went wrong, say Horny had miscalculated and Vinnie had found a way to make her stay and do the picture.

The scene I was remembering was a huge break-up moment. The heroine, desperate to escape a lover she felt was drowning her career, picks a fight by making outrageous charges against the poor sap…just another case of art imitating life.

"I know," I said. "I was something of a monster. I can see that, now."

Her eyes widened, just a momentary flicker as she recognized her lover's dialogue from the *Purgatory* script. I had, after all, read for her to help her learn her lines.

"I mean," she said, shifting her line of attack, "you became so unreasonable. Everything was you, you, you. You're bloody career, your new car, your big dreams of becoming a real writer."

"I know," I repeated. "I was such a selfish brute."

Her lines were still from *Purgatory Passion*, but mine were from an earlier picture, *Lardon Estates*, a story of *lust's labors lost* set in the 19th century. Vinnie's historical epics generally involved different costumes and accents and lots of obligatory half-naked scenes where men and women tried to figure things out, the grouping for understanding just an excuse to bring on the tits-and-ass. Over the years, I'd become something of an expert at bedroom breakups, and by listening to the scornful comments from the actresses, had picked up a few useful ideas, hints as to the complicated workings of the female mind.   *Sad but true, almost every quotable bit of wisdom I knew about women I'd learned from the movies.*

Seeing the conversation wasn't going as planned, Joy threw off her covers and made her way naked around the room. Her movements were deliberately ordinary and her expressions subtle, nothing telegraphed, but I knew her the way a rabid Baptist knows the Bible. It was the great Joy Benefeté fishing through her wardrobe of characters. I pretended not to watch, but I couldn't help myself. She was fascinating, as always, on screen or off. She moved with a touch of slink, Catwoman looking for Batman, Cleopatra on the prowl around the pyramids, thirsting for live meat. *What was she thinking?* In the next moment she might be a wide-eyed virgin, balancing a water jug on her head on her way back from the well. Or perhaps Lady Macbeth, all ingrown emotions and ready for the stabbing. That's the problem with being an actress; it's hard to try on new faces without letting it show.

"What's wrong, sweet?" I asked, trying to sound innocent and maybe even concerned.

"Oh, nothing," she said. "I'm just having one of my moods." She glared out the window at the rain and the swollen river rushing by. After a while, she dialed in sweet and lovely but tough-as-nails Amanda Smythe of *Softly The Willows* and came back to bed. She lay on her back, knees up, and stared at the ceiling. The wheels were clicking, alright. The anger had softened and she took on Amanda's vulnerable look, or maybe that of a lonely lost teenage girl, run away from home to find herself selling her body on the mean streets of the big city, and for a brief moment finding herself in the arms of a kind stranger who just might be good-hearted enough to whisk her away to a new life together.

"I always wanted a cottage like this," she said in a small, reflective voice. "But somewhere in the mountains near LA. Maybe Lake Arrowhead or Big Bear."

"That would be nice," I said, trying for calm neutrality.

"We could do that, Mattie!" she said, turning excitedly toward me and propping her head on one arm. "You and me, like Huck Finn and Mandy or whatever the crap her name was, living off nuts and berries and lettuce in the wilds."

"I think they have a Jack-In-The-Box in Big Bear," I said. "And maybe a Taco Bell."

"Come on, Mattie!" she pleaded in her most convincing tone. "You know what I mean!"

Unfortunately, I did know. A bit further down in the *Purgatory Passion* script, the heroine suckers her lover into believing they could get away to a bright future together, living somewhere in the mountains...just before she runs away with his arch-enemy, a rich guy who is poised to steal his go-go internet company.

"I'm not good at living off the land, Madge," I said. In *Purgatory Passion*, the lover and the rich guy face off at the mountain cabin in a rolling sort-of duel that involves knives, axes, clubs, broken beer bottles and finally an actual confrontation with real dueling pistols at point blank range.

She sighed and turned away from me. I could see out of the corner of my eye that she was staring at the wall, trying to figure out her next move. I knew she had feelings for me...at least, the lust was real, and probably somewhere deep in her screwed-up psyche, she actually liked me. Respect, well, that was a different thing. My ex saw love as a game of war, and the winner was the one who slipped away at the precise moment the beloved other came to expect they might stay.

After a while, her fingers began to move over my body, touching and circling and building desire in me as her hands made their inexorable way to the organ she had, in earlier times, referred to as *Havoc's heaven*. Aroused and drowsy, we made love a third time, moving on the bed to where we could lie at ease and kiss and stroke each other, she giving sweet attention to Havoc's once again stiffening *rod of paradise,* while I gently explored the warm and pliant

194

folds of Madge's *lovely orchid garden.* We made our way, fingering and lingering and licking and tenderly mouthing as we moved through the ancient dance like a slow and beautifully rich orchestral movement that somehow was tinged with sadness and the hint of inevitable loss. After the music of our passion faded we lay close together, our arms around each other's hips, and she pretended to sleep while I listened to the ebb and flow of the sweeping rain and thought about our lives and how we kept coming in and out of each other's arms and I wondered if there was even the slightest possibility of any hope for the two of us in the future. *Probably not*, I thought.

After a time, she pushed me on my back and moved on top of me. Although I wasn't half the man I'd been a few hours before, she caressed me and then lowered her hips over mine until she once again took me inside and her warmth flooded over me. You have to understand, Joy was as close as I've ever come to meeting an insatiable woman. From experience in our earliest times together, I knew what this was about. She called it our *late night love song,* and said I was the only man she'd ever found who could actually sing it with her. Once she had me aroused enough, she would keep me excited inside her for hours, somewhere east of sleep and west of blissful climax, a sleeping male sex doll that could be guided close to ecstasy without leaving the shores of desire. At that moment, she had me in such a state, and I don't know how long she moved over me while I went in and out of sleep and blissful joy and back to sleep again.

At that moment, I wanted to stay there in her embrace forever, but since the sheets of driving rain had no answers for concerns such as these, and since we were, after all, only mortals who couldn't stay in heaven forever, our weariness slowly became heavier and heavier and we eventually drifted off to sleep.

The next day, when I finally woke to the soggy light of a mid-morning in Portland, the first thing I did was reach across to her pillow to confirm that it all hadn't been simply a dream. And, though it is the cliché of all silver screen romance clichés, you will not be surprised to hear that Peanuts, my dear once-and-again but never forever lover, was nowhere to be found. It seems that the wanting and dreaming and I-will-love-you-forever stuff had vanished with the night. There was no note, no fond farewell other than a small, hastily drawn heart sketched in red lipstick on one corner of the bathroom mirror. I felt an empty ache, but I had to nod in acceptance when I saw it. Knowing something of the complicated business that was my ex-wife, one single generic red lipstick heart seemed the most appropriate gesture.

"I told you we'd be together before this shoot was over," Peanuts had said with a throaty note of triumph in her soft voice. At that moment we had been lying together under her bed sheets, and there was no way she could possibly have been wrong about her prediction. That had been somewhere in the middle of our blindly blissful few hours of passionate understandings. But the next morning, in the cold grey light of day, I had to admit with a rueful glance at my rumpled self in the mirror, she hadn't said anything about living happily ever after.

CHAPTER 22

The morning after my unwise roll around the star's cabin with the star, I packed my things and caught an Alaskan Airlines commuter run south to LAX. The flight made a stop in San Jose, and since it seemed like a good idea, I got off there, rented a car and headed south out of town, intending to drive the rest of the way to Los Angeles. I made my way south through heavy traffic on the 101 and took Route 152 east through pungent Gilroy, the garlic capital of the world. I had a late lunch at the Casa de Fruta and continued on up the winding road over the Pacheco Pass. The road snaked into the steep green hillsides, topping at the St. Luis Reservoir before dropping toward the Central Valley and Interstate 5, the most boring road that exists anywhere outside of Kansas.

I was running on autopilot, now seriously regretting renewing my intimacy with Peanuts. I couldn't really call it a relationship any more, even though that's how it had felt when we were together. Seeing her again made me realize how much I had missed my ex, though I'd filled my life with film production busy work, and there were months on end when I hadn't thought about her. And now, after one rash and reckless night, I had her scent, her touch, her feel—her everything—around me like a warm blanket.

This was not good, because it wasn't real, it was a distracting mirage. Madge Sacknall, my once-upon-a-time beloved Peanuts, had given me up to chase fame and fortune. She had become the highly sought after major actress known to the rest of the world as Joy Benefeté, and though she might have dropped in for a night of romance (read, 'roll in the hay'), even a fool-for-love like me could see that this wasn't the beginning of a new phase in our lives. .

I pulled off the 5 at Promontory Point, a hillside stop overlooking the irrigation canal our ingenious California forefathers had cut through the valley, bringing water south to broad patches of land that had been cleared for farming squares of giant vegetables and broad stands of fruit and nut trees. I was thinking back, reviewing the past few weeks Joy and I had spent working together, and that last passionate one night fling we'd enjoyed together. Before coming together on *Softly The Willows*, we'd seen each other around town a time or two, but actually we had been divorced for nearly a decade. I kept telling myself I was different now, I could keep our professional lives separate from any personal relationship we might share. But at the root of my feelings, I wasn't sure of anything.

Women, I decided, had an advantage over men, in that they instinctively understood the man-woman thing. They knew that intimacy, even a fast lay in the bushes, changed everything for the man. There was a sea-change, an emotional upheaval, and after the tides of passion retreated, nothing left behind would be the same.
That was why women always knew when their guy was having an affair. They didn't have to reason it through—they *knew.* But when you added to that my ex-wife's appetite for stardom, it spelled a recipe for

disaster. Not personal ruin, and not general chaos…just disaster for the emotional life of one Matthew Havoc.

For once I was actually happy that Julia—the girl I'd hoped might replace Peanuts in my heart—was lost somewhere in the vast nothingness that was the middle of China. There would be no way I could hide what had happened between Peanuts and myself from Julia. It wasn't fair—Bertrand's granddaughter, my lovely sprite Julia—my *pumpkin sweetie pie princess,* as crazy old Bertie himself had dubbed her—had left me, jumping our little boat-for-two just as had Peanuts. And now here I was feeling guilty about the way I'd acted towards not one, but two women. I blew out a breath and shook my head in self-disgust. *Hollywood Havoc,* I thought to myself, *isn't it about time you got yourself a serious life?* The wind was riding in from the north, but unlike the words to the old Peter, Paul & Mary folk ballad, there was no answer a-blowing' in with it.

The leading edge of the cold front that had brought rain to Portland two days earlier had followed me south, and a chill wind rippled through my open jacket as I leaned against my rented Ford Mustang and watched the empty nothingness of the Central Valley. Maybe that would be my life, going forward, a cold and empty vista. That seemed too melodramatic, even for me, and so I snorted a derisive little laugh. I found myself studying the distant layout of the irrigation system, the smaller trenches leading off from the main canal like branches from a long tree trunk, and how these trenches themselves divided into still smaller cement brooks that led to individual fields. A world of details…show business was like that, only maybe running backwards, thousands of separate threads of input that came together to create one giant stream that was any individual movie production.

Joy was gone again from my life. She was gone, and she wasn't coming back. I had to face the hard reality; what I saw before me was Berger Royal and an endless string of B-pictures to fill my days, the flow of the mighty river of show business.

` I was going to have to fling myself into my work with a renewed vigor, to work as hard as I'd done the last time, ten years before, when Peanuts and I had ignited in a furious explosion that had separated us and sent our separate lives careening in opposite directions. As for my nights, well, they would have to take care of themselves. I'd been the original love 'em and leave 'em guy—Hollywood Havoc, good for a party and a night on the town, and sure to be gone in the morning. It was only fitting that, after a decade of separation, Joy had given me a little dose of the same medicine. A cold spatter of rain hit the windshield of the car and I retreated inside as the cold wind picked up a swirl of dust from the gravel cut-off where I'd parked.

I pulled back on the 5 and after a few minutes got ahead of the cold front. Even with a twenty minute stop for steak and eggs at Harris Ranch, I stayed out front of the rain. Traffic heavied up again as I reached the San Fernando Valley, but I was able to pull into LAX just as the orange-red orb of the sun sank below the Pacific horizon off to the west past the airport runways. I paid a king's ransom to get Vinnie's Explorer out of long-term parking, but instead of heading for Sea Garden Cove, I threw my luggage in a room I rented at the Beverly Hills Hotel and headed over to Berger Royal. By this time it was eight at night. I flashed my pass and my famous winning smile at the frowning Raleigh Studios gate guard and parked in Vinnie's spot near our building.

Nobody was in the office so I let myself in. In my absence, Vinnie had mounted posters from Keg's War, Dragonfly Madness, and Beam Me Up on the walls behind his favorite chair in his office, and the runner on the long wall in the conference room was set with half-poster size black-and-white sketches for the Carnage Days Ads.

The sketches were like an instant refresher course in development madness, an update of all the wrong, bad things one mustn't do in developing a motion picture, not if you wanted it to turn out good, or even decent.. A robed Moroni looked out on us with a blank, beatific stare, a big, sloppy Three Dog Night hot dog in one hand and a semi-automatic pistol in the other. The logo now read, Carnage Daze.

I looked over the six inch high stack of loose papers piled on the conference table where Marc usually worked. Easy to see, *Our Man From France* had been busy. I poked around for a bit, but the script was going to need a major overhaul rather than a brief tune-up. I set the whole mess down where it had been before I disturbed it, and called it a wrap, retreating to the hotel room I'd rented.

Bright and early the next morning, I caught a long, hot shower to wash the last of Portland and *Softly the Willows* out of my body and mind, and suited up in a pair of my desert tans, adding a Goofy bandanna around my neck for a touch of color.

Vinnie grinned when I walked in, "Hey, Hollywood, look at you! I haven't seen a get-up like that since Lawrence of Arabia."

"Keg's War, more like," I said. I pointed to the poster on the wall behind his desk. Keg was swinging on a vine, carrying a pretty Oriental girl to safety across crocodile infested waters with his usual stoic charm, while bad Asiatic troopers behind him lit up the night sky with tracer bullets. The shirt and pants I wore were close imitations of the originals, but the bandanna was an exact match—in fact, Ben Dabney, who'd played the indomitable Horace Keg, had given it to me after the wrap. It had taken four washings to get his signature, signed in ball point pen, out of the fabric.

I turned Vinnie's attention to one of the new poster sketches, "Carnage Daze"

"We changed the title," Vinnie said, wrinkling his nose at me. "Marc's idea."

"It is a good idea?" Marc said in his odd, questioning way. He looked up at me as if I'd been there yesterday, instead of on a month long sabbatical.

"Somehow appropriate?" I shrugged.

Vinnie hid a smirk. Marc could call it The Nerds From Machu Picchu, for all he cared, so long as the checks didn't bounce.

But I could see it hadn't been all sweetness and light in my absence. Marc Fraper gave me a weary look across the shiny black granite slab of the big conference table and nudged the plump and disheveled pages of the script in front of him, pushing them a few inches in my direction. .

"So then we have it all here, then?" he asked.

He looked over at Vinnie, who'd insisted on us getting together first thing, *So that Havoc could catch up.* Well, nobody knew, but the night before I'd Xeroxed the whole mess, and I'd gone through everything a time or two before I turned out the lights. So, as we gathered around the big black granite slab for coffee and bagels, I had a pretty good idea of where we were…or weren't. I snagged a blueberry bagel and a cup of bitter coffee and settled in. Script continuity being what it was, I started at page one and fired the first of a thousand questions.

"You've got frickin' War and Peace here," I said. "What ever happened to 118 pages?"

"What one hundred what pages?" Mark sounded genuinely confused.

"It's a little long?" I suggested. I lifted the messy batch of papers, hefting them for weight. "Feels like about four hours and thirty eight minutes to me."

"Well, that is your business to pare it down?" Marc said.

I looked out the window, wondering if Joy might not come back to save me with another location assignment, maybe this time in Siberia or even Canada. But lightning never strikes twice in the same place; at least it didn't that time, so I had to content myself with the script at hand. The silence lengthened as I speed=read the first few pages.

"Why is Moroni wearing his white robes in the opening credits?" I asked finally.

"The symbolism is obvious?" Marc said in his customary questioning way.

"Well, I see that," I said. "But then what's the arc of character? Moroni's supposed to be a normal guy at the beginning."

"Well, ahh, so, yes…but I am thinking he must perhaps have the beginnings, the potential for the oncoming madness…?"

Vinnie raised both hands and flapped them in surrender. "Okay, okay, I get it, Havoc. Marc, we gotta can the white robes in the opening shots." Vinnie was so quick to run up the white flag right from the start that I knew he was counting on me to pull some sense out of the madness. *Right—all I had to*

do was cut three hours out of a five hour script.
Vinnie was grinning at me. He nodded once, sure
he'd passed his benediction on to me by mental
telepathy, and then he took three bites to devour half
an onion bagel slathered in cream cheese. Talking
with his mouth full, it sounded like he was saying, *Be
cub shli wear uh whi tie o sub.* Translated, "He could
still wear a white tie or something."

"You are saying what?" Marc asked.

"Vinnie says, lose the robes," I said. Moroni
gets to wear a white tie in his opening scene. Nobody
wears white ties, so it's already a little odd. Nice
foreshadowing of trouble to come, Vinnie."

"Thank you," Vinnie nodded gravely, just
another noble Lord of Old passing great wisdom down
to his young knights and merry men gathered about
the round table.

Marc frowned, but Vinnie smiled happily and
we moved on. Introducing Moroni's robes early was
a simple bad idea, but in script writing the bad ideas
compound themselves, and by the time we were ten
pages in I had dozens of concerns with matters far
more conflicting than style and fashion. Fraper had
rewritten Moroni as unlikable and thoughtless. His
friends, instead of being insensitive and waggish (as
Marc now was portraying them), were originally
simply trying to be helpful. So when Moroni starts to
come apart, there's no reason to care for him...or for
them, for that matter. Motivation and script continuity
being the complexities they are, I led us carefully,
wading through the stinking swamp that Marc had
created and pointing out the dead ends, the
quicksand and the impassible spiny bramble bushes
as we went, hopefully missing nothing. Marc
defended every one of his changes and additions as
script enrichments, and even with Vinnie's secret

alliance coming to my aid now and then, the going was murderously slow. After several hours of defending this or that atrocious idea—all of which caused us to bat the little Frenchie about the head and shoulders for budgetary excess, out-of-character actions and European artiness (this last from Vinnie, who thought he ought to throw in a few jabs if only because the vile European film buyers were always crapping on Berger Royal films as *lacking in true filmic artistry.*

"Most of our flicks don't even play over there," he complained, grumbling as he stomped around the conference room as if Marc, himself, was personally responsible. Vinnie had cracked open a small glass of cream cheese with little bits of pineapple preserves in it, and was using his penknife to apply a generous layer to a cinnamon raison bagel that had somehow escaped his ravenous maws earlier.

"Let's get on with it," I said, giving him what I hoped was an appropriately bleak look. "Only three hundred pages to go."

"Some of them are only half pages with scribbles, *n' est pas?*" And there I had it, the answer to Marc's peculiar English inflections, the French way of saying *Is it not so?*

"Right. Should go real fast from here on," I said, feeling illuminated but not particularly unburdened.

By the time we broke for a quick lunch at noon, our little French bankroller looked exhausted. He shouldn't have been that tired, we'd only been going at it for the one session. I called a half-hour break. Marc disappeared somewhere and I pulled the blinds in my office and zoned out for a quick nap. Even so, I was back at it fifteen minutes before anybody else returned. Mark showed up looking guilty and Vinnie came back from the studio cafeteria resentful about not getting his nooner with Gloria.

For all that, Vinnie was my ally, and he was easy. I placated him with sub sandwiches from Dan's Subs that I had messengered in from Woodland Hills in the West Valley for a late afternoon snack. I got Marc the giant 12 inch meatball sub because I thought it might slow him down and make him sleepy. I had number 11, the six inch salami and cheese. Vinnie had a giant meatball sandwich, same as Marc. He ate his and half of Marc's, too, so there went my devious plan. Around four-thirty, Vinnie had his feet up, his head back and mouth open, and was snoring so loud his secretary peeked in to take a look, knowing that sometimes stroke victims make snoring noises when they're really already dead. Vinnie's secretaries were all teen-age high school dropouts, hardened kids he picked up off Sunset Boulevard to give a shot at show business. They looked of dubious hygiene, they stole from him, worked when they felt like it, could hardly answer the phone and generally lasted under two weeks. Vinnie didn't care. He'd been born poor in Brooklyn and got into the biz when a theater owner hired him to stand in the lobby and nab kids trying to sneak from A to B to see two movies for the price of one. He said it was his way of giving back to society. Still, in less than a day, Marc, Vinnie and I had managed to pull apart the entire script. By this time the loose pages were all on my end of the table. We yelled and debated and walked around in stormy silences. When anything was decided, the loose pages were handed, tossed or flung in my direction, and I made a few quick notations and reassembled them as best I could on the fly. Carnage Days was now Carnage Daze, and we were all feeling a little dazed, but there were no longer any major holes.

And, as important as anything else, I'd gotten it back down under 130 pages. I would brush it up a few more times over the next couple of days just to make sure we didn't get embarrassed on the set, which usually happened when some actor or actress, trying to make it big in Hollywood, would point out a hole big enough to drive a cement truck through.

By this time, the script itself had become a colorful affair, with pastel colored Post-it notes in blue, pink, green and common yellow on nearly every page, and the pages themselves, with replacements from previous revisions, were now more colored paper than white originals. Some of the pages themselves had been snipped and taped on new sheets of pink paper carefully labeled A, B and C through the alphabet, then aa, bb, cc, and finally one or two AAA, BBB and CCC.

"You gonna eat the runt end of that sandwich?" Vinnie asked, yawning as he rubbed his eyes. He was pointing to the remains of my hard salami and cheese sub.

"All yours, Vinnie," I said, sliding it across. "Sleep makes you hungry, huh?"

"Don't be a smart-ass, Havoc," he said.

Marc eyed him warily, a worried look on his face.

"Don't worry, Marco," Vinnie snorted. "I already had my quota of heart attacks for the year."

Marc looked away. His face reddened and he was suddenly busy, fussing with the script. That wasn't the reaction I'd expected. He looked more than tired. I caught a fleeting look at something else. Just for the briefest moment, he looked immeasurably sad. I thought to myself, *Something is going on with the Frap-man.*

He'd been a busy little beaver while I'd been gone, and when the gods of motivation and continuity finally froze him like a bug in amber over his computer keyboard, he'd resorted to jotting his ideas on a yellow notepad, ready for my return. Once our sessions got going, he'd fought like a madman for his ideas.

But by the time Vinnie woke up, toward the very end of our story meeting, he was quiet and even restrained. Vinnie saw we were getting on okay and left for a belated nooner with Gloria…never mind that it was nearly five in the afternoon. I was able to talk Marc out of Moroni's symbolic white robes in a few other scenes, though he insisted our hero don them after he goes truly nuts and takes off in a helicopter in a mad attempt to crash into the high rise office where he once worked.

Still, I thought I sensed something more problematic in the Frenchman. Marc, who had seemed so open and emotional when I first met him, had grown an outer shell of privacy during the time I'd been gone on my Oregon adventure. I figured it was private stuff. Maybe he was the guy who wasn't getting any sex, or maybe I should just butt out for a while. We had work to do, and Marc was going to have to unscramble his own problems, whatever they were.

CHAPTER 23

Whatever else might come of my life, I was back at Berger Royal. The green vegetation along the Willamette River and the meaningful dialogue of *Softly The Willows* was fading fast. Actually *Softly The Willows* and my mad and crazy night of ecstasy with Peanuts was already a week in my past, which is to say that was now ancient history. I had already shifted my gears. Once again, I was Hollywood Havoc; I worked for the tricky and devious Vinnie Berger and we were silver screen moguls, talking *big on the screen*.

Willows didn't need me across town where they were posting. And, Peanuts wasn't hanging over the editor's shoulder, either. She had left me a brief call, saying she missed me and our night together had been one for the ages—but, if you could believe The Insider, my ex had dashed off to the French Alps where there still was excellent snow at the higher elevations.

I did get a call from Arnie Control. The only real reason he called was to get right the number of days I'd worked, so he could correctly fill out the forms that he was turning in to the guild. But he gave me a brief update, more or less in passing, making sure I understood it was just a courtesy, producer to a writer/director who had gotten lucky for a few months but now was no longer on the payroll or even in the charmed circle of "A" list talent.

The film editor, Arnie said, had conferred with Rags and was assembling a director's first cut. Rags himself was already viewing the daily progress from monitors strung over his hospital bed. He'd declared he was going to be fully available in a month in spite of the outraged protestations of his doctors and his physical therapist, all of whom insisted he was still in great and imminent danger of losing his reattached leg.

Arnie made it clear that I was out of the loop, which for me was a good thing because Vinnie was now fully loaded, and both he and Fraper-the-Clapper were itching to *begin the carnage*, as Vinnie was fond of saying.

In the last two or three years I'd been taking over more and more of the day-to-day responsibilities at Berger Royal, and I knew Vinnie had been secretly pleased that I'd been out of town. It gave him a chance to dip his hand back into the nuts and bolts of production, to show he still had the right stuff. But, detail work being what it was, I think that joy had worn off in a day or two. Still, to his credit, he'd ground along and handled the dirty work that normally would have been mine.

"You won't be surprised to hear that I signed Bret Hanley," he said the next day as we gathered around the familiar conference table, eating Krispy Kream Donuts and swigging steaming cups of coffee poured from a big container I'd brought in from the closest Starbucks.

"Cool," I said. I wasn't surprised. Bret had been Vinnie's off-and-on preferred director over the years.

Marc gave him a sharp glance. "You did not clear this with me."

"Marco," Vinnie said, "you get your name above the title. I get to pick the director."

For the moment, I thought Fraper-man was going to have a heart attack, but he held back whatever he was about to say. Finally he sighed and shook his head.

"But—I thought a *French* director…"

"Marc, remember what happened when Billy Friedkin married Jeanne Moreau?" I asked.

"I do not remember anything of zat sort…"

Vinnie merrily jumped right in. "She dragged him over to the artsy-fartsy side, and she did it all in the name of the European gods of cinema. You know, Cupid and Dunder and that wine-guy." But then, Vinnie went from casual to dead-serious. He thumped one fist on the granite and gave me a look of pained surprise, granite being one of the Almighty's few stout inventions that wouldn't yield to his will. "And what happened was Sorcerer, a terrible, rotten remake of Wages of Fear!" He couldn't get back at God, but the Frap-man was right here in front of him.

"But…" Marc was searching for the logic in a diatribe that basically didn't have any. Vinnie didn't give him any time to fish around, either.

"But nothing, kiddo. The only French director worth his ass was Michelangelo Fellini."

"*Federico* Fellini," Marc corrected him, sitting back with a scornful twist to his lips. "And he was *Italian*."

"My point, exactly," Vinnie said as he reached across me to snag another of the cream-filled donuts. "Meanwhile, we got Bret Hanley."
Bret Hanley was a survivor. He probably acquired his longevity in Vinnie's good graces the same way I did;

Bite your tongue, swallow your pride and get on to the next set up.

Admittedly, he had a tougher row to hoe. Vinnie's admiration for his directors always took a dip when the critical reviews came in. Since he saw the director as the captain of the ship, they were responsible for critical disasters, of which we'd had many over the years at BR pics. We could launch a project with unbelievable crap dialogue weighing it down and huge holes in the story structure, and when it was panned as *merde* in the trades and went over like a lead balloon at the box office, in Vinnie's mind it remained still and always *the director's fault.*

"His credentials are the finest, then?" Marc asked.

"You can look him up. IMDB him, or look on the Directory of Members at DGA.org," I advised.

Vinnie waggled his fingers at us on his way out the door. "Nooners wait for no one," he said as the thick plate glass swished shut behind him.

"So, your opinion is what?" Marc asked me.

"My opinion is, my opinion doesn't count." I wasn't about to defend Brent Hanley's string of so-so B movies. If you look at Bret like he's a guy trying to stay current with three alimony payments and a big mortgage on a five acre spread in Ojai, his choices make some sense. But if you're a serious director trying to build a career in Hollywood, you can't be so desperate for the work that you take anything that comes along…but listen to me talk, the pot calling the kettle black.

"Marc," I said. "I have no shame."

"What this means, this?"

"It means I like to do good work, but I'm compulsive, I have to be working, doing something. Many of us are like that. I don't work at Universal or Sony, I work at

Berger Royal. I do "B" pictures because nobody offers me "A" pictures.

"Except your...Peanuts."

"That's right," I agreed. "And that's why I tell you Bret Hanley is a good director, probably lots better than his credits."

He didn't say any more, but his look remained dark and troubled, and what I'd said didn't seem to solve any of his deeper problems, whatever they might be. What I had told him about myself was true. I'm compulsive about my work, and I have to be doing something. Maybe working all the time keeps me from serious thinking about my devastated love life, and from finishing that total mess of a novel manuscript, Loose Days In La La Land, that I'd been writing practically since my life first crawled out of the primordial soup. But it didn't explain why, after Marc left and everyone else had gone home, I was still holed up in my small office next to Vinnie's at Berger Royal. It's all very well to push real life out of the way when there's work to be done. But once I had to set the script aside, I couldn't figure out how I was going to survive the next day, and the day after that.

Shamseen Usudman had put a hit out on me, as the gangsters like to say. I'd foiled his plans, stolen some of his money and, last but not least, killed three members of his family. True, that last had been in self-defense, but I didn't think I was ever going to be able to argue to that defense in Shamseen's court of opinion..

Somehow we had gotten through the day without any more blowups over the script revisions. For one thing, Vinnie left for his late afternoon nooner, and that helped. I retreated to my office and worked on story continuity, and before I knew it Marc was at the door, bidding me good evening.

"It's nothing personal?" he said.
"You mean our argument about Bret Handley?"
"Oui...non...I mean everything. It is all...you know,
business. We do as we must, and have to. It is so,
no? '
"Right, Marc. It is so. It's just show biz." I waved him
off. "Don' t worry, pal. I'll see you tomorrow."
But I nearly didn't.

CHAPTER 24

The minutes ticked by and I still didn't get up out of my seat and leave my office. I tried to get back to *Carnage Daze,* but found I couldn't concentrate. My mind kept wandering back to Peanuts and our night in the cabin by the river. I was starting to think maybe I should shut down and leave the office for the night. I had things to do. For one, I really had to get down to Newport to inspect my condo. Everything of my personal life had been there before the fire, and I wondered how much remained. Vinnie had given a glowing report on the work his wife had done, and Bertrand had called to say I could pick up the new keys at his place, but of my books and screenplay manuscripts and the manuscript of my version of the *great American novel,* I had no idea how much had been saved or simply thrown out as trash.

I couldn't let Shamseen scare me away from my own life. I should be getting on down to Newport Beach, driving up the little hill from the guard shack at the entrance to Sea Garden Cove and taking an approving look at the work everybody had done. But there I was, feet up on my desk, thinking about driving at dusk on the freeway and wondering who would be the next to move alongside, pull out some sort of automatic pistol and take the next pop at Hollywood Havoc.

And sometimes, when you are thinking about trouble, it actually comes looking you up. There was a faint swishing noise, and a slight change in air pressure in the room. Someone had just opened and then closed the front door of our office. *Or had they?*

Everyone had left Berger Royal. I'd been alone for over an hour. Had I actually heard anything? I jumped to my feet and thought to run out to see who it might have been. But then I thought I heard a dim, indistinct hum that might have been the elevator. The overheads in my office were off. I'd been working by the light of a desk lamp and my computer monitor. I went to the window and cracked the drawn blinds a bit so I could see the entrance below.

After a minute, a dark figure hurried out the door and walked quickly away toward the parking lot. The night illumination at the studio left much to be desired, and so I couldn't make out who it might be, or even if it was a man or woman. *Somebody small,* I thought, *somebody with quick, light steps.* I turned away from the window, thinking *What would Horace do?* Horace Keg, the man of action, would rush down the stairwell and overtake that person. I actually took a first step to leave the office before my second thoughts overtook me. *Rush out there to say what? To do what? Other indy production companies had offices on our floor. Suppose it was somebody dropping off a script? Suppose it was somebody from our office who had dropped by to pick up a significant other and then had seen he or she had left, and so also departed unannounced?*

I went back to my desk and put my feet up. And that's when the overhead lights throughout the rest of the building went out, plunging the outer offices into darkness. *Seven thirty,* I thought to myself. *Of course. The overheads go out automatically at seven thirty.* But I couldn't lose that little frizzle of apprehension that was running up and down my spine.

I sat there for five minutes, and then another five. I couldn't help it. I was frozen in space and time. My cell phone sounded and I must have jumped a foot. It was the familiar Bugs Bunny/Road Runner phone tone, and it was Vinnie, wondering how I liked my rebuilt condo.

"I'm still at the office, Vinnie."

"Yeah, I figured as much." He hesitated, Vinnie chewing over options. "I shouldn't tell you, kid, but it's a surprise party to celebrate everything going back to the way it should be. You better get your ass on down south or Old Bertie will eat all the pizza."

"Christ!" I hung up the phone, folded my laptop and slipped it into my carry case…and that's when my harried glance settled on Horace Keg's night vision goggles sitting dusty and neglected on a nearby shelf piled high with scripts.

I sighed, took a deep breath and set down the case. I clicked the switch on the side of the goggles. The batteries still had juice in them. I turned off the remaining light in my office and strapped the goggles on. Consciously, I couldn't tell you why I did that. I do remember I was thinking *There are no coincidences.*

The room around me lit up in a fluorescent green glow, the objects outlined with ghost-like halos. *This was paranoia gone wild! I had a party to get to and I was fooling around in spy-world!* But I managed to shake off my impatience and move slowly to the doorway. I left my office and shuffled out into the reception area, hoping the night guard or the janitors wouldn't come in at that moment. I made it to the big glass doors with our regal signature BR on the front, and still I saw nothing. Disgusted with myself, I ripped off the goggles, plunging myself into darkness. That was a stupid mistake, and I paid for it, grouping my way back in my office and tripping over some boxes of left-over production gear. I went sprawling to the floor. I got to my feet and, after some more blind feeling around in the near total darkness, snapped on my desk lamp. What a mess! Keg's canteen punctured with the bullet hole, Keg's big combat knife, Keg's web belt with the grenades and the ammo clips, Keg's picture of his lost loves, My Tuan and Tuy, Keg's can of Silly String...*Silly String*! Now maybe that was the most tenuous of connections, but, after all... *There are no coincidences!*

I turned out the light, put the goggles back on and went back into the other room, spraying the Silly String as I went. The fluorescent goop sprayed from the can, looking to my eyes like some sort of magical, glowing spider web...no big deal until I was nearly at the glass front entrance to our reception area, and then it made a little two inch high tent running parallel to the main doors. And that's how I found the taut, nearly invisible wire that ran low to the ground and was stretched across the main doors.

It ran a few inches above the tile and directly across the path I would have to take to exit the building. Vinnie was big on potted plants, and the wire was wrapped around a brick tucked behind the palm on the left hand side, and on the right ran into one well of a large cinder block lying sideways on the floor, this one nearly out of sight behind a struggling ficus plant.

I turned on a light at the receptionist's desk, and what I saw was enough to make me go back to my office for a big beam flashlight from our earthquake survival kit. It was an antipersonnel mine, innocent as an aluminum soft drink can and full of shrapnel deadly at up to thirty feet. I could never keep them straight, but we had used reconstructed blanks in Keg's War and so I knew it was probably an M14A or M16A. And, being in a cinderblock that it could turn into deadly chunks of cement, there was little chance I would survive a detonation.

I couldn't just step over the wire and be on my care-free way. One of the studio guards making his routine rounds would trip on it and be blown to hell just for doing his job. But maybe I didn't have to... I actually knew how the mines worked, sort of.

We'd strung some look-alikes for the jungle prison escape scenes in Keg's War and set them to go off with a flash and a bang. We must have rigged four dozen and triggered them at the right moment with no casualties among cast, crew or curious native onlookers. I could see the hole on the firing mechanism on top of the can where there had been a safety ring with a pin in it. It was in what the manuals called *active standby mode*. Once that safety pin was pulled out and the device charged by pulling the tripwire taut, all it took was a footstep into the wire, and I could see if the lions actually lay down with the lambs... or if hell was hotter than Las Vegas in August.

I retreated into my office and called Halliburton Rooks on my laptop. Rooks knew all things military. He would know what to do.

I went through the black box procedure and typed

HOW DO I DEACTIVATE LAND MINE?

Almost before I'd finished typing, Rook's lightning response came streaming back at me.

WALK AWAY IF YOU CAN.

I typed

NEGATORY. MUST DEACTIVATE.

DESCRIBE MINE.

LOOKS LIKE A COKE CAN WITH AN IRRIGATION RAINBIRD SCREWED INTO THE TOP. WIRE ACROSS DOORWAY, BRICK ON ONE END, MINE ON OTHER.

ANY SORT OF SAFETY PIN?

I'LL GO LOOK.

SEND ME A SHOT.

I found a metal ring with two prongs—that had to be the pin—discarded in the nearest ceramic pot. I took a picture with my cell phone, uploaded and flashed it back to Halliburton.

PIECE OF CAKE, he typed back. *WELL, MAYBE NOT. YOU TAKE BLURRY PICTURES. I'M THINKING ITALIAN OR FRENCH. EURO-UNION KNOCK-OFF OF THE M16A...MAYBE... GETTING THE PIN BACK IN WILL BE A LITTLE PROBLEMATIC. I CAN BE THERE IN SIX HOURS.*

GOT TO DO IT NOW.

CALL ME ON CELL. I'LL TALK YOU THROUGH IT.

SOUNDS GOOD TO ME.

YEAH. NOBODY LIKES TO DIE ALONE.

I went back to the land mine and peered at it while calling Rooks.

"So, what do I do?" I asked.

"Well, if it's French, you have to let up on the tension on the wire a little bit and that should align the holes so you can slip the pin back in."

"Okay," I said. But when I let up on the wire there was a deadly click.

"I heard that," Rooks said. "That means it's Italian. You have to go the other way. Pull it tighter."

"You're sure about this?"

"Well, you know," his chuckle was thin but unmistakable over the phone. "After three scotches, everything is BOOM."

"You've had three scotches?!"

"Doubles," he said proudly. "Come on, do this thing."

So I pulled harder and the entire firing mechanism came off in my hand.

"Hal, it fell apart."

"Must have been a dud. Dump it in a land fill somewhere."

I looked closer at the small can. It appeared to be empty, except for a small note rolled up inside. I opened the note, and read, "I want my money back."

It had to be from Shamseen Usudman. Shamseen had tried to take Vinnie and Bertrand on a scam, but things had gone wrong for him and I'd ended up with millions of his ill-gotten gains.

"It's a note from the terrorists," I told Hal. "Usudman wants his five million back."

"That much. We wondered about that. How'd you get so good at hiding money?"

"Vinnie taught me."

"Yeah. That would do it. Well, you better get to your party."

"Is there anything you don't know?"

"My personal life's a shambles. I guess I don't know anything about women. Rooks off in the East."

With that he clicked off and I was on my own.

CHAPTER 25

Needless to say, the drive back down south to my condo was one long paranoid voyage through the unknown. I don't know which scared me more, the old couple puttering along at 45 in the passing lane or the guy in the black Honda with the hip-hop thudding through the air space as he zoomed past on my right. I tried to calm down by thinking about my recent misadventures as a movie plot gone bad. By sorting through the happenings, perhaps I could find the flaws in my logic, and see where the story had gone wrong.

The old, hard facts, what we call the *back story,* was easy enough to fill in. In his younger days, my batty old neighbor, Bertrand Berke, had been in the import-export business. Desperate for business, he'd taken on a deal with some Nigerians to import a boatload of oil. But the deal had soured, the oil turned out to be a boatload of salt water, and Old Bertie had stripped the boat of everything that he could in an effort to get some of his investment back. Fortunately for the health of Southern California, one of the articles Bertrand took was a cement truck lashed to the deck of the boat...a cement truck with a heart of uranium that Shamseen Usudman and his organization was plotting to detonate in Los Angeles.

I first became involved because Bertie was out of town when I ran across two Nigerian thugs who had broken into his condo, which was located next door to mine. As batty old Bertie was nowhere to be found, they decided to kill me, instead. I escaped and managed to double-cross Shamseen Usudman, who turned out to be a mysterious Nigerian with Middle Eastern connections. In the end, various agencies of the U.S. government became involved, and the uranium was air-lifted to Nevada. But I still had $5 million of Shamseen's money, and he still had his undying hatred of America.

But here the story line gets muddy: His attempt to pitch me down an elevator shaft had failed, as had several other attempts at my life. He hadn't been interested in getting his money back then. Nobody had said, "Give us back the 5 mill or we'll kill you!" That inconsistency bothered me, being the storyteller I am. Now, when he could just as easily have taken me out with a land mine, he sets up a fake bomb with a threatening note. Something else was at work here, some threads to the story I couldn't even begin to understand.

As I drove south past the Commerce Casino, I went back over the evening, reviewing in my mind the little I did know. I'd been working late, and I'd been alone. Marc, I was sure, had been the last person to leave the office. The shadowy figure I'd seen hurrying away from our building could have been Marc…but that didn't make any sense. Marc had a pile of money invested in Carnage Daze, and he and Vinnie needed me to make that picture happen. Vinnie and I called him a sneaky cheese-eating surrenderist, but that was just us being stupid Americans, somewhere in our black hearts we knew you can't hold a nationality against a person. Marc wasn't very good as a story editor, but he seemed like a decent enough guy, and he had no motivation to kill me.

And so the time flew by as I mulled my way south on the 405, took the off-ramp at Jamboree and drove toward the ocean and Sea Garden Cove. I made my way past the guard gate and up the small, winding road to our cul-de-sac, and arrived about a half-hour too late for the party. The only one remaining was Bertrand, sitting in my dad's old chair, Soul-Sucker, which had been refurbished in dull maroon. The doomed souls carved in oak wood at shoulder length still wailed with open mouths, though the one on the left looked a little crisped by the fire.

"You're late," Old Bertie said. "You disappointed a lot of people, including Marsha, who did such a great job here."

"Who?" I eyed him suspiciously.

"Marsha."

He waved his wine glass around, and I was glad to see it was nearly empty. And, indeed, Marsha had done a good job.

"Wow," I said, taking in the book lined walls and the built-in desk in my study. "I should be grateful, but I can't get over the fact that your old buddy, Shamseen, tried to kill me again tonight."

"Phlag!" He said. "That's ancient history."

"Bertie-"

"Don't interrupt, Matthew Havoc. Young people have to learn to listen and not break in on the considered thoughts of their elders."

I took a deep breath.

"Okay. I'm sorry."

"You should be, " he grumped. "Got any more pizza?"

"Bertie, I just got here."

"Well, how about breakfast then?"

"You have to come back for that. It's only ten at night."

"Oh," he said. "Now you got a special time when you're serving?"

"No, but I just got home."

"Vinnie had his crew stock your place with food," he suggested.

I went out to the kitchen and found a new pan and knocked in six eggs and slopped in some milk. There was a used bottle of Caribbean Picapeppa sauce in the refrigerator, so I laced the eggs with that and cut in a half stick of turkey kielbasa for good measure.

Bertrand nodded his approval, watching closely to make sure I didn't make any mistakes.

I shoveled us out each a plate full of eggs, and we sat across from each other at the kitchen table. He was wearing one of my Keg's War t-shirts.

"That shirt's four sizes too big for you," I said.

"Christ, you got 200 of them in your garage," he said. "I'll give you some CrazyWear shorts for trade."

"I'd die first," I said. Bertie had invested in a bankrupt clothing company with designs so outlandish he couldn't even give them away to third-world nations after typhoons and earthquakes.

"You'll die when you hear this next one."

"Oh, boy," I said with a sinking feeling. "You and Vinnie got into my liquor cabinet."

"You don't have a liquor cabinet no more," Bertrand said. "You got a wine refrigerator."

"You and Vinnie didn't get to talking movies, did you?"

The last time that had happened, the two of them had nearly brought down a biblical rain of fire on the Southland.

"Uhh, no, 'course not," Bertrand said, hurriedly standing and brushing the scrambled eggs off his t-shirt. "Getting' late. Look around, all the nice stuff. Marsha, she fixed you up good."

"You keep saying 'Marsha' in that way you have…"

"Yeah, you know, Vinnie's wife."

Bertrand, the old dog, was now on a first-name basis with Vinnie's wife. That couldn't be good.

"Oh, boy," I said.

"Well, gotta scoot," he said, heading for the front door.

I tried to slow him down, "I notice the commie condo committee got my new front door the right shade of puke."

"Thank Marsha," he said over his shoulder, "she dealt with them." He stopped at the front door, "Say, you don't think I'm too old for a gal like her, do you?'

"Bertrand, you're too old for the Queen Mother of England!"

He gave me a puzzled look. "How old is that?"

"A hundred and ten, at least."

"I was serious, Matthew," he chided. And with that, he was gone.

"That's what I was afraid of," I said to the empty doorway. Bertrand wasn't very big on closing doors behind him, but that wasn't my real problem. Since his wife had died, his personal life had been a mess. When the Nigerian scam artists weren't keeping him busy, he was chasing some black widow from the local church grief club, a gathering that seemed to have little other business than encouraging old ladies to prey on addled gentlemen of means.

For some odd reason, red wine and scrambled eggs were starting to feel appropriate for that hour of the evening. I wandered around, picking up paper plates and wine glasses and looking over the job

Marsha had done redecorating my place. I was impressed. The Sea Garden Cove Condo Committee had made sure everything was reconstructed exactly as it had been, but she had made it turn out looking good.

My study had suffered the least damage, and my row of screenplays, thick and rumpled with water damage, was back on the shelf. Uncomfortable Soul-sucker, now in maroon velveteen, waited for the unwary to take a seat, and my Nolan Miller chair was poised in front of the blank computer screen. Even Loose Days In La La Land, my attempt to escape from BR by becoming a real writer of literature, was gathered together in more or less the same mess that it had been before. I had a new computer, most of my zip disks, CDs and DVDs still worked and, as my black box connection with Rooks was on his end, I had my password and that should still be in order.

So I was back in town and back in business at good old Berger Royal and everything should have been peaches and cream, only it wasn't. I sat in Soul-Sucker and mulled where I was at. I felt spooked and outside my game, like a guy who usually plays blackjack and finds him suddenly tossed into a game of poker where the stakes are life and death.

I was the cat who'd used up too many of his lives and I walked around looking for the next crane to fall on my head and the next mine to blow me up. I'd always been a fairly carefree person, but no more. From now on I was going to act with the realization that there were thousands of ways to kill a person. There was no way I could be ready for everything, but I was going to try.

CHAPTER 26

Over the next few days, Dad's old army buddy Halliburton Rooks did his part by sending a man over with a fancy electronic de-bugger and a few new side arms. I now was the proud owner of a big Smith & Wesson 9 mm and a smaller hide-out Beretta. I tried to get into the preproduction work on Carnage Daze, but it was routine compared to real life where a big time terrorist had unknown assassins trying to frag me. There was plenty to think about, and nobody to talk it over with. Julia was off in the Orient, seeking enlightenment. Peanuts, never one to look past her own problems, would just say I was crazy and I should get on with *whatever.*

Back from the Swiss Alps, she phoned with progress on *Softly The Willows.*

"Rags shows up in a motorized wheelchair," she said. "He said to say *Hi,* and to pass on that you did a good job, standing in for him."

"That's a good thing," I said, distracted and not really listening.

"You're relieved that he's back, aren't you Mattie."

I didn't deny it. Without some check, she would be constantly pressuring the editors to hold on her close-ups.

"But you shouldn't be."

"Why's that, Joy?"

"Because we're not sleeping together."

I don't know why, but I felt a sudden rush of relief.

"Why is that, Joy?"

There was a pause, and then words came tumbling out of her like a schoolgirl in the confessional.

"It's you, Mattie. It's you, it's you. I can't get you out of my mind."

There it was, the world handed to me on a platter. Only Peanuts was high-maintenance, and I had to concentrate on staying alive.

"It was just the madness of the moment, Peanuts."

"That was the night of a lifetime! You know it was!" Her voice went up a notch or two. My ex didn't like to be contradicted or denied in anything. The only thing I could do was be open with her.

:"Shamseen is threatening to kill me, Joy. I can't pull you into my mess."

"But...then...you're not saying we weren't meant for each other?"

I guess you could say I was somewhat of an experienced hand at calming the tigress. *Offer her what she wants, and, sooner rather than later, she'll change her mind.*

"No, Joy. I'm not saying that. Just finish the picture. I'll get Shamseen off my back, and we'll talk when everything calms down."

"It was a night to remember, wasn't it, Mattie?" Her voice was small and needy as a lonely little girl's.

"Yes, Madge," I said. "I'll never forget it."

Her editor interrupted on her end and she said she had to go and look at a scene before they carted Rags back to his room at Cedars Sinai.

Even after his own misadventures with Shamseen Usudman, Vinnie only half-believed anything I told him. With Vinnie, it was all about story, and if he couldn't use it on *Carnage Daze*, he didn't want to hear about it until we did a movie with a terrorist plot. That left my nutty neighbor, Bertrand Berke. But even old Bertie was full of secrets, distracted by some secret new deal.

"No time for your foolishness, now," he growled, chomping into a ham on rye sandwich he expropriated from my plate. "I've got real business going."

"What, with Vinnie? Tell me about it."

"Not a chance, Mister Blabbermouth."

"Blabbermouth?! I've been out of town for months!"

"It's not even a big deal, but there's a little money in it for Vinnie and me."

"Well, this time try not to take Southern California down with you."

"See why I don't hang around here?" he asked. "Negative. Everything too negative."

"I thought it was because you're stealing my ham sandwich, you cunning old thief," I said. But I was talking to myself, as he'd already made his way out my front door.

I went to the refrigerator and retrieved the other half of the ham sandwich. But I wasn't hungry, and I just sat in my kitchen, trying to figure out my wreck of a life.

We movie story people are supposed to have life all figured out, but all I knew was that life kept moving forward, and I had to keep step, one foot at a time, just to keep up. I felt lonely, though I have to confess I was confused about whether I missed Julia or Peanuts more. I know there were times when I found myself thinking about the one, and times the other. I know I *liked* Julia better, but Julia was gone, gone, gone like yesterday's daisies, with about zero chance that she was ever coming back. Of course, Peanuts was never actually here for me either, but she had found a way to worm herself back into my life, and my radar sixth sense about women, weak as it was, kept telling me I hadn't seen the last of her sly wink, her perfect breasts and her scheming tricks.

So I'd been sitting there for a few minutes, and just about when I had figured out my life was a complete mess, Bertrand returned.

"Thought so," he said, scooping up the sandwich from in front of me. "Don't these come with any dill pickles?"

At least, I still had my work. Just as Vinnie was happy to show the world he still could get in there and do a picture, I think it bothered me that he'd gotten so far along without me. I was Hollywood Havoc, and yet, the truth was, Hollywood could get along just fine without me.   But I decided it wasn't going to get the opportunity.   It was as if I heard the distant roll of drums, my call to action...although I well knew that action at Berger Royal was less the storm and thunder of Hector Berlioz and more the happy clatter of Bob Marley. Whatever it was, I wasn't going to dance to the tune of Shamseen Usudman. Screw him; I had a picture to make.

CHAPTER 27

That's the thing about show business—you never know what's going to happen next. And so, the next morning when I got in to the office at eight Marc and Vinnie were already pacing around the big conference room, alternately staring at the multi-colored schedule laid out on one wall and yelling at each other. Well, not actually *at* each other as if they were angry, but more to point out some urgent matter that had to be attended to. I could see their problem right away. The making of any film can be analyzed as the synthesis of three streams of input: There's the time line, the money line and the talent. And the less you have of any of the three, the more of the other two it takes to make up for it. Here, Vinnie and Marc clearly were running out of time. I took a closer look at the new schedule Vinnie's secretary had push-pinned to the wall and my eyes widened.

"Don't pee your pants, Havoc," Vinnie warned.

"Vinnie," I yelped, "You can't schedule the big outdoor action stuff up front!"

"Why not?" he asked, eyeing the particularly fresh donut rolls with the raspberry centers that he'd brought in from the Boulangerie, the latest find in his endless search for the world's most perfect bakery.

"It could still rain! That would ruin us!"

"Aww, Hollywood. It hasn't rained in weeks! You still think you're in Portland!"

"I think it is not going to rain?" Marc piped in his own questioning opinion.

I gave Marc the glare I reserved for do-gooders and street-corner saints with their hand out, "Oh, great—everybody's a weather man!"

"Don't be such a chicken-shit," Vinnie grumbled, the amusement obvious in his voice, at least obvious to me. "Come on, Havoc. Let's roll the dice on this one. The mornings have been foggy. Maybe we'll get some moody crap, like those Nam Copter shots we got in Keg's War."

That reference set me back a little. The helicopters rising through steam off the Mekong river with a red ball sun in the background had been pure poetry in the dailies and for a brief time had us talking about an Oscar for cinematography …until the reality set in that we were Berger Royal and we didn't win Oscars, we made B grade pictures and the critics used our handouts for snot rags.

Sometimes I wonder how Vinnie and I have lasted this long. As film producers, we have vastly different methods of operation. My style is, I like everything buttoned down to the last button, while Vinnie is more free-wheeling and spontaneous, the original Vinnie Berger *Oh what the fart, let's shoot some more footage and we'll fix it in edit* school of filmmaking. It didn't matter when I was the new guy working my way up through the ranks, but now I kept finding loose ends, scraps of deals on the back of hamburger wrappers, crumpled receipts in the trash can, publicity memos unsent that might have served the picture weeks ago but now were almost too late. That sort of thing.

"I like it, we shoot the big scenes first?" Marc half-declared and half-questioned.

"Well, it's your money, Marc."

"*Our* money," Vinnie corrected me. "And we are good shepherds guiding our little flock of dollars through the perilous production…err, path." He sounded like he was quoting from one of the lectures he gave film students at Loyola Marymount, USC and CSUN in the Valley when he didn't have anything else going. He said it was a great way to meet new talent. Translation: to pick up starry-eyed young co-eds.

I threw up my hands.

"Okay, I give up. We shoot the big scenes downtown first. You want me to book the Coast Savings & Loan building?" I was actually reaching for the phone, thinking, now that we were committing to a date, all we needed was for somebody else to slap down an advance and ruin our plans.

"Already had the UPM do that," Vinnie grunted.

That raised my eyebrows. "Who wrote the check?"

"Don't get your balls in an uproar," Vinnie said. "Coast people agreed on good faith. You got three days to get a check over there."

"Why would they do that?"

Vinnie shrugged. "They got their problems. A lot of vacancies. I guess they need the money."

I knew what kind of problems they had. After a while, dead bodies in an elevator shaft start to smell. But that wasn't my immediate worry.

"Okay," I sighed. "When do we shoot?"

"Three days," Vinnie said. Marc nodded happily, looking at me from behind the thick lenses of his wire-rimmed glasses. Since he'd come on board, I'd thrown out my own wire-rims in favor of the horn-rimmed owl look. We stared at each other, a pair of dueling myopics seeking advantage in the fuzzy world of film scheduling where nothing ever turned out exactly as planned. A few days was a stunningly short time to prep for a major action sequence. I couldn't think of anything to say.

"Hey," Vinnie assured me. "No problem. We been working here while you been spreading the peanut oil up north. Hanley and the UPM have blocked out the days and times." He indicated a separate board with multi-colored strips representing day, night, indoor, outdoor, and the all-important action montage. "Bret's over there right now. I talked to him five minutes ago. He's up on that patio you found—great job, by the way."

I figured I'd take one last shot at common sense. "Vinnie, what if it rains? Come on, humor me…what if?"

He took a big bite out of a roll and a little red squirt of raspberry hit his shirt at stomach level.

"Well then…" I could see he was thinking about it, probably for the first time. But he was Vinnie Berger. He made decisions; he didn't change his mind. "Well, then, we shoot in the rain. Jesus, kid, quit worrying. Didn't you just get back from your watery baptism in the Oregon monsoons?" He turned to Marc, "He got laid, too, didn't I tell you?"

"Yes, and you know this?" Marc, who didn't seem to have any joking side or light-hearted humor to him, still couldn't believe the famous star Joy Benefeté and I could ever be an item.

Vinnie gave him a hearty slap on the back and his wire-rims nearly went flying off.

"Come on, Fraper—look how serene he looks, like a little altar boy who's had his nuts shaved."

I flipped Vinnie the finger, but his response was a big guffaw and a friendly wave of dismissal. I didn't even try to deny it. After our years together, he had me down pretty well. Or, more likely, he'd had a side bet with Peanuts and she'd called her old boss to gloat and collect. The collapse of my moral stance was probably worth a few thousand to her, money he'd gladly shell out.

"Vinnie, that's not the point," I protested. "*Softly The Willows* was written for Oregon in the winter." I waved at the scheduling boards, "But *Carnage Daze* here doesn't call for even one drop of rain."

Marc looked us over speculatively. "Rain, you know, a good thing potentially, very symbolic of mankind's troubles, don't you think?"

"Oh, yeah," Vinnie agreed, giving me his innocent, wide-eyed school-boy look, "*Raindrops keep falling on my head...*quintessentially symbolic."

He was rubbing the stain on his tan shirt with a napkin he'd dipped with grape juice he got from a small cooler where we kept snacks and soft drinks.

"No, Vinnie," I said. "Club soda."

"Huh?" He looked at me like I was crazy.

"Grape juice doesn't take out raspberry stains. Club soda takes out wine stains."

"Oh. I knew it was one of those."

He stopped spreading the big purple stain and started taking his shirt off. I raised my voice like a short order cook, "*One Chop of Death* golf shirt, please! Triple X Large. Hold the onions and mayo!"

"One extra. Extra, extra large, coming up!" Vinnie's secretary's amused voice floated back from the next room. "Over easy, of course." A moment later she came running in with the replacement shirt, which he began to pull on over his head.

"Okay, Vinnie," I said. I grabbed my notes and headed out the door.

"Hey, where you going? You haven't even had a donut."

"Script revisions," I said. "I'll be in my office."

That was the beginning and the end of my brief last stand against their crazy decision to start filming at once. I decided to stop talking about how little prep time we had and just be there to contribute what I could and pick up the pieces when it all came apart.

CHAPTER 28

Need I say how badly I slept that night? Peanuts called after midnight, just after I'd finished a few mushroom calzones and beers with Bertrand and shooed him out the door.

"Mattie," she said in that sexy, softly purring, slightly slurring voice that meant she'd been out drinking on the town. "How's about I get the service to drive me down to your place for a little *Havoc Heaven*?"

"How's the edit coming, Joy?"

"Is that a yes, Mattie?"

"No, that is not a yes! I have to work tomorrow, and it's already way past witching."

"Oh, super-pooper, come on, give a girl a little touch of madness, sweet Mattie."

"Joy, we're grown-up, responsible people. We did get separated for a reason, remember?"

"I can't seem to remember right now," she said in a husky whisper. "It's all blocked out by the image of you ripping my panties off in our little cabin by the river. That was just last week, wasn't it? Surely you haven't gone old and grey and limp in a few days?"

"Let me be the bad guy, here," I said, trying for a firm voice-of-command that I didn't really feel. "You and I called it quits because we couldn't stand each other."

"No," she said. There was a long pause, and she didn't say any more.

"No? What do you mean, 'no'?" That was news to me. She'd always insisted we share the blame for our split, 60-40 my fault, and I'd always thought it wasn't worth arguing over. *Done is done; let's get on with the rest of life.*

"We got separated," she said in that low, throaty way of hers, "because my goddamn career got so important to me that I forgot about what we really had…I little piece of heaven. And I don't mean Havoc's Heaven…well, that too, but so much more…"

"Joy, you've been clubbing in Beverly Hills, right?"

"Slumming in the Valley," she chuckled.

"Okay, but the point is, you've had a few, you're lonely and you don't want to be alone right now."

"It's more than that, Mattie," she said.

"I know you think you owe me, but you don't. Joy, we're even. You enriched my life. You gave me great pleasure. You continue to be my friend."

"Your *best* friend, right?"

"Yes, of course, your very best friend." I was just agreeing to be agreeing. I thought we'd gone from open hostility to an uneasy neutrality. The sex we shared in the cabin was a bonus, but I could hardly be called the exclusive recipient of her urges and desires. I would say it was more like winning five grand with a California Lottery Scratcher, maybe something called RIGHT PLACE, RIGHT TIME.

"You're always there for me, Mattie. You never let me down." I heard her yawn, and for a moment thought she'd fall asleep right then and there, with me still on the line. But then I heard her voice, small and warm and sleepy.

"I'm going now, my dear sweet best friend. Imagine if you can for now my lips just gently kissing the tip of heaven, and maybe a moist little lick, with the rest to come for later."

"Okay, Madge. Goodnight," I said.

"This thing isn't over between us, Mattie...no, no, no, Mister Havoc...not over by a long shot. It is only the beginning..." And then she did hang up, leaving me with a thousand questions.

So how do you go to sleep after turning that down? The truth is, I didn't. Something didn't seem right with Peanuts, and I couldn't figure out what it was. We had always been straight with each other—I would describe her attitude toward me as brutally frank, particularly when she thought I was standing in the way of her career. Me...well, the way I saw it, my survival in our relationship had depended on my flexibility, my willingness to dodge and dart. I had been motivated to make it work; Jack Havoc and his missus had never ducked out when times got tough. But after Peanuts had walked away and filed for divorce, I'd finally been forced to the realization that she had a different set of values.

And now, barely turned thirty, she was in fresh full bloom, and particularly now that she was proving she really could act, better offers would be coming in. "B" pictures, the tits-and-ass sex-taculars that had launched her career, were a thing of the past. Vinnie and I no longer had anything she could use.

So...why was she hanging around now, and what was all this 'best friend' business? With our long (by Hollywood standards) history of push and shove, I suspected she wanted—here you may insert, 'felt she needed'—something. But for the life of me, I couldn't figure out what it was.

I tossed and turned for a few hours and then sat up and watched stilted old black-and-white movies on DirecTV, admiring the revolution Stanislavski had inspired in acting. At about five the next morning, I stretched and threw on some running togs and jogged for a few miles through the fog along Jamboree. I came back to my place to shower up, and made a double latte in my Rancilio Silvia, that I'd had the *Softly the Willows* production clean-up crew ship me down from Oregon. And I still didn't have a decent thought on what was motivating my ex wife to phone me in the middle of the night and whisper sweet nothings in my ear.

By the time I showed up at BR Pics the next morning, Bret Hanley and his boys had nearly finished blocking out their shots. I pounded out the final script revisions, and hung around hoping for a crisis I could solve, something impossible that Vinnie had forgotten and only I (with my unique experience and vast book of contacts in the biz) could correct, but the day crawled by and nothing like that came up. Meanwhile the countdown was on and we only had one more day left until the actual *Carnage Daze* shoot was to begin.

Famous directors like Hitchcock and Sturgis worked with an art director weeks before shoot day, sketching out scenes so the director could firm up how he wanted to shoot the scene. Berger Royal Pictures, on the other hand, generally bypassed the expense of having a professional artist storyboard anything. Vinnie would rather see that money in his pocket, and couldn't be convinced any other way…that is, until Marc Fraper insisted on having the helicopter scenes worked up for *Carnage Daze*.

In a way, it was still somewhat Marc's money, so Vinnie shrugged and called Boris Rascalova, an old friend of his with a quick wrist who made a living bouncing around the studios.

Boris showed up within the hour. He was a short, stocky Russian with a spade beard, and he spoke in terse, nearly unintelligible bursts of tough guy talk, like a Chicago truck driver on speed. Marc went on for some time, waving his hands expressively and talking about the symbolism of the helicopter rising like new hope through the mists of early morning.

"Yeah, I could do that," Boris nodded. "Get out of here and let me work."

"You need anything?" I asked.

"Russian tea would be nice," he said. "And get me Hanley."

"Hey, this ain't the Russian Tea Room," Vinnie grumped, but he backed down when Boris stared at him with his dark eyes.

"That's a joke, you see, Boris," Vinnie explained.

"Yeah. Now get out," Boris said.

He and Bret Hanley had worked together before, and soon the Berger Royal conference room walls were pasted with quick shots of a strange looking helicopter rising past the alarmed faces of L.A. police and the general downtown public, the helicopter darting between the high rises near the Coast Savings Building, the crazed happy look on Moroni's face as he sat at the controls of his helicopter (in Marc's latest version, Moroni is an ex-army helicopter pilot who has been doing traffic reports for morning news), the chase as two police choppers took off in hot pursuit.

They didn't seem to mind my being there, so I sat quietly in the conference room, munching on a beef and bean burrito I bought off a taco truck and chugging a Snapple Peach Iced Tea. Boris and Bret were at the other end of the table, Bret waving his hands in graceful swoops and Boris excitedly scratching on a large art pad on his lap.

"What kind of helicopter is that, anyway?" I asked.

"French," Boris said, not bothering to look up from his drawing.

"Marc's idea," Bret added. "He flew one in the French military."

"Marc can fly a helicopter?" Wonders never ceased. I hoped he was better at it than he was at fixing scripts.

"You are surprise, yes?" Marc himself said, returning from lunch, and emboldened that Boris had allowed me to enter his artistic inner sanctum.

"Amazed," I admitted. "The L.A. cop choppers are easy; I can get them in a flash…but where we going to get this one?"

"Vinnie lined it up," Marc said. "It is an Aerospatiale SA.315B Llama, and it climbs at an extremely rapid rate. I will have to throttle back, so the police can keep up?" That was classic Fraper, still making questions out of his statements.

"YOU are going to fly it?!"

"Yes, of course?"

I could see getting the whole truth was going to be like pulling teeth. I hate it when that happens. You just know something's not right, but you don't know exactly what, and no time left to figure it out. That had been happening a lot to me of late.

"Great. And where did Vinnie get this fantastic, fast-climbing helicopter?"

"He got it from me," a familiar, grumpy voice said. It was Batty Old Bertie, my next-door neighbor—and he was returning from lunch with his new best buddy, who happened to be my boss, the head of Berger Royal Pictures. The only thing I could be grateful for was that Bertrand had left his Crazy Wear shirts and sweat pants with their zigzag designs and eye-popping colors at home in the boxes in his garage. A few buttons were out of place, but, on the whole, he was dressed entirely decently, at least for him.

"The helicopter you stole from the oil tanker?" I asked.

"*Took*, Matthew," he corrected me. "I *took* the helicopter in exchange for services rendered and fees paid."

"This is absolutely crazy!"

Vinnie gave me the wide grin he uses whenever he's able to pull one over on anybody. "No it isn't, Matt. We had it certified. It's all checked out, ready to go. Marc's had me up in it several times. I'm convinced. He's a really good pilot."

"There it goes now," Bertrand said with a note of pride in his voice. From our third floor windows I could see the helicopter, which was sitting on the flatbed back of a truck that looked suspiciously like Fat Boy. The entire rig was heading out the front gate of the studio.

"You fixed up Fat Boy!"

"Yup!" Vinnie grinned.

"And we're renting her to the production—for the going rate, of course," Bertrand said piously, glancing over at Marc.

"When we're done, we're going to sell the unit to Hollywood Rentals," Vinnie added.

"We'll squeeze them damn Nigerian turnips yet!" My crazy old neighbor added.

It was enough to make my head spin; after our near call with nuclear disaster, I'd hoped I'd never see Fat Boy again, and yet here it was, rigged for the key action scenes in *Carnage Daze*. Dazed, indeed—I was the one beginning to feel daffy and out of the loop.

Fat Boy slowly maneuvered between lanes of parked cars as it crabbed its way out the front entrance of the studio. We were looking at it from a down angle. From what I could see, Llama was a metal skeleton of an aircraft with a clear bubble up front, skids underneath and an exposed turbine engine on top behind the main rotor. Metal tubes criss-crossed their way back to the rear rotor. A bright red elongated tube was mounted underneath between the twin skids. That cylinder looked dangerous and forward thrusting, like a napalm pod or a wing-tip gas tank. The three red-tipped blades on the main rotor were collapsed back and tied down so the rig could make its way through the streets.

"What is that big red thing underneath?" I asked.

"Spare gas tank," Marc shrugged. "That's the way it came. *Jamais* look a gift horse in the mouth?"

I would have loved a closer look, but Fat Boy had already lumbered around the corner and was gone.

"Where they taking it?"

"Downtown," Vinnie said. "We're a go for tomorrow morning."
I wasn't sure why that bit of news startled me so badly. Once again I had the feeling things were moving too quickly. I wanted some more time to catch up.

"Tomorrow! What happened to next weekend?" I'd been pushing to delay the shoot a few days, as the weather looked sketchy.

"We got an okay with the permits, so we jumped on it!" Vinnie threw his arms wide in triumph. "We had the crew on standby. They're ready to go!"

"It is all stunt doubles, so we need no actors?" Marc added.

"Hey, Johnny Mountain says it ain't gonna rain." Bertrand added the topper with a final note of triumph. After all, Johnny had been accredited by the Meteorological Society.

Vinnie glowed and walked around the room, looking for stray donuts somebody might have forgotten. The gods of filmmaking were smiling on Berger Royal Productions. It was entirely too much enthusiasm for me. I was eager to get away, but Vinnie called me back as I was making for the door.

"What, you leaving? It's only 3 o'clock in the afternoon. Bret wants us to go over the sketches."

"I want to see for myself what you did to Fat Boy." Actually, I wanted to inspect that dangerous-looking red cylinder everybody seemed to be taking for granted.

Vinnie's face broke into a proud grin and he slapped me on the back, "Pretty good conversion, huh?" He didn't wait for an answer as he steered me back into the conference room with his great bear-like paw. "You'll see it plenty, come tomorrow morning. I tell you, she jumps like a bird, Havoc!"

There was no way out of it, and, actually, there was plenty of serious planning to get through. We chewed over angles, direction of the sun. and the distances between the various buildings. It was going to get crowded up there, with five helicopters churning through their various assignments at the same time. We had Moroni's Llama, two chasing police helicopters, the main camera helicopter and a second overhead camera helicopter, and they all needed clear lanes, as well as secondary options if something went wrong. Then we had the positions of the stationary cameras, the chief ones being on the patio on top of the Coast Savings Building and shooting from the windows and rooftops of several nearby buildings.

Our little preproduction meeting provided for me a somewhat surrealistic scene. My goofy old neighbor Bertrand winked at me as he accepted a Cuban cigar from Vinnie and relaxed in one of the big leather conference chairs with BRP stamped in gold on the high backs, soaking it all in like an executive producer (which, in a sense, he was, as he was making a financial contribution to the production.). It didn't make me any more comfortable that Bertrand had confided over a big slab of mushroom calzone that, thanks to some rejuvenating blue pills he'd gotten from a geriatric doctor, he was now involved in furtive liaisons with Vinnie's wife Marsha.

"Maybe you could have that thing do a loop-de-loop," Bertrand growled at me. Somehow, he was now seeing himself as a *Hollywood idea guy*. And in my batty old neighbor's mind, I was the fellow who would translate his golden notions into cinematic action.

I decided to make old bat-brain's suggestions Marc's problem.

"Marc, you're the expert. You can make your Llama do a loop-de-loop?"

Marc frowned, looking at me as if I was making fun of him.

I shrugged innocently and pointed at the source of the suggestion.

He shook his head, No, pursing his lips.

"We make it go like this, spin, spin, spin?" he said. He indicated he could make it whip around like a top. "You like something of excitement like that?"

It wasn't exactly what he'd visualized, but my batty old neighbor nodded excitedly, fairly glowing that he had contributed to the film.

"Hey, Bertie, you're gonna be there, right?" Vinnie asked.

"Wouldn't miss it," Bertrand said, flicking the long ash from his cigar on the black granite tabletop.

"Call's gonna be brutal," Vinnie advised. He raised his voice, "Melody, get Bertrand a room downtown. Get him an early call, say four or four thirty."

And, just like that, batty old Bertie had become a Hollywood mogul. I led a strange life, but somehow at the moment I couldn't think of anything stranger than that.

CHAPTER 29

By the time we broke off our production meeting it was after rush hour, and I didn't get back to my condo in Newport until nine that night.   I bypassed dinner, grabbed a few cans of Red Bull from the refrigerator and marched into my study without bothering to check the mail or the answering machine.

I was on the line to Rooks in under a minute.

VINNIE PLANS TO FLY HELICOPTER TAKEN FROM OIL TANKER SCAM IN SHOOT TOMORROW MORNING.

My dad's old intelligence agency friend's rapid-fire answer spilled across the screen.

HELLO TO YOU, TOO. WHAT KIND OF HELICOPTER?

SORRY, I'M A LITTLE AGITATED. IT'S AN AEROSPATIALE SA.315B LLAMA.

FAST CLIMBER. DEVELOPED BY SUD-AVIATION FOR INDIAN AIRFORCE FOR USE IN HIMALAYAS

IT SEEMS TO HAVE AN EXTRA TANK WELDED ON UNDERNEATH. SHOULD I BE WORRIED?

ABOUT NUKES? I DON'T THINK SO. LLAMA COULDN'T LIFT THE WEIGHT.

I couldn't think of anything else to ask. If that helicopter couldn't carry a bomb, maybe I was paranoid, suffering as Vinnie had said, from "post-nuclear depression syndrome." Then Rooks was typing again:

WHO'S GOING TO FLY IT?

MARC FRAPER. FRENCH FILM PRODUCER. EX-FRENCH MILITARY, HE SAYS.

ISN'T THAT A BIT EXTRAORDINARY? I MEAN, DON'T YOU HAVE STUNT GUYS FOR THAT?

IT IS AND IT ISN'T. VINNIE WILL DO ANYTHING ON THE CHEAP. AND MARC IS EAGER TO DO THIS.

HEARD ANYTHING FROM SHAMSEEN USUDMAN?

NO. ALL QUIET SINCE THE LAND MINE.

MAYBE HE'S ON TO OTHER THINGS.

YOUR MOUTH TO GOD'S EAR.

HOW'S THAT?

JEWISH PRAYER OF HOPE.

OH, RIGHT. THE HELICOPTER SHOULD BE OKAY. WE'LL HAVE A MAN THERE, ANYWAY. FOUR O'CLOCK CALL, RIGHT?

Rooks knew all about the call. He probably knew about the helicopter, and Fraper as well.

DO YOU KNOW EVERYTHING?

DIDN'T KNOW THAT PRAYER OF HOPE. ROOKS OUT IN THE EAST.

I signed off. HAVOC OUT IN THE WEST.

     I poured myself a small brandy and tried to go to bed, but I just tossed and turned. I looked at my watch. It was nearly midnight. I'd had my friends re-wire my phones, and I saw that Bertrand was at 82 calls for the day, evidence that he was still dancing with the scam artists. And that's when Peanuts called again.
     "Mattie…" her voice was soft, but hesitant.
     "I don't do phone sex, Peanuts. I mean, I do, but I'm not very good at it."
     "Nooo…not that…"
     "How's *Softly the Willows* going?
     Her voice brightened a little. "Really, really good," she said. "And it looks like Rags isn't going to lose his leg. He might limp a little, but that's it."
     "And…you're okay?" I asked.
     "Well…that's the thing," she said. The next sentences came out with a rush. "I think I'm pregnant. I think those crazy, impulsive things we did made a baby."
     "Joy, that only a week ago. You couldn't possibly know—"
     "You don't know what I know, Matthew Havoc. Men don't know anything. I'll tell you one thing; you're the only man I've been with since we started *Willows*."

She meant it to be reassuring, but I felt a little bit like the last passenger to hop on the train. I didn't want to say the wrong thing. I didn't want to hurt or insult her. But it was a crazy conversation. Women don't just know they are pregnant. And Madge had done this to me before, not once, but several times. And, I knew she'd been to an entire platoon of gynecologists, and the general diagnosis was that the odds of her getting pregnant was a bit like finding a sperm in a haystack.

"It may be nothing, Joy," I said. "You know we've been here before."

"You're not mad at me?" Her voice sounded small and uncertain. That was the thing about my ex. Underneath all the passion and thunder, under all the grasp and greed, she was just like everybody else— uncertain, and wanting to be loved.

"Madge, how could I be? It's always been *you and me, kid.* This is us. We don't get mad about the serious stuff." '

"Oh, Mattie, I knew I could count on you!" she said.

"Don't worry about it," I reassured her. "It's only been a few weeks. You're under a lot of stress, finishing *Willows* and everything, and we both know from experience that it's too soon to be thinking about this. Everything's going to be way okay. You have to believe that. You have to be tough, like Amanda Smythe...or better, tough like the Madge Sacknall I fell for all those years ago..."

"You're right, I'm just being silly," she said. "Thanks for talking with me, Mattie. You're always there for me. I feel better now." And without another word, she snapped the cell phone shut on her end. I called her back, but the number I had had been discontinued, something she did about every other week. That left me with a thousand new questions, and no way to get the answers.

I sighed and threw on a pair of Dockers and a *Dragonfly Madness* T-shirt, the one with brave Tran Le's fists cocked and flaming, looking like he'd just returned from hell with a vengeance. The chill night breeze was blowing in off the Pacific, so I pulled on a green rip-stop jacket a member of the SWAT team had worn in *California Climax*, and my trusty Keg's War hat. *Worry wasn't making me any prettier*, I thought as I squinted at my reflection in the hall mirror. Ten minutes for a stop for a grande percent latte at the Starbucks on McArthur Boulevard, and I then was on the 405, headed back north toward my fate, whatever that might be..

CHAPTER 30

Well, okay then, Hollywood Havoc, I said to myself as I pointed one of Vinnie's Explorers north toward downtown Los Angeles. *Okay, suppose Madge is pregnant.* The fact was, *if* she was, and *if* she said it was my baby, I wouldn't question it. But in my ex-wife's world I didn't really think that would matter. There would be no joyful moment, or even a conversation about what we might call it. Joy Benefeté was born and alive, and wouldn't be moving over for a squalling little infant. The woman I knew would have that little thing scraped out before it got to be the size of a pea. *Nuisance, sure. Maybe a few days to recover.* And then, *To horse and a full gallop on after those distant mirages that were her golden dreams.*

But…suppose she *wasn't* pregnant? It didn't fit any story or script we'd ever rehearsed together, or any film I'd seen of hers since we split. Maybe she'd found something new—a new project with a part for a successful businesswoman who suddenly finds out she's pregnant. I felt I was on to something. *That was entirely like Joy.* She had practiced her roles on me so much over the years that I never could be sure what was real and what was a complicated fiction in her mind. I knew that to somebody outside the business that might seem twisted and even deranged, and certainly not normal, but I also knew that was the way many serious actors thought…and certainly Joy had been no exception. She could be an absolute monster, playing lines in her head when all I wanted was a straight and simple answer. And she never, ever admitted to what I saw as her fatal addiction to acting. There were times when I'd even thought that, some fine day, she might drive a car over a cliff, a tragic moment even though contrived, just to see what it felt like, to get it right in her head. *Crazy, right? Welcome to the life and times of Hollywood Havoc.*

And, thinking in that vein, I asked myself *What was all that best friend stuff?* We certainly had never been what anyone could call real buddies. How could a person be best friends with someone, if you never could tell whether she was feeling something real or just feeling out her next role in a movie? Her attitude of late only made sense if one assumed she was working on a new part in some dramatic relationship flick. I even came up with the log line: *Glamorous movie star has to come to terms with abortion when her best friend, an ordinary guy she's known since high school, accidentally knocks her up one night at their drunken class reunion.*

Well, no matter what, I knew the outcome of that movie. Madge Sacknall, driven by her inner demons to reach the Hollywood heights, would never break stride to drop a baby.

But…enough of that. I had a more immediate problem of my own, a complicated mess with five helicopters flitting dangerously close, in and out and around the shiny, mirror-glass windowed skyscrapers of downtown Los Angeles.

It wasn't yet two in the morning when I pulled the black Explorer with the BR Pictures logo magnetized to the panel on the drivers side into the parking lot where we were holding our rendezvous.

The riggers and the vehicles guys were already there. As luck would have it, Old Holtzinschnab (Old Holtz for short) and his son Young Holtz were going over the Llama when I got there. They had fanned out the blades and were wrenching them into the locked position. I knew the Holtz father and son from California Climax; we had crashed many a car together in the period of a week and a half.

"Havoc," Young Holtz said. His father simply nodded. The Holtzinschnabs were long on mechanical ingenuity but short on words. BR Pics used them a lot, so I was used to it.

"Ready to go?" I asked, indicating the Llama.

They both just nodded.

"Where's the fuel tanks?"

"Tank," Young Holtz corrected me. He pointed to a square metal container as big as two bales of hay that was positioned right behind the plastic bubble.

"Why do you need that spare one?"

"Came with the machine," Young Holtz said.

"Empty," Old Holtz added.

I looked around, but the lot was empty. Over an hour and a half yet until the caterers would show up. After that the crew would straggle in, arriving in ones and twos.

"You sure it's empty?"

"Was yesterday."

"Could you humor the producer?"

"Heard you was seeing shadows," Old Holtz grinned.

"You're going to make me hit an old man," I grinned back.

"That would be a mistake," Young Holtz grinned. I knew he was right about that one. The old man had to be 75, but his chest was broad as a barrel and his arms were thick and hard as oak limbs.

256

"Well, please, then."

"The magic word," Young Holtz said.

"Think he means it?" Old Holtz asked.

"Benefit of the doubt," Young Holtz said. They nodded once to each other and moved to the side of the long red tank slung under the helicopter.

It took some fiddling with a monkey wrench, but after opening a breather valve, liquid came from the tank in a rush.

"Scheista gevalt!" the older man muttered under his breath.

"Gasoline," his son said.

They wanted to discuss how it could be possible that the tank had been filled, but I didn't think we would have time for that.

"Can you drain it?"

"Yah, for sure." The old man said.

"And replace it with water?" I saw the puzzled look on both their faces. "Ballast," I said. "It has to be a certain weight."

"We can do it…"

"Now. I need it done in the next 20 minutes."

"Okay, Matthew Havoc. Okay." The older man gave me the look that said it would be difficult but it would be done.

"Five hundred dollars, here and now." I pulled a roll from my pocket and peeled off five bills. "Five more if it's done before another soul shows up on this set."

That proved to be the proper motivation. Young Holtz improvised by draining the drinking water tank that was on the back of a small blue pick up truck; that took care of about half the contents of the evil red cylinder. He drove away in the direction of a local gas station, returned with the tank ready for a refill, and in under a half hour, I paid them another five bills.

"Now," I said, "fill that red tube thing with water before anybody shows up and I'll give you another thousand."

Sometimes it's good to be the guy with the spare change in his pocket.

CHAPTER 31

Vinnie, who had a sixth sense for the caterer's truck, showed up at 3:40, ten minutes after it arrived.

"Had to wait for HIM," he grumbled, pointing to his car as he shaped his mouth around a donut that was still warm from the oven. Bertrand was sitting in back of Vinnie's Expedition, rubbing the sleep out of his eyes and pulling on his shoes.

I walked over to see how my neighbor was getting on. Vinnie snagged a cup of coffee and his second donut and came ambling along at my side.

"Told you it wouldn't rain," he chortled.

"Last of the big-city gamblers," I said.

"I told you!"

"Yes, you told me. Foggy, though."

"Aww, that'll burn off."

"You hope." We came to a halt by the side of Vinnie's dark green Expedition.

"How goes things, Bertrand?" I asked

Bertrand seemed to be having trouble with the zipper on his pants.

"You should have worn Crazy Wear," I suggested. "It doesn't have zippers."

"Punk kid," he grumbled. "I should have turned you in to social services."

He finished his zipping chore, took the donut out of Vinnie's hand and gnarfed a big bite.

"Nobody takes my donut," Vinnie said, more surprised than angry.

"We're partners," Bertrand said. "What's yours is mine." If he only knew how untrue that was, but he didn't appear to have a clue. He stared at the hustle around him in amazement. "You film people actually work for a living."

"It's a revelation, isn't it," I said.

"It's a good thing. I'd hate to be partners with a bunch of shirkers."

"Shirkers?" Vinnie, who'd begun to walk away for more donuts, started to protest.

"Careful," I warned. "What's yours is his."

"Where's our little French beauty?" Bertrand asked.

"You mean Marc or the helicopter?"

Bertrand glared at me, "The helicopter, of course."

I pointed it out. "Ready for take-off." I looked at Vinnie, who was still watching Bertrand eat the last few crumbs of his donut. Now was as good a time as any. "Who's going to fly with Marc?" I asked.

Vinnie shrugged, "One of the AD's, I suppose."

"I want to do it."

He shrugged again, "Hey, it's your life." He gave Bertrand another frown, and headed back for the donuts.

"Okay with me. Ask the Director."

I ran off to find Bret Hanley, who was arguing with one of the camera helicopter pilots over how much fog was too much fog.

When I spelled out what I wanted, Bret grinned, "Is this some sort of death-wish?"

"Thrill-a-Minute Havoc, that's what they call me."

"Have at it, Maniac," he said, doffing his black Greek fisherman's hat and giving me a mock little bow. "You'll need some sort of dark jacket. Talk to continuity and get over to the wardrobe van."

I knew Bret would agree to let me fly with Marc, and he'd done so almost without giving it a second thought. He was about to be super-busy with eight cameras running simultaneously. I'd served as his assistant before in the blurred flurry of assignments made necessary by the Berger Royal method of production-on-the-fly. My going up meant he'd snagged an extra pair of hands away from the producer's assistants, a useless bunch to his way of thinking.

By 4 o'clock the fog continued to thicken until the buildings that surrounded our main building were just vague shadows, but the entire crew was assembled, that is to say, they were all present and scurrying around loading film and making sure equipment was ready while they swigged burning hot coffee and gulped down donuts from a seemingly endless supply.

Somewhere in the gathering madness I reported back to Vinnie.

"You think we should call it off?" I asked.

"What? You crazy? This is gonna be great!"

Some of the color drained from my face. I forgot whatever I was going to say next, because Vinnie's wife Marsha, looking fresh and neat as if she'd just come from a hair salon, was heading for a closer look at some of the helicopters—squired on the arm of none other than my neighbor, batty old Bertie!

I guess my mouth was hanging open. I didn't know what I was going to do next—maybe rush over, kidnap Bertrand and lock him in the gaffer's van. I tossed a quick glance at Vinnie, but he stopped me with one brief negative nod of his head and a look off into the distance. *Bertrand was fooling around with Marsha, and Vinnie knew!*

Vinnie spoke while still looking off into the distance, his eyes not meeting mine.

"There was a time I would have killed any man..." His voice was soft, and trailed off. He seemed to gather the words, and he started again, "Marsha says he's cute and harmless."

"He is not harmless, and he is not cute! You're forgetting this is the guy who nearly wiped out Los Angeles!"

"Yeah, yeah," Vinnie waved me off as if that was past and, hence, of no consequence, "Suppose they are fooling around?"

He turned to look at me, and the slow smile that crept onto the corners of his wide face made me appreciate the messy but human complexity that was my boss. He answered his own question, "Well, then, that would make Marsha feel even more guilty about her secret bank accounts and her small shack on St. Kitts that she doesn't think I know about. Takes the pressure off, you know?"

"I guess," I said, simultaneously giving him a short laugh of relief and a doubtful shake of my head.

"On your toes," he warned, "Here comes the happy couple now."

"This is so—exciting!" Marsha exclaimed.

I had to reply that it was. Bertrand approached Vinnie and handed him a napkin-wrapped donut.

"Raspberry filled," he exclaimed in triumph. "Your favorite kind!"

Vinnie thanked him and accepted the gift, and they wandered away with Vinnie, who walked them through the action of the coming scene. Moroni's helicopter, the lithe little Llama, would take off first, followed by the S.W.A.T. chase helicopters. I had wanted sleek army cobras for these, but the budget couldn't stand it, so we had two lumbering old Vietnam era HU-1B choppers. In a way, it was better, because they had open sides with gun mounts, and would film more dramatic for the chase scene, at least the way Boris and Bret had sketched it out.

The police pilots who would be manning the two chase helicopters showed up, as well as the two men to fly the camera copters. Soon all five were revved up, and even with the engines idling, the thudding *whup* sounds from the slowly rotating blades made it difficult to hold a conversation. Marc was the last to arrive.

"Marc! Where have you been?! We were ready to get a replacement!"

I walked over and handed him a half-and-half.

"Café au lait," I said. "A last drink for the doomed man."

He gave me a haunted look, "What is that the meaning of?" I assumed for once it was a real question.

"It is the meaning of have some coffee, you idiot Frog."

"You don't know anything, Matt Havoc." He spit the words out, suddenly angry to the point where he was shaking.

I took his arm. "Hey, Marc. It's me, Havoc."

But he pulled his arm away, threw the coffee on the ground and walked over to his helicopter. The Llama was idling, the big overhead rotor cutting swirls in the fog immediately overhead.

"Marc, you have to get ready," I yelled. "Where are your white robes?" But even the mention of Moroni's symbolic white robes, which Marc had raised such a fuss over, didn't slow him down.

"I'm coming with you, you know," I called after him.

"Merde," he muttered over his shoulder.

Young Holtz hopped from the pilot's seat when he saw Marc coming.

"She's fired up and ready to go, Mr. Fraper," he said.

I'd warned the Holtzinschnabs father and son to say nothing about switching the gas out of the auxiliary tank, but I walked over to make sure neither of them blabbed to the Frenchman. And that's the only reason I was close enough to get on the helicopter with Marc, because he fired up the engine and, without bothering to check any gauges or even strap himself in, he took off.

There was a moment of panic, people scurrying in frantic chaos, like when some kid kicks an anthill. Crewmembers were running and screaming, both towards and away from us. *Wait! Stop! What are you doing, you fools? Jesus Christ! Idiots! What, we taking off already? But I got no film in the magazines!*

Bret Hanley yelling, "I didn't say ACTION yet!"

And over it all, Vinnie's booming command, "Shut it off, you god-damn crazy *fromage* eating Gaullist idiot!"

It was at least an hour too early. The backup that Rooks had promised was nowhere in sight—at least, I hadn't seen anybody. The police were a joke, just looking on like this was some part of the production. I couldn't blame them; they'd been hired to keep away the curious and the gang-bangers who might want to take a piece of us.

Whatever was going to happen, I was going to have to do it myself. As the crowd looked on in stunned amazement, the engines roared and the whir of the blades took on a higher pitch—and the Llama rose in front of me in a swirling cloud of dust.

I guess I see too many movies, and it's easy to confuse the happy world where everything turns out alright with the real everyday world where cars run off bridges, buildings burn and collapse, robberies go wrong and in all these situations real ordinary people get hurt, maimed and die. *No matter.* Horace Keg would have dove for the nearest skid of the rising helicopter to save the world for freedom and democracy…and, absurd as it seems, so did I.

I took three steps, reached chest high and grabbed for the rising machine, catching the nearest of the skids in both hands. Surprise, surprise—the skid was slippery with gasoline or oil, and almost immediately I slipped to where I was hanging by one hand. Meanwhile the Llama, true to its reputation for climbing performance, was on its way up, and in what seemed like a twinkling we were over a hundred feet in the air.

It felt like my one arm would be longer than the other until the day I died, which would be today, unless I got my act together and did something positive. Somehow—I'll never know exactly how, though I suspect it had something to do with the superhuman energy generated by pure fear—I managed to get a second hand grip and pull myself up to a standing position with my feet on the skid. The startled expression on Marc's face was almost worth the effort. He waved me off with a sweep of his hand, as if that fierce gesture was going to convince me to leap 250 feet to my death. He couldn't do any more as he had to stay at the controls of the helicopter.

I pulled myself into the cockpit and put on the headset.

"Where are we going, Marc?" I yelled.

"You don't need to shout?" he said still locked in his desperately incorrect overtones even as death loomed.

"Where are we going?" I asked again in a more moderate tone as we shot upward and the deepening fog swirled around us.

"Will they not kill my wife and daughter?" he asked, the note of despair clear in his voice.

"Shamseen Usudman?" I asked.

He nodded grimly.

"What are you going to try to do?"

"Is that not the tallest building in Los Angeles?"

"Yes, but you can't take it out."

"Why can I not? I have the calculations. I know where to hit it?"

"If you can find it in the fog."

"Don't you think the fog is sent by God? They can send up jets but they won't be able to find me."

"Marc, you've got to go back down."

"What chance of that is there, Havoc? You would do the same, to save the ones you love. It's my life, it's one building. Now it is early. Surely, no one is there?"

"Wait a minute! Just stop a minute and listen to me!"

He kicked some levers and we hovered in mid-air. Things looked familiar, and for a moment I couldn't figure out why. Then I saw we were at the same elevation as the patio on top of the Coast Savings Building. And I saw something else; in addition to the camera crew positioned there, there was a man with a rifle pointed at us.

"Marc, you can't take down the building. You think you did everything right, but there will be no explosion. I switched water into the big red tank."

266

"What? You didn't? This is not to believe?"

"And I had most of the gas drained out of the regular tanks. We're running on fumes up here, buddy."

"But…how did you know about this?"

"I know Shamseen Usudman. And I suspected you because of your Mid-eastern connections. You have to bring this helicopter down—now!"

His eyes were wide and frantic as they darted from me to the tallest building in Los Angeles and back again. I'll never know what he would have done, but at that moment Halliburton Rook's rifleman made his move. He saw he had a clear shot at Marc, and so he took it.

Fire leapt from the muzzle of the rifle on the patio, and Marc jerked backward in his seat. A spray of red blossomed from his chest, and he slumped forward over the controls.

The Llama hung in the air, spinning slowly counterclockwise about itself. It wouldn't stay there long. *It was time for Hollywood Havoc to leap into action!*

Impossible? Maybe, but when you're life hangs in the balance, you don't think that way.

I'd fooled around in the cockpit of Horace Keg's Huey 1-B, nearly crashing the damn thing before the stunt pilot slapped me away from the controls. Nothing here was the same. The HU-1B was a lumbering beetle; this was a nimble little dragonfly.

I tried to lean Marc's body out of the way. The Llama veered right and headed for the patio. I tried to lean him back the other way, but it was too late. The rotor blades bit into the awkward façade of the building and exploded into a thousand metal shards. The Llama settled down with a bone-jarring thump as it came to rest on the lip of the patio.

I didn't have my seatbelt strapped, and so I was tumbled out of the chopper and across the patio like a like a skittering piece of fat on a hot commissary grill. I was skinned and scraped and bruised, but lucky to be alive. The Llama teetered on the brink for a moment, and then started to slide off the edge.

I caught Marc's gaze in that last moment before he disappeared forever. He may have been in shock, but that grim stare was clear enough. I was responsible for the death of his wife and child, and his own death as well. One withering look that would last me until eternity, and then the Llama slid back off the edge of the building with a grinding squeal. There was a long silence, and then a crash far below.

CHAPTER 32

Later that afternoon, Vinnie and I finally found a moment we could be alone. The reporters and the police were gone for a bit, and we'd ordered in big, hot bowls of Chinese Corn Chowder Chicken Soup messengered from Crown Wok in Woodland Hills in the Valley. Vinnie slurped his soup and gulped big bites of lemon chicken. He was a fat tub of mixed emotions, so on edge that I was worrying about the arrival of his next heart attack. No producer likes death on the set, and it didn't happen very often on a Berger Royal production. On the other hand, the footage had been incredible, and he couldn't stop talking about it.

"Fantastic! You should have seen it! Llama went up into the goopy fog with you hanging on by one hand!"

"You're not going to use that footage?" I asked.

"Are you kidding, Havoc?! It was sensational!!"

"Yeah, but a guy died-"

"Come on, Hollywood—what better tribute? You can't have him die in vain."

That was Vinnie; he saw everything in terms of the picture. He saw the look on my face.

"What? I mean, I'm sorry about the Frapperman and all, but I'm the one who told you French Cinema people are all screwed up, didn't I?!"

When he put it that way, I didn't see any way not to use it. Homeland Security came out against it, of course, but they backed off when Vinnie started in yelling about the rights of free speech in the land of the free and the home of the brave, and threatening to go to the press. It was a good thing they backed down, too. Vinnie had duplicate negatives struck and sent someplace overseas. I knew that, if they pushed him hard enough, he'd have the picture finished overseas—a huge publicity bonanza guaranteed to bring in a gigantic box office.

"I'm sorry about Frapper, really, I am," he repeated. "I'm gonna miss the little guy with his funny way of talking." And then he shrugged, getting as philosophical as he ever might, "But, you know the guy brought it on himself. Frickin' French symbolism! Ain't it ironic that the one time it works it's by accident? I tell you, Havoc, the secret is and always will continue to be *Get it big on the screen!*"

Vinnie was right, too, about being able to manipulate what he referred to as *the death footage* so that it worked in *Carnage Daze*. Bret and Boris found a way to insert a few shots establishing an actor wearing Dockers and a forest green rip-stop jacket just like mine. In fact, we didn't even have to buy them; we had a half dozen in storage, left over from *California Climax*. You never see the pilot when the helicopter comes crashing back down to earth, so our editors cut the footage to look like Moroni and the man in the rip-stop jacket both get off on top of the Coast Savings building.

The days after what the trades referred to as *Berger Royal's helicopter incident* were long ones, with us trying to film the rest of the picture and the police and the FBI coming and going. Everybody had to be interviewed at least twice. The rifleman turned out to be an FBI marksman, alerted by my old friend Halliburton Rooks. Marc would yield no more clues to help us track down our deadly enemy, Shamseen Usudman; if the bullet to his chest hadn't killed him, he was dead on contact when the Llama hit the wide cement apron at the street level. At least, in his honor, Vinnie convinced me we had to shoot the opening scenes of the movie with Moroni trying on his symbolic white robes.

A few nights later, I answered three phone calls. The first came at about 10 o'clock while I was watching the news reports chew over once again the tragic scenes. Vinnie had released tantalizing snippets of footage of the helicopter rising with me hanging on by one hand, and of the crash into the top of the Coast Savings building. The footage that he provided ended just as the helicopter was teetering back and forth, and you didn't know what was going to happen next. They would be re-running it for weeks.

My second call was from Shamseen Usudman, himself.

"We've executed them both," he said in a quiet voice, "The wife and the little boy. She begged for him, so we shot him first. And you, Matthew Havoc…you're directly responsible for their deaths."

The actual word of their murders hit me like a stone. I'd been through plenty of violence and several near-death experiences in the past few years, all because of Shamseen. But you never get used to cruelty…at least, I don't. While my experiences in the crazy world of rock-em-sock-em movies had kept me alive so far, I knew it was nothing more than luck.

And the deeper truth was, Marc's ending and the fate of his family had been weighing heavily on my mind. The best way I could work it out was that I was in a war, and in war there are no easy choices. You simply try to make the right hard choice and go forward. The closest to war that I'd experienced was Keg's, a war fantasy I'd co-written with Vinnie. But I'd read a lot and talked with my father about it, as well. I think I had the essentials down. The same principles that held true any other time also applied in times of terrorism.

Shamseen, I figured, had called me to score what psychological points he could. Maybe he was thinking I was a weak, silly American, full of politically-correct nonsense and ripe for the picking. That was his mistake. He wasn't going to find any soft targets lying around the Havoc house.

"Murders, you mean." I replied coldly.

"Whatever," he said.

"Not, 'whatever,' Shamseen. Murders. You murdered them. And don't think you can spread the guilt around. I never knew Marc's family. I have no images of a loving wife or a sweet son to keep me awake at night. I didn't kill them. You did."

I was going to hang up, but I thought of something else. I don't think of myself as a vindictive person, but in addition to multiple attempts on my life, this man was trying to cripple me emotionally. He deserved whatever he got. People who live in glass houses shouldn't shoot target practice indoors, or something like that.

"On the other hand," I said, "I did have a hand in the death of your sister and your two nephews. But I didn't kill them, either. I had no choice, but you did. You sent them to their deaths. Their blood on your hands. Did you love them very much, or don't you care at all about anybody? Were their deaths simply another sacrifice to your cause, whatever the hell that might be?"

There was a long pause on the other end of the line. When he finally spoke, it was with a voice dipped in hatred.

"I underestimated you, Matthew Havoc. It won't happen again."

He hung up and almost immediately the phone rang again. This time, it was a screaming rant from a voice I couldn't recognize, calling me every obscenity from the original Tinseltown production handbook of vile names.

"Who is this?" I finally asked when my irate caller stopped for a breath of air.

"Michael Blastowitz, you uncaring son of a bitch!"

"What's the problem, Michael—lose Peanut's luggage in Portland?"

"You asshole—I got her the biggest eight figure picture deal this town ever saw for a woman!"

"Goodie for you. And?"

"And, you stupid fool-pig-idiot-bastard, *you* got her pregnant so she turned it down!"

And, with that said, he hung up on me.

By the next day the rumors were all over town and the phones at BR Pics were ringing off the hook. And the day after that I read all about it in the Hollywood Reporter. Super-star Joy Benefeté had turned down the lead in a megabucks new Warner Brothers tragic-comedy and had been whisked away to her retreat in Southern France to have a baby. The father was reported to be Berger Royal Productions executive Matthew Havoc, to whom she had been married, and with whom she had recently worked in Portland on the filming of his screenplay adaptation of a Miriad Breech novel.

When the reporters had caught up to her on her departure from LAX, someone reminded her that Matthew Havoc was an ex-husband.

To which my dear familiar Peanuts happily responded, "No, you must have it wrong. Let me give you a scoop, darlings. I never signed those final divorce papers. Why would I divorce such a sweetheart of a guy? It's our baby, and Mattie and I are still happily married!"

And with that, she had walked the length of the blue first class carpet like the mega-star and thief of love that she was, and boarded an Air France plane…a big silvery trans-oceanic passenger jet that had taken off at just about the time I was dangling one-handed from a helicopter swiftly rising into the pre-morning gloom of downtown LA.

I am Hollywood Havoc, producer of schlock "B" movies for Vinnie Berger's Berger Royal Pictures, also the husband of Madge Sacknall, otherwise known as world-class superstar Joy Benefeté, and to some few close friends as Peanuts. I am told I am soon to be the father of her child.

And somewhere, the gods of show biz are gathered around a huge table in some cavernous and airy production place. They are puffing celestial cigars, chewing on an endless supply of divinity flavored donuts, and tickling their nubile, ready and willing cherubs. And, I am certain, all this as they look down on the tawdry, tattered dreams of Tinseltown, and laugh at me.

THE END

ABOUT THE AUTHOR

During the Vietnam War, John Klawitter was a military intelligence spy with a Top Secret CODEWORD clearance. He worked at a SE Asia branch of the National Security Agency's so-called 'Puzzle Palace'. Back stateside and having been awarded an Honorable Discharge and an Expeditionary Forces medal, he began his career as a cub copywriter at the Leo Burnett Advertising Agency, working on such national accounts as Kellogg's cereals and Nestles chocolate bars. He became a do-it-yourself filmmaker and won many awards, including an EMMY, for his political documentary work. Advancing over the years as a Hollywood writer, producer and Directors Guild of America director, as well as a member of ASCAP and The Authors Guild, he has authored over a dozen novels and non-fiction books, including the highly regarded HEADSLAP: The Life & Times of Deacon Jones, HOLLYWOOD HAVOC: The Trouble With Fat Boy (EPIC Author's Award 2009 for Best Action-Thriller Novel), and TINSEL WILDERNESS (EPIC Author's Award 2009 for Best Non-Fiction Book). His trade paperbacks are available from Amazon, B&N and the rest of the usual suspects.

E-books of his titles are available in all formats from www.double-dragon-ebooks.com. Information on upcoming novels and film projects available at www.johnklawitter.com.

John Klawitter

John Klawitter

www.ingramcontent.com/pod-product-compliance
Lightning Source LLC
Chambersburg PA
CBHW071124170626
46809CB00002B/485